FROM ANCIENT
SHADOWS

FROM ANCIENT
SHADOWS

Wayne Trebbin, M.D.

To order additional copies of this book, contact:
Xlibris
844-714-8691
www.Xlibris.com
Orders@Xlibris.com
831203

1

The creature was hunting. Its eyes darted to and fro, picking out details through the dark predawn mist with preternatural acuity. The air was still, and there were no sounds of nature. No birds cried out, no leaves fluttered, and yet the creature could feel the fear eroding through the core of its prey. The prey had no idea what was stalking it, but it sensed the creature's presence.

The creature sniffed. It was closer. It carefully placed one foot forward, then another. It stood still again, and sniffed the moist cool air once more. It craned its neck forward, and listened. The heart of its quarry was pounding, and the predator could hear it. Its hearing was beyond acute, but so were all of its senses; it was, nonetheless, despite its considerable advantages, an assiduous hunter: thorough, vigilant, intelligent and relentless.

The full moon rendered everything in shades of blue, silver and gray. The mist dimmed the details. Despite this the hunter could see enough, and it knew that its intended kill could not. The stalked heard nothing, and could see little, but it knew…it felt the danger approaching. It knew time and space were closing it with destiny quickly, and it wanted to run, but did not know which way to go. Its muscles were tensed, ready to hurl it this way or that at the first perception of a corporal presence, but none materialized. It would take virtually nothing to make it bolt at this point. Its wide-open, widely dilated eyes flicked about with the adrenaline laced jaggedness of near panic.

The hunter took several more careful paces forward, ears pinned back, then froze. Its victim was in sight. A dim dark form, but there it was. Another step forward, and a large bird hurled itself into flight from bushes forward and to the right of the creature. Its great wings churned the air into sound, and it let out a frightened cry diffused by the mist.

The hunted sprang up a few inches, realized the source of the sound, and went down low again, immobile, hoping it was still unseen. Its heart pounded terribly fast.

Of course, it had been seen. The creature was behind it to its left. It was down wind to its intended kill, and even if it were much closer the other animal did not have the acuity of hearing, sense of smell or peripheral vision to gauge its nearness.

Another few paces placed slowly, carefully. Now there was nothing between the two but medium height grass. The prey was not as fleet of foot as its hunter, and it would be over soon. The moment was…now!

Several dozen muscles galvanized at once, and the predator literally hurled its body through the air in a powerful leap. This was followed by another, and the distance closed quickly. The hunted knew instantly that the end game had begun. It, too, snapped into action, retreating diagonally to the attack, guided only by the increased sound of movement through the grass, the direction of the sound confused by the thick moisture in the air.

A little cry escaped the terrified victim. It imagined the attacker looming over it at the crest of a pounce, and it zigzagged, changing its direction by forty-five degrees. The predator countered, and was now measuring and timing what would be its final spring.

Somewhere the bird that had been flushed a moment before cried out, and in the otherwise quiet predawn the affect was startling. The prey dug its feet in to start reversing direction at the sound, and the predator had not anticipated this. It made its killing leap, but because of the prey's momentary cessation of forward movement it overshot its target.

The quarry got a full view of the carnivore. It was a sight of such emotional magnitude that all the poor victim's cognitive functions crunched to a halt. Neither plans nor concepts formed; just a mindless and overwhelming passion to flee. It took no measure of terrain, or its foe anymore. It was now a thoughtless biological bundle of feelings, the sensation of which was akin to forest fire.

Get away, get away…that was all it knew, except for a near tangible wish not to die.

The predator wheeled and lunged at the prey. A miss. The foot race was on. It was brief, and in less than three seconds the predator had its victim in its grasp. The victim twisted and turned, screaming, trying to shake its attacker off. The predator bit the side of the victim's shoulder, sharp teeth sinking easily into the soft, tasty, living flesh. The prey screamed again, but continued to twist its body and flail at the attacker. The predator drew on the glands deep in its cheeks, and spit a fine spray of poison into the victim's face. The spray covered the victims left eye and cheek, and burned terribly. The sclera of the eye and the surface of the facial skin were quickly corroded, and the poison began to enter the victim's nervous system. The two fell to the ground, entangled in their embrace of carnal finality. They rolled and screamed, one in terror and one in triumph. The creature's mouth again bit into the victim's body, this time in the abdominal flank, and again the creature's oral glands contracted, emitting their poison.

The prey regained its footing for a moment, and tried to flee, this time dragging its attacker, but the hunter shifted its weight savagely, torquing their bodies, and spinning them both to the ground again.

The prey cried out, and was surprised to hear it as pinched and pitiful, not enraged and terrified. The toxin was working very fast, and adrenaline was causing it to surge through the body faster than would have been the case without the autonomic response.

Again, teeth tore flesh. There was more writhing, and the dance of death tore and dragged apart the grasses beneath them.

The hunted lay on its back and side, unable to move, the paralysis of its arms and legs complete. Although in extremis, its breathing had slowed unnaturally, and it could not cry out at all.

The hunter paused over the soon to be killed and cocked its head to examine it. Then it bit deeply into the victim's throat, clamped its teeth, and pulled back and to the side hard. It reveled as it swallowed the flesh and drank the blood. Passion rose quickly to crescendo.

2

The doctor's fingers moved carefully as they closed the final knot. The long intravenous catheter was now snugged securely to the skin. Before applying the dressing, the doctor stood up, shoulders moving to try to shift the paper sterile gown, then turned to the table placed across the bed, and reached for a small syringe. The physician pulled back the plunger, drawing air into the syringe. In a moment it was attached to the external end of the catheter, and the doctor's right thumb pushed in the air. The balloon at the end of the catheter deep in the circulation of the patient's lung, wedged into the small capillaries, and inflated with little resistance. The doctor's eyes shot to the monitor above and to the left of the bed. The broad wave pattern below the cardiogram reading had changed abruptly, and now showed low amplitude waves.

"Good wedge," said the nurse on the other side of the bed, her eyes also fixed on the machine.

"Yup," said the doctor. "What do you think...wedge about 32?"

"UmmHmm."

"Okay, let's give lasix forty milligrams I.V. now, and start a lasix drip at ten an hour. If the urine out put doesn't pick up with that, increase the rate to fifteen, and call me. Okay?"

"No problem, I'll go get the bolus now." The nurse, in blue scrubs with large, black letters spelling MICU stamped on them, turned and left.

The doctor stretched slightly. She applied a dressing, then spoke to the patient.

"Mr. Cutter, we've put that line in okay. It suggests you have too much fluid on board, and that's causing your lungs to fill up. That's why you're

---

having trouble breathing. That can happen after a heart attack like yours, but we have lots we can do for it."

The patient, an obese man of fifty two, nodded. The doctor could see the polite smile behind the misted oxygen mask.

"You sure I really had a heart attack?" he asked.

The doctor nodded, smiled slightly, and gently put a hand on the man's shoulder. "Yes, you did. That's why the fluid has backed up in your lungs. That's called congestive heart failure, but I hate that term because it sounds too scary. People hear heart failure, and they think their heart has totally shot. That's not necessarily true in general and it's not true in your case. We're going to give you some medicine to get some of the extra water out of your body, and that ought to make your breathing better."

The man nodded, and closed his eyes, the sedating morphine taking him once again.

How many times has this guy been warned, the doctor mused? How many times was he told: quit the cigarettes, take your medicines, lose weight? How do cigarette manufacturers look at themselves in the mirror, anyway, in the morning when they brush their teeth and not want to cut their own throats? Death for dollars.

The doctor knew the patient's wife and children, had heard him talk about his dreams for them, and looked at their pictures on several clinic visits, admiring each time the wife's beauty, the younger child's elfin smile and the intelligence in the older one's eyes. The doctor turned, head shaking from side to side slightly.

The beeper under the doctor's protective surgical gown went off. The doctor pulled off the gloves, the fingertips of which were bloody, then pulled off the gown itself, rolling it up, and dumping it into a wastebasket while heading out of the patient's cubicle. She pulled the beeper out of its holder clipped to her waist, pressed a button and read the message. There was a nursing station island in the middle of the intensive care unit, on which a bank of monitors reported the heartbeats of every patient in the unit, and three computer terminals gave quick access to lab values and much of the patients' records. There was a phone on each side of the island, and the doctor sat down in front of one of them. Off came the surgical mask, which was quickly dispensed into a near by trash barrel, and four finger strokes later the phone started ringing on the other end. After the second ring a voice answered.

"Doctor Michaels?"

"Yes?"

"It's Matt. You coming to the luncheon conference?"

Matt Collins was the indefatigable chief resident of the internal medicine service. Efficient, smart and poised, many hoped he would eventually stay on as part of the attending staff at the hospital.

"Yes, I am. Is everyone there already?"

"Ready, eating lunch and waiting for you." He gently stressed the last word turning the sentence into good-natured chiding.

"Be right there."

Damn, the doctor thought, hanging up the phone, late again. It was a continued frustration for one made nervous by tardiness.

The doctor left the ICU, crossed the hall, and entered the surgical area. Quickly finding the female lounge, she pushed open the door with the palm of her right hand, and went into the changing area. She opened her locker, quickly stripped off the scrubs she had been working in while in the Intensive Care unit, tossed them into a nearby laundry bin, and put on a conservative white shirt and gray skirt. As a cardiology fellow she always felt a little out of place using the surgical lounge to change, but it was convenient, and that was key given her usual schedule. She pulled her long white lab coat out of the locker, and slipped it on. Fixing her collar, she quickly looked in the small mirror on the inside of the locker door. Her golden brown hair was neatly pulled up in a bun. The bridge of her slightly turned up nose bore two small red marks where the thin metal piece of the disposable mask had pinched down on it. She shrugged, and turned, walked briskly to the lounge door and pulled it open, then entered the main corridor, walking in rapid cadence towards the elevators.

Though pressed for time, she looked forward to giving the talk. The subject was cardiac arrhythmias, and the audience would be made up of interns, residents and medical students.

Doctor Janis Michaels had, all her life, enjoyed being the center of attention. It had helped move her to succeed in sports and in the classroom. She liked excelling, and had finished college summa cum lauda. In medical school she had been in the top ten percent of her class, which bought her a berth in a very prestigious medical internship and residency. There was no hesitation on her part in choosing to do a fellowship after that, and cardiology had been an ideal fit for her abilities and predilections. She enjoyed understanding how things worked rather than simply memorizing lists. The physics and electro physiology of the circulatory system gave her a vast sea of mechanisms to understand and the potential to chart new waters in what she dreamed would be a productive academic career in the near future.

She was enthusiastic about her field of interest, and articulately outgoing in public. This made her a naturally popular instructor to the medical students and house officers who generally made every effort to arrange their schedules to allow them to attend her lectures.

She pulled out the thumb drive she had tucked in her white coat pocket, and mentally flipped through her slides as she walked: v tach, a fib, bifasicular block, W.P.W, and others, This would be a good intermediate level talk. Each arrhythmia had a corresponding brief case history, and she would keep things lively by calling on the members of her little audience around the lunch table in the residents' lounge.

I hope Dad's not there she thought to herself. At her last lecture the senior Doctor Michaels had made a surprise visit joining the group for lunch, and markedly dampening the pleasure she usually took in giving these conferences. He was a wonderful man, with kind eyes behind rimless glasses, and she loved him dearly, but he was a nationally known member of the senior faculty, he was the Chief of Medicine, and he was her dad, all of which conspired to put her teeth on edge while delivering her talk.

As she approached the door of the conference room she heard the voice on the public address system announce "Code 8 Emergency Department… Code 8 Emergency Department."

Security. Someone in the E.D. must have pulled a nutty. Belligerent drunk, some kid on PCP, domestic fight…it could be any of a number of things. Janis was glad she was not on duty down there, and even more was glad she was not a security guard.

Her left hand grabbed and turned the door handle to the resident's lounge, and as the door opened she was greeted by a faint sweet smell of warm soup. She glanced at the tureen on the table, and checked out the large salad with chicken slices next to it. Beverages and cookies were at the other end of the table. She would eat after she delivered her talk.

Janis smiled at the group of students, residents and interns sitting around the central table with a few forming a broken second row.

"Hello," she said as she placed her thumb drive on one end of the central table, and reached to pull the projector towards her. Without being asked, one of the medical students rose, leaned forward, and pushed the projector toward her.

"Thanks," she smiled at him. She turned her gaze to the group at large, who was acknowledging her arrival with smiles, and a few counter hellos.

"How are you guys doing today?" she asked them.

Again, a scattered, muffled array of responses all basically indicating that everybody was fine. No one actually stopped eating; long hours and short breaks had taught them all to do that.

"Okay, today, we do some arrhythmias," Janis began. "I'll start by presenting you a briefcase, and then let's see what you do with it." Her eyes darted to the clock at the back of the room, and her mind pleasantly played with the thought that she would be seeing Philip in a few hours. Philip Skorian was her boyfriend of a few months. He was fun, but her feelings for him were mixed. While he had a good heart, he could be full of himself, and she found him a strange paradox of generosity and egocentricity. He was driven, that was for sure, and he aggressively pursued both his career and his hobbies. This afternoon they were to go sailing on the river near the hospital. Janis loved sailing. Her father had taught her when she was a little girl. When she and Philip sailed together, if he got too bossy, she would amuse herself by telling him to stick it, watching his crestfallen face, while she took over. She was a better sailor than he was.

Philip talked easily, laughed easily and people generally were charmed by him. He deftly concealed some selfish tendencies with his quick smile and the twinkle in his eyes. Janis often thought he was perfectly suited for what he was doing. He was in his 8th year of surgical training, with the goal of being a high-powered thoracic surgeon. The surgical residency here was grueling, and, quite frankly, Janis had to admit, people in it had to have their share of narcissism just to endure…or was it masochism?

This reverie transpired as her eyes moved from the clock back to the class.

"Okay, the first case is an eighteen-year-old male who comes to the E.R. complaining of a rapid pulse. You look at the vital signs, and see that his pulse is 150, and his blood pressure is 100/60. He looks anxious and is not diaphoretic. What do you do?"

A female intern of Indian extraction was the first to raise her hand.

"Yes Savita."

"I would early on ask him about drug use."

"Okay, keep going."

"Obviously I would be interested in cocaine, but we would also have to consider amphetamine, and others."

"What about too much coffee?" a student asked.

"Sure," Savita said, turning to him. "Caffeine could do that. I'd also want to know about anabolic steroids."

"Why?" Janis asked, knowing the answer.

"Cardiomyopathy."

"Good."

The questions and answers continued for a few more minutes; then Janis turned on the computer in front of her, and clicked on her first slide. It was an EKG showing a fast regular rhythm.

"Did this guy have recent prolonged travel or an injury?" asked a second-year resident.

"No, but I bet I know what you're going to say." Janis smiled faintly.

"P.E.?"

"Yup, what would a discussion of tachycardia be without someone mentioning pulmonary embolism?" She paused briefly, her look kindly. "No, no recent anything that would suggest that. Let's look at a preceding cardiogram taken by the kid's primary care doc...turns out this has been a recurrent problem." She clicked on her next slide.; this one had a much slower rate.

"This shows him when he's not having the tachycardia. Do you see anything noteworthy here?"

The room was quiet for a moment, then Savita chimed in, "Are those delta waves?"

"Very good." Janis' finger pointed to a little deflection preceding each of the major waves. "These are pretty subtle in this case, but you got it. So what's has this guy got?"

"WPW," came a few replies from the group.

"Wolf Parkinson White syndrome...okay. Does anyone want to tell me about retrograde and antegrade conduction in this ailment?"

A discussion of the underlying physiology went on for a few more minutes, and then they began another case. By the time they finished the fifth case the hour was up. As the group thanked her, and she collected her travel drive, Janis heard again the call for Code 8, in typical hospital fashion being sounded twice from the loudspeaker.

Wonder if it's the same thing going on down there, she wondered silently. She thought about lunch, but as she turned to move towards it her beeper went off. She pulled it from its clasp at her waist, and pressed a button as she peered at the little screen. In her mind lunch dimmed and faded away. Consult in the I.C.U.

Okay, she thought, I'll go there now, and hopefully still be able to get everything done in time to meet Phil. She quickly left the conference room, moved down the corridor, and was pleased when one of the three elevator doors opened before she could press the button. An older obese lady and what must have been her grandchild in a stroller exited the elevator, and then Janis entered. She looked at the only other person in the car. He was leaning against the rear wall, looking over an index card of notes.

"Hi Matt," she said, smiling.

"Hey Janis," the chief resident replied looking up from his notes, and smiling back. "You involved in that ruckus in the Emergency Department?"

Janis frowned. "No, but they've called security twice. You know what's going on?"

"A nurse told me there is some kid down there who got violent. I don't know the details, but it sounds like she made a mess."

"A kid?"

"Not a child. I think it was a teen. A female, but apparently she was strong enough to make them call for reinforcements."

The elevator stopped. "I gotta go," Janis said looking up at the number of the floor. "Have to see a case in the I.C.U. Where are you going?"

"I'm curious about super girl in the E.R."

"Careful."

In a moment she was pressing the electric pad on the wall to open the door that led to the corridor in which the intensive care unit was located. She entered the I.C.U. directly. She doubted she would be doing a procedure, so there was no need to put on a new set of scrubs. She moved towards the dictation area near which which sat the unit secretary. She flicked on the computer and found the record she was looking for. She noted what room the patient was in, and let her eyes dart in that direction. She saw an elegant looking elderly woman with silver gray hair pulled back into a twist at the back of her head.

"Okay," Janis said to herself. "Let's see what's going on." She tuned out the sounds of ventilators, nurses, buzzers and other sundry indicators of modern healing. As she adjusted herself in her seat her beeper went off again. She pulled it into her hand, pressed the button, and read the page.

"Doctor Michaels please call Dr Michaels ext 4453" Janis smiled at the redundancy, and warmed to the call. Dad. She reached for the phone on the desk, and lifted the receiver from its cradle moving it to her ear. She punched in the four numbers, and waited as the phone rang.

"Hello. This is Dr. Michaels," came the solid, controlled voice on the other end. "Can I help you?"

"Hi, Dad."

"Jan." His voice lifted.

"What's up, and where's Melinda?" Melinda, the senior Dr. Michaels' secretary, always answered his phone.

"She went off to copy some papers I have to send to the dean's office. Listen, Honey, I was wondering if you might like to have dinner with me tonight. My treat."

"Jeez, Dad, I would love to, but Phil and I are supposed to go sailing later, and then I have to get home, and work over the data for my project." Janis was working on publishing two small but interesting papers.

"Hmmm, sailing. I remember the time when there was only one man you would dare go sailing with."

Janis could imagine his kind smile on the other end of the line.

"Listen, Dad, the guy's a surgeon. I don't really want to be with him, but I have to go to save his ass if he screws up out there again." Again, she could feel his smile.

"You've been seeing quite a bit of him. Is this turning into something?"

"Oh, I don't know. I have too many things on my plate now." The father could translate the words, and knew this to be daughter-speak for "don't push, Dad. I love you, but I don't want to get into this now." He respected this, and backed off.

"You busy?" he asked.

"Oh yeah, but that's my life."

"Okay, sweetie, I'll let you go then. How about breakfast tomorrow in the cafeteria. 6:30?"

"Deal. Love you."

"Talk to you soon. I love you too," and he hung up.

Janis put the receiver back in the cradle, feeling a pang of regret over having said no to her father. Then with the click of the mouse she opened the patient's chart, and read the name: Mary Logan.

This was an eighty-five-year-old woman who entered the hospital complaining of chest pressure radiating to the left side of her jaw. She had a ten-year history of diabetes mellitus and a twenty-year history of hypertension. She did not drink alcohol, and had quit smoking twenty years ago. Father died of stroke, mother died of cancer. Two siblings, one deceased from cirrhosis and the other recovered from a stroke like episode. The lady took half a dozen different medicines. Allergic to penicillin. Widow. Profession: retired professor of English romantic poetry.

Cool, Janis thought.

No recent travel, no pets, only surgical history was a gall bladder removal fifteen years ago. Review of systems showed a few minor things, but nothing of much import.

Janis' eyes moved onto the admission physical exam. Blood pressure 150\95. She moved onto to the Emergency Department note. About twenty minutes after arrival the patient's blood pressure had fallen to 85\50.

Bet she had an inferior or posterior M.I., Janis mused, and found the EKG done on arrival.

"Hah, there they are," she whispered softly, looking at the negative deflections in leads II, III, and AVF. "Flipped T's. Not diagnostic, but suggestive."

The patient had received a liter of normal saline I.V., and the pressure had come back up. Janis turned back to the physical exam. Lungs: clear. Heart: soft murmur at the apex. Abdomen: soft and nontender. Liver and spleen: normal, no abdominal masses appreciated. Mild swelling in both lower extremities, but no signs of phlebitis.

So far pretty straight forward. Next the labs. No anemia, good. Electrolytes normal, but the potassium was at the lower limit of normal. Okay. Kidney function maybe a little impaired. Blood sugar moderately elevated. Cardiac enzymes up!

So, my friend, you've had a heart attack. I knew it. Well, if there is nothing else going on, I think you ought to be okay. She began to read the progress notes. Problem on day two…post infarction chest pain. That's not good. Only lasted for a few minutes, and relieved with the second nitro. Recurrence a couple hours later relieved this time with only one nitro.

Okay, let's take a look at you.

Janis opened the door of the little glass walled room. She walked directly to the patient's cubicle, its curtain drawn back, and the patient in clear view.

The lady looked at Janis and smiled. She had gray intelligent eyes and thin lines on her face that gave testimony to a legacy of easy laughter and intense concentration. An intravenous was taped to her left forearm, and a green oxygen tube encircled her head. She wore the usual hospital jonnie, and the bed covers were drawn up to her waist.

"Come in dear," she said to Janis.

"Hello, I'm Dr. Michaels. I'm the cardiology fellow, and your doctor asked my team to see you."

"A female fellow, interesting use of words" the patient mused, smiling again. "A fellow, that means you're in training, right?"

"Yes, it does. I'm a fully trained internist, and now I'm training to be a cardiologist. But don't worry, the fellows here always present their cases to a staff cardiologist who'll come by to see you with me on rounds later."

"Oh that's okay," the woman soothed. "The more brains on my case the better."

Janis smiled, then launched into a series of questions to gather more of the woman's cardiac history. She asked about cholesterol, how well she had done controlling her diabetes over the years, exercise, and a myriad of other points relevant to the consultation.

"May I examine you?" Janis asked after a few minutes, placing a small note pad and pen on the bedside table.

"Of course."

"Would you turn your head this way?" Janis asked, gently pushing Mrs. Logan's head to her left. She examined the patient's neck veins. "Now the other way," and she looked at the other side. Janis placed the second and third fingers of her right hand on the woman's carotid artery, taking note of its intensity and the speed of its rise and fall. Next, she took her stethoscope out of a side pocket of her white coat, and positioned the earpieces in her ears. Briefly cupping the head of the scope to warm it, she placed it first over the patient's left carotid artery, and listened, then placed it on the other carotid. She heard no bruits, the murmur like sound that would indicate atherosclerotic narrowing of those large vessels to the head.

"Okay, let's check out the ticker. I'm going to untie the back of your jonnie." With the patient still reclining in the bed, Janis reached behind the base of her neck and undid the cotton ribbons tied there. The jonnie loosened, Janis slipped her stethoscope under it, and carefully listened for the sounds of illness. There were none of significance save for the murmur, and that didn't seem like any big deal.

The exam went on a bit longer, and when she was finished, Janis pocketed her stethoscope, and sat down on the edge of Mrs. Logan's bed facing her.

"Well, you know what I think Mrs. Logan?" Janis said, smiling.

"Call me Mary, dear."

Janis' smile broadened. "Mary, I think you're going to be fine. I don't like the fact that the pain came back a couple of times, but we have options for that."

"Like what?" there was nothing challenging or frightened in the question, only interest.

"The most aggressive case scenario would be a cardiac cath."

"My husband had one of those."

Janis nodded.

"Unfortunately, he had to have a bypass, and died of complications." The elderly lady's gray eyes misted a bit for a moment.

"We're not going to let anything bad happen to you. How long were you married?"

"Sixty two years. He's been gone three now. How I miss his kindness and his good looks. We met in graduate school, and both went on to teach at the same university."

"Do you have any children?"

"Oh yes, four. Of course they're all grown and scattered all over the country now. My son is coming in this evening. You might get to meet him."

"I would love that." Janis replied. She liked this articulate, educated woman. Though old, her voice was clear, and her thoughts quick. She had known love and loss. She had given a whole career to teaching the beauty of words and symbols to others. And she was still lovely, with her high cheekbones, high forehead and haunting eyes.

"I'm going to go write some brilliant words of wisdom in your record now," Janis said, holding the patient's hand briefly. "I'll probably see you later this afternoon when we make cardiac rounds. I'll be with another cardiac fellow and Dr. O'Brien, the staff cardiologist on service this month."

"It was very nice to meet you Dr. Michaels. Thank you for your help." Janis smiled at her, and gave her a quick wave by quickly flexing the fingers of her right hand as she rose from the bed.

Once again seated at the desk in the glassed-in room, Janis opened Mrs. Logan's chart in the computer, and began to type.

3

It was time to feed again. Once a month for the few days when the moon was at its fullest the creature's appetite would rise, and it would hunt. In between it would lie in hiding, resting, waiting; but when the hunger came it could not be resisted. Because it was predicated on a lunar cycle it was important for the creature to gorge, and it was common after a good hunt for it to feel bloated, heavy and lethargic for days.

It could hunt most animals, but it preferred members of the herd. Sometimes, but not often, they could be a challenge to bring down, and those times gave the creature pleasure, but most times they were stupid and frightened, and there was no exhilaration of the chase. Still, they were the creature's favorite. The taste of their flesh was very pleasing, their marrow sweet, but their blood; oh their blood was exquisite. It tasted different from that of all the other types of prey in the world, and was worth suffering a tepid hunt.

The stalker and its kind preferred temperate climates, and over time had hunted all over Europe, North America and parts of Asia. The species was very ancient, and had been present since before the early days of man. It had always been composed of solitary, secretive hunters on the move. It mated rarely, perhaps once every twelve hundred to fifteen hundred moon cycles. This, and its long gestation kept its population small, which was good, because there was always plenty of game available as a result, and the herd gained no collective memory of the terrifying occasional entity that sometimes culled their number.

This month's hunt was of particular importance to the creature. It was feeling the first stages of the reproductive urges in a new breeding cycle, and it would need nourishment as it changed in preparation. Already

---

it sensed another of its kind nearby, and both had come to know that the preliminary scents were auspicious. Mating could be dangerous. The species was purely carnivorous, and had no communal loyalty of its own. A creature misunderstanding the signals of another at its own mating time could be severely injured or even eaten itself. Competition was its way. It competed with the world around it, and it competed with itself. The result was that over eons the species had become refined, intelligent and ruthless without love. This applied even to its young. While females would usually keep their young with them for a few years after birth, if times became hard, with insufficient food, then without remorse a mother would often not hesitate to bite its young through the neck, and add it to its own energy sources.

The hunter's urge to reproduce, once commenced, was insistent and unremitting. It was not propelled to copulate immediately, rather it moved through a series of irresistible urges that defined behaviors long proven successful to its survival. First it required increased internal protein and calorie stores. This was needed for the profound physiologic stress and body changes that would accompany the long pregnancy. The hunt would need to be refined during this period of time. There would be more killing, and it was of paramount importance that the herd not be panicked by the escalating carnage. Picking off loners, the hunter's usual method of victim selection would not be adequate during this time. It would move into the herd, hiding in crevasses and dark places, moving like a shadow in the background, a chameleon that blended in, not by changing color, but by contorting its shape to mold into its environment. In this manner, during the correct time in the lunar cycle, it would glide along with the herd, watching, waiting, listening. Its eyes would move continuously, unblinking, lest they miss a fleeting instant of vulnerability in its quarry. In this mode, no member of the congregated food source was beyond attack. The bulls were more of a threat than the cows or calves given their superior size and strength, but none of them were very dangerous when taken by surprise and overwhelmed with an explosion of courage vaporizing violence. It was the shock and violence of the hunter's attacks that often made it unnecessary for it to compress the glands in its cheeks and eject a spray of poison through its gaping mouth lined with serrated, pointed fangs.

The second urge in the mating cycle was the selection of a post coital nest. This would, perforce, be a carefully chosen, inconspicuous enclosure. Natural formations were preferred, but, if necessary, the creature would fashion its own shelter. The proper choice and preparation of the nest was critical, as it would house the creature during its dormancy while gestating, the most vulnerable phase of its life. Discovery at this stage would lead the creature to complete and utter vulnerability to attack.

Next the rutting process would begin. This was preceded by the male and female beginning a careful search one for the other; each tentatively selected by the other some time prior. At first the search was by scent, and by a dim awareness of the other's thoughts. As the predators drew cautiously closer to each other over the ensuing few days, they would begin to emit high-pitched sounds in a frequency range inaudible to the hunted. Ultimately, guided in this manner, the two aroused beasts would find each other. They would begin to circle each other cautiously for hours, facing each other as they did this, occasionally baring their fangs and emitting hissing noises. When the actual act of copulation itself occurred, it was quick and bloody, each beast leaving its linear clawed markings, carved during clasping, on the other.

Finally, the female hunter would seek sanctuary in its redoubt made formidable only by its new, implacable inhabitant. There the creature would disappear from the world. In like manner to its post gorge lethargy, it would partly burrow into the ground leaving only its head and neck exposed. Unlike the post gorge state, it would completely lose consciousness until birth was eminent, thus conserving energy and insulating its body somewhat to changes in ambient temperature. It would emerge to give birth.

Now the hunter craved meat. It drooled a little saliva as it thought of the sweet taste of blood. It wanted blood, large quantities of it. The need was imperative. The need was immediate. The moon was full.

It had begun to mingle with the herd, and, as usual, the lesser animals had no idea as to what was among them. The problem was that this current cluster of the greater herd was densely populated, and there was a real hazard to bringing the game down in this circumstance. In numbers, if properly rallied, the prey could pose a hazard. Encirclement was the most feared maneuver. In sufficient numbers the potential victims could overcome their fear, and overpower an encircled hunter insufficiently experienced to avoid such a circumstance. Such misfortune could result in severe injury or, rarely, even death.

No, the stalker would need to be clever.

Stealth, unobtrusive presence, and an unflagging capacity for patience mark all successful predators. This one had the added advantage of intelligence. Equipped with a full set of feral instincts, this creature and its kind could also reason. Its memory was excellent, and it possessed analytic ability. Although it had no written communication, on the rare occasion of peaceful encounters with its own type, it could exchange ideas with a complicated set of vocalizations and gestures; and so, in that manner, it had developed its traditions.

Today it had been watching the young and the elderly with particular intensity. But the females were watching the young closely, and the elderly were scarce. Furthermore, the considerable congestion of beasts continued to change its spontaneous formations confounding the stalker's attempts to anticipate the positions of victims.

It was hungry. It was angry. It fought to control its growing impulse to simply hurl itself into an attack and bring down its game.

There were many scents today. The creature could smell the total herd, of course, and within that could differentiate reproductive age males and females; it could also detect the odor of refuse. There was something else now, however, that had not been there before. The scent was familiar. At first the new scent was mild and evanescent. But as the creature continued to move it got stronger. Now it was recognizable; it was the smell of carrion. Some of the hunted had died on their own, and others were ill. The creature preferred living prey, but hunger could drive it not only to eat the dead, but even the decomposing. This was such a time.

4

"Oh, Lord," Janis groaned as she once again peered at a message on her beeper screen. Consult in E.D. ASAP. What the hell do they mean ASAP? Is it Stat or not? From the threshold of the ICU, where she was about to leave, she walked back to the secretary's area, went behind the counter, and sat down in front of a telephone. She picked up the receiver, and punched in the four numbers. On the fifth ring the unit secretary in the E.D. picked up the phone.

"Emergency Department, Katherine speaking. How may I direct your call?

"This is Dr. Michaels. You guys called me?"

There was a brief pause, then, "Yes Dr. Michaels. Just a minute please, Dr. Smith would like to speak with you."

A vague unpleasant sensation briefly stole over Janis. Mark Smith was a taciturn, nasty tempered physician who complained incessantly about his work and his colleagues. His greatest talent was to expedite disposition of E.D. patients. He wanted them worked up and out as fast as possible. In and of itself this was not a bad thing as it prevented the Emergency Department from backing up, but Smith's style left a lot to be desired. He rode verbal roughshod over anybody he perceived to have the temerity to disagree with or otherwise obstruct his plans, and his work ups could, at times, be superficial. Janis was not looking forward to the conversation.

"Janis?" there was no warmth in the voice from the receiver.

"Yes, hi Bob."

"I've got an odd one for you down here. A Jane Doe, teenager, with a severe bradycardia, but good B.P. Problem is I don't feel safe sending her out with a pulse this low. Bp's okay…about 110 over 60."

"How low is the pulse?"

"20"

"Really."

"I didn't call you to bull shit you." His voice was without tone. "You want to come down here to see her, or what?"

Janis felt her face color a little, but did not reveal her ire.

"Any family history? Ingestions?"

"Look," Smith's voice was taught now. "I have a full E.D. here, and you can come down and do your own history." He hung up!

For a moment Janis stared at the phone receiver in disbelief. A quality she had always hated in herself was to first blame herself when someone else treated her badly. She was reflexly doing that now, and, annoyed, she willed herself stop it. This guy was an ass hole. She wanted to punch him, but knew she never would. She had been perfectly appropriate in asking a few questions. It was expected. She thought of things she could say to the jerk, but nothing fit. She was further exasperated when she put the phone receiver down, and could feel a slight tremor in her hand. Adrenaline. She was angry.

She left the unit, walked briskly down the corridor, and ultimately came to the bank of elevators. She poked the down arrow button hard several times. Janis was thinking about the case she was about to see, weighing possible causes, and trying to fend off the distracting irritation at Smith's behavior.

Teenager with a pulse of 20. That was a severe bradycardia, and the kid was probably going to need a pacemaker if nothing reversible was found. Congenital heart block? Possible. Ingestion…always a good choice with this age group…but what? The patient couldn't be terribly sick if Smith had even thought of sending her out. So why does she look good with a pulse that low?

The elevator door opened, and she got out. A few brisk paces, and she turned to go down another corridor that led to the Emergency Department. At the end of the hall she swiped her ID card through the slot on a lock so she would not have to be buzzed in, and the door opened automatically with a pneumatic sigh. Before her stretched the E.D. It was a new wing, and state of the art. The main corridor was a long thoroughfare with patient cubicles along its right side. On the left were a series of counters making up individual nursing stations. There was one for surgical, one for medical and one for pediatrics. Midway down the corridor on the left was a hallway that led to an x-ray suite and two operating rooms for trauma. A little further, also on the left, was a short hallway where the doctors' dictation room and a kitchen were located. A bank of cardiac monitors was suspended at eye level from the ceiling near one of the nursing stations. Scattered along the main hall were two "crash carts" each containing drugs, a larygoscope, intubation tubes and other sundry items to aid in cardiac resuscitation. There were two cardiogram machines, some chairs and a couple of I.V. poles as well.

Equally impressive as the scenery was the activity. Everyone seemed to move with purpose. Each nursing station had a unit secretary taking off orders, making phone calls, and otherwise assisting the doctors, nurses and technicians. All the nurses and physicians wore scrubs. The physicians, for the most part, wore long white coats with their names embroidered in blue above a left chest pocket, despite the fact that all hospital staff were required to wear photo ID badges clipped to their clothing. The nurses wore short length jackets made of the same fabric as their scrubs. Everybody's pockets contained sundry items to aid them in tending to the never-ending river of need that flowed by them every day. Most carried their stethoscopes draped around their necks for quick access. Technicians moved from patients to medical personnel and back to patients again carrying out some of the more mundane tasks of the Emergency Department.

Janis walked to the middle nursing station, and the pert Asian unit secretary looked up.

"Hi Chaou," Janis smiled.

"Hello Dr Michaels." The woman's Vietnamese accent was not subtle, but it added charm to her engaging soft voice and happy, twinkling eyes. Janis knew her from many visits to the E.D. where Chaou worked with unflappable cheerfulness and competence. Her shoulder length, rich black hair and her smooth features belied her fifty years.

"Can you tell me where the Jane Doe is," Janis asked.

Chaou thought for an instant, looking up and down the hall.

"Room 7, Dr. Michaels,"

"Thanks."

Chaou smiled and nodded.

Janis walked to Room 7. Before she could enter, a figure from within the cubicle flapped aside part of the curtain, stepped out, and let the curtain return to its original position protecting the patient's privacy. The person was a nurse in her twenties with green eyes and blond streaked brown hair. She moved with assurance, and when she saw Janis she smiled.

"What's up, Janis?"

"Hey, Sharon. Is this the Jane Doe with the slow heart rate?"

The nurse nodded. "Let me talk to you before you go in there though."

Sharon Calder and Janis had worked together on many cases, and Janis always felt comfortable with her. The nurse had distinguished herself for being able to calmly handle many problems simultaneously in diverse areas, and was often called upon when a situation was particularly difficult. She was involved in assuring nursing education activities in the hospital, and sometimes personally gave in-services and other talks to the nursing and technical personnel. All of this contributed to her deserved reputation as a valuable resource person. Janis always paid attention when she spoke.

"Okay. What's up?"

"I think she's on something, or else there's some serious psych problem here." She paused, but Janis said nothing. Sharon cleared her throat, and continued. "She hasn't said a word since she came to us. She was found by a bunch of house keeping people on break while they were having a little party, listening to a boom box on Clark 3. They said that she was wandering around there without a stitch of clothing on. When we tried to start an I.V. here, she got belligerent."

"Was she one of the code 8's I heard a while back?"

Sharon nodded. "She was both of them, actually. The first was when we tried to put in the I.V. She pushed the tech, and apparently scared him, he says, with some sort of facial expression." The nurse made a crocked grimace meant to be sardonic, and Janis looked puzzled. "He wouldn't try again unless he had a security guard with him. He never did get it in though. She continued to pull her arm back every time he tried, he stayed spooked, and finally Smith told the tech to back off."

Smith, Janis thought. The kid has the pulse of a sick ninety-year-old, and he chickens out of an I.V.

Sharon went on. "We let the patient cool off, and then tried to put on monitor leads, which we should have done before placing an I.V. and then it got worse. The patient slapped the techs hand…hard, then flipped the EKG machine over. It broke! There were two security guards here then, and they wanted to put her in restraints, but Smith said no."

"He did?"

"Yes, but I think he might have been right, because she quieted right down then. She just got back on the stretcher, and looked at us. We paged psych before we called you. Problem is, the E.D.'s been wild today, and I think way too much time was wasted because Smith kept hopping from one patient to the next."

Janis pursed her lips as she thought. Basically, nothing had been done for the patient. Maybe that was best for the moment given what had happened, but time could have been critical here.

"Did you sedate her?"

"Well, that was the plan, but she won't take anything P.O. We can't even get her to open her mouth a crack. And nobody's has been hot to give her a shot. I've only been here a little while, but I think that's pretty lousy."

Janis agreed. That was 'pretty lousy'. Essentially, the patient's care had been allowed to come to a halt.

Janis nodded, and smiled at Sharon. "Wish me luck," she said, and pulled back a half of the curtain, stepped into the cubicle, and slid the curtain back behind her.

The remaining hospital guard stood against the wall farthest from the girl, who lay on a stretcher. The guard was gray, about sixty, and had a belly that hung over his garrison belt. His heavily lined, drooping, plethoric face was grim. His eyes flicked furtively to the doctor as she entered, and then quickly back to the patient. Janis wondered where they got these prime specimens for the security "force." Then she turned her attention to the patient.

The back of the stretcher was elevated about sixty degrees, and with two pillows the girl sat nearly upright. She was clad in a hospital jonnie, but it was untied in the back and it had slid down her right shoulder.

What had she been doing on Clark 3? That floor was home to the laundry, the morgue, the pharmacy and the renowned security department. Probably drugs. But entering the hospital naked? Did Sharon mean that literally? Janis' eyes scanned the cubicle, but saw no bulging plastic hospital bag, draw string pulled tight to hold the patient's personal belongings. No clothes.

The doctor's eyes went back to the patient. The girl looked to be in her late teens. Her hair was short, brown and uncombed. She was thin, and at first glance could have been taken for scrawny, but she wasn't. Her muscles, while not at all bulky, were well defined and toned. The patient was filthy. She had dirt smudged in various places in varying intensities, and there was a feral smell in the room. It was obvious that the nurses, usually very fastidious about such things, had been prevented or been too intimidated by her to clean her up. One of the things that struck Janis, and gave her some concern was the girl's color. She was extremely pale. It was not the color of one who had simply protected herself from the sun, but a sickly ivory-like waxen color. It was wrong. Anemia Janis surmised, but there was something about the appearance that just didn't quite fit this, and the diagnostic impression did not sit comfortably with her.

The doctor's eyes moved to the patient's hands. They were delicate with the exception of the fingernails, which had all the appearance of small claws. They were a deep purple in color, and they were thick. Obviously, Janis thought, these had to be acrylic applications done in some punk adolescent style. Ugly.

The girl's face also was remarkable. Her lips were thin and tight and of a burgundy- like color that gave them more the look of being a slash across her lower face than a functional anatomic structure. Her nose was small and non-descript, but her eyes were eerie. They were slitty, with gray irises, and they glittered notably. To Janis they looked cold. They were death eyes, and against her will Janis shivered.

"I'm Dr. Michaels," Janis said, a little tentatively, not coming quite as close to the patient as she would ordinarily have on introducing herself.

The girl had fixed her eyes on her the instant Janis had entered the cubicle. Her look was cold, intelligent and calculating. This child was obviously alert. She may have been looking for drugs on Clark 3, but Janis doubted she was on anything now. She was neither too up nor too down, just very alert. There was no fear that Janis could discern.

"I'm from the cardiology department, and the staff here asked me to check you out because your pulse is kind of slow." Janice smiled at her, but the patient remained impassive.

Abuse victim? Janis wondered. Some sort of posttraumatic shock syndrome? She moved to the stretcher and rested her hand on the raised guardrail. The patient's eyes were instantly on the hand, and Janis, picking up the signal as troubled, quickly removed it.

"Are you uncomfortable?" No answer.

"Can you understand me?" It occurred to Janis that maybe the patient did not speak English.

"Habla Espanol?" No response. "Ruski?" Again, no response, but this time Janis felt a touch of relief, as that had pretty much exhausted her Russian vocabulary.

Autistic, Janis postulated. That fit, and with that beginning diagnostic impression, Dr. Michaels set about trying to find a way to examine the patient without frightening her.

Slowly and very gently, Janis reached for the girl's hand. She touched it, and the patient flinched slightly, but her slitted gaze never left Janis' eyes, and she allowed the touch. Carefully, the doctor placed her index and middle fingers on the teen's pulse, and then raised her other arm so she could look at her watch while she counted the heartbeat. A full minute passed, and the count was twenty-two. Janis had hoped that there had been some error, that the heart rate would now be normal, but such was not the case. She noticed the patient's skin felt cool in her light grasp. She reached for the patient's forehead. The girl shrank back a little, then froze and let the exam proceed.

Poor kid's terrified, Janis thought. She wondered what the temperature was, but doubted anyone had succeeded in obtaining a reading.

Next, she gently tented the skin of the patient's forehead using a gentle pinching motion to see how fast the skin would snap back to position when released. This gauge of skin turgor was important in assessing her hydration status. Janis was expecting dehydration and was surprised when the skin briskly returned to normal. She wanted to look at the membranes in the mouth to see if they were moist.

"Let's check inside your mouth," she said, doubting comprehension as she gently put downward pressure on the girl's chin with her thumb and pantomimed opening her mouth. The patient clamped her jaw shut, pursing her lips tighter.

"Okay, we won't force it," and Janis moved on to check the veins on the side of the girl's neck for volume, but she was sitting up on the stretcher too erect for the exam to be very meaningful.

Janis, still with slow deliberate motions, removed her stethoscope from where she had placed it in the right-side pocket of her white coat. She held it in front of the girl so she could see that it was not frightening, then placed the earpieces in her own ears. She slipped the head of the stethoscope under the patient's hospital gown, and placed it at four different sites on the front of the young woman's chest, pausing to listen to the heart sounds carefully at each site.

"So far so good, honey, but your pulse is slow," Janis smiled. The patient showed no emotional response. Janis moved the stethoscope to the patient's back, and applied it to the skin. It was easier to do here, since the jonnie opened in the back.

Audibly Janis drew a series of deep breaths to suggest to the patient that that was what she wanted her to do. There was no response. As she opined how else to approach this, Janis became aware of the P.A. speaker in the E.D. coming to life.

"Code Blue I.C.U.....Code Blue I.C.U......Dr. Collins, Dr. Reddy, Dr. Piano, and Dr. Michaels I.C.U. stat......Dr. Collins, Dr. Reddy, Dr. Piano, and Dr. Michaels I.C.U. stat."

Janis's own pulse responded, and she was instantly hyper-alert.

"Sorry, honey, I have to go," she said to the patient quickly and softly. "I'll be back as soon as I can." Her beeper went off. As she hurried out of the room she grabbed it quickly, pressed the button, saw that it was the same code call, and quickly turned it off.

"Dr. Michaels?" Chaou's musical voice called from the nurse's station. "They just..."

"I heard it Chaou. Thanks." She was jogging now, heading down the corridor toward the door by which she had entered the Emergency Department. Chaou pressed a button, and it automatically opened for Janis to pass without pausing.

There was commotion in the Intensive Care Unit when Janis arrived. She was a little breathless, having forsaken the elevators for the stairs in an effort for speed. Savita Reddy, the intern from the luncheon teaching conference and Tom Piano the second-year medical resident working with her this month were already there. Entering the unit at a run from the other end, white coat flapping was the Chief Medical Resident, Matt Collins. The code cart was pulled several feet from where it was usually tucked away along the wall, but it had been abandoned mid- retrieval and had not been moved to the bedside of any patient. The intern and second year resident were in a tight group with two staff nurses and the nursing supervisor talking in animated but hushed tones.

Probably a false alarm, Janis thought. She hated false alarms. It was like when she used to run track in high school, and they had to be called back to start again. All that adrenalin and nothing to do with it. Maybe it was a D.N.R. instead that they didn't know about. At any rate, eager to know what had transpired, Janis walked briskly up to the huddle of medical personnel.

"What happened?" she asked.

"Patient in 408 coded," the supervisor said flatly, looking at Janis. The doctor's face flushed, and she felt a hollow feeling in her chest. That was Mary Logan's room.

"Mrs. Logan?"

The supervisor nodded.

"I was with her just a little while ago. Why aren't we coding her?"

Tom answered, "There's an order 'Do Not Resuscitate' in the chart by the attending, and the D.N.R. is also mentioned in the admission note. Apparently, the patient also had a living will that says the same thing." The supervisor, in affirmation, was nodding again as he spoke.

"She didn't seem so bad when I saw her. What happened?" Janis was not aware that her posture had slackened, and she was frowning.

One of the nurses responded, "It's not clear what happened. Her rhythm strip just shows her going from a normal sinus rhythm with a few atrial ectopics to V. fib." She produced a long narrow strip of paper, recording the terminal events, and offered it to Janis, who accepted it, and checked its whole length quickly"

"She's gone?"

The nurse who had given her the rhythm strip nodded.

"We've got to go. We have a problem we have to get back to upstairs," said Tom Piano, looking at his intern. Savita nodded, and Piano added, this time addressing the group, "Do you need us for anything?" The supervisor shook her head, and the two house officers left. Matt Collins hadn't said a word, but was standing, leafing through Mrs. Logan's chart.

For reasons she did not really understand, Janis walked over to Mrs. Logan's cubicle. Someone had already drawn the curtain shut to prevent viewing by other patients or their visitors. Janis pushed it out of her way, walked over to the bedside, and looked down at the lady she had known only briefly, but had already begun to like. Mrs. Logan's laugh wrinkles at the corners of her eyes were all but erased in her atonic state, and her lips were a sallow pale color now. She was totally still.

Dr. Michaels sighed, turned and left the little room. Then she left the unit.

5

When Janis returned to the Emergency Department, Chaou smiled at her.

"Back already?"

"Patient didn't make it."

"Ahhh," Chaou responded softly, making it sound like a sigh.

Janis noticed that the security guard with the big belly had moved to the nurses' station where he was seated, sipping coffee from a Styrofoam cup. His expression was still sour, but his posture made it clear that he was happier away from the feisty teenage patient in room 7. Janis looked towards that room, and saw Sharon, as she was about to enter it. The nurse gave her a smile and a quick wave, which Janis answered with a similar greeting. Then the nurse disappeared into the room.

Janis headed toward the bank of cardiac monitors suspended from the ceiling, backed up to get a better view when she got there, and checked Jane Doe's heart rhythm. It was a regular, steady 28 beats per minute.

A loud, nondescript clattering noise suddenly came from room 7. Janis looked over her shoulder quickly, and a second noise, sounding like something ricocheting off the wall came from the same direction. Before anyone could react, Sharon was hurling herself out of the cubicle. She exited leading with her right shoulder as though she were trying to break through an invisible obstacle in her path. Both of her hands were covering her eyes, and dark red fluid was visible between her fingers. She was screaming.

The Emergency Department exploded into action. The security cop shot out of his chair, sending it backwards on its coaster wheels. Predictably his coffee spilled on the desk, but he gave it no heed, rushing towards the injured nurse. Another nurse and Dr Smith poked their heads out of different patient cubicles, saw the obvious disaster, and hurried to enfold Sharon. A tech carrying a stack of laundry turned to the sound, and dropped it in a scattered pile at her feet. Chaou stood up to see what had happened, and her jaw went slack at the sight of the injured nurse.

Seeing that Sharon was quickly being attended to, Janis headed toward Room 7 to check on the patient. Smith had already entrusted Sharon to the nurse who had gone to her with him, and was now also heading towards room 7. The two doctors arrived at the curtained entrance at the same moment, and with neither waiting for the other they entered shoulder to shoulder.

"Where is she?" Smith said to no one.

"I don't know," Janis answered anyway. She was worried the patient might also be hurt. An old chrome metal Mayo tray, salvaged from another era, and typical of operating rooms and older emergency rooms lay tipped over on the floor by a wall. The sheets on the stretcher were in great disarray, but supported no current occupant. Fresh spots of what appeared to be blood were also on the sheets and on the floor.

"You think she attacked Sharon?" the male physician asked; this time addressing Janis. She shook her head.

"It doesn't seem likely if she's not here. Did anyone see her leave?"

At that moment Sharon felt the hair prickle on the back of her neck, and a tsunami of chilly foreboding that she didn't understand washed over her. Her senses were on high alert. She had a feeling, intense, cold and gnawing, but she could not quite identify it. She felt compelled to turn, and did so.

Her eyes were drawn towards the ceiling, and her pupils dilated as her pulse quickened with startled disbelief. She drew a breath in past her vocal cords, making a sort of inverse sighing sound. Smith, his attention captured by Janis' movements, turned now too, and startled by what he saw, took a full step backward, his heart leaping into super drive. "What the hell," he said, his voice a soft, throaty, mystified grumble.

6

Scent was what had led the creature to the location of the carrion. Fresh kill was always favored, but these were special times: the rutting season was approaching, and the moon would be at its fullest for only a brief time. A good deal of feeding was required now, and biological drives were in control. Whether the prey was living or dead was of little importance at this point.

In all its hundreds of years of life, the creature had been a shrewd hunter. It would choose its kills carefully, weighing risks and advantages. It greatly preferred hunts made in the open. However, when pushed, it would, on occasion, enter a den of one of the prey and kill it, and if there were a mate or its brood present it would feed on all of them. The stalker had never entered a hive. A hive housed too many of the prey, and there would be the risk of encirclement. In all of its encounters with the herd the hunter had never experienced the terrible state of encirclement by members of the herd. It was one of the few situations in which the creature or its kind could be overpowered by them. It knew such disasters had occurred; such stories were in its tradition, but the creature was smart, and instinctively eschewed any hunt that was likely to bear risk of any significant magnitude. The game had simply always been too plentiful to make risk taking very necessary.

The hunter was now, however, in an unusual situation. Its hunger was intense and unremitting, its craving hormonally driven and reproductively linked, and the lunar time for feeding was short. The current segment of the herd was too congested, and isolated; weaklings could not be easily sequestered from the cluster and brought down. Carrion would be relatively safe, for there would be no terror, no struggle, no noise. The herd would be unlikely to notice if this were done carefully. So the creature made a hitherto unchosen decision. It took a reasonable risk and entered a hive! It was the hive from which the smell of the dead emanated.

Entering undetected had been easy. There was a small, unobtrusive opening near the ground, and the stalker was able to wriggle through it. Its body had been designed, by evolutionary mandate, and was wonderfully adaptable to twisting and contorting in ways that allowed it to hide in dark crevasses and fit through small apertures. This flexibility made it stealthier and more elusive than most predators, and the hunter was using this gift now.

When it entered through the hole it fell a few feet. Its quick reflexes allowed it to turn, cat like, so that it landed on its feet, its flexing knees and hips cushioning the impact harmlessly. It was in a large dark space. The hunter's eyes adjusted quickly, and it smoothly, quickly assumed a ready crouching posture. Head held still, shoulder muscles tensed and ready, it took in its surroundings. There was a noise. The creature had heard this kind of sound before. It was quite distant now, rhythmic and odious, and on the occasions when it had been heard before it was always in association with the herd. The creature did not know if these were bodily noises of the prey or some type of exogenous associated phenomenon. It had learned long ago not to care either, as the sound never seemed to pose any danger.

The smell of food was stronger now, and the hunter began to move. Its steps and general body movements were graceful, quiet, stealthy. It moved rapidly to a wall in the chamber, blended into the shadows, and keeping low moved like an unseen breeze to the opening of what appeared to be a passageway. That led to a stepwise incline with more illumination, and following the scent the creature bounded up it silently. The incline switch-backed repeatedly. While the summit of the incline had not been reached, the scent told the creature that it must stop and push through a thin wall that obstructed an entrance to another passage. It did so, and there was even more light in the new passage, but the creature saw no breach where the sun was able to enter. It pondered this for only a brief moment, and then moved on, favoring what shadows there were. It could see a passage intersection ahead, and bolted to get beyond it. The strange noise, first detected a moment ago, was near and loud now, coming from the junction's left limb, and it made the hunter nervous. The creature wanted to quickly get beyond the mysterious sound it didn't understand. Three long bounding leaps, and it was passing through the intersection where it made a serious mistake. It hesitated with curiosity, looking left toward the noise, and to its horror found itself in the grasp of one of the prey.

This had never happened before. Immediately other prey were all around it. A group of bulls would have been the worst situation, but the current encounter involved a mixture of bulls and cows. Nevertheless, the creature knew the danger was real, and it knew that the next few moments would determine its fate. It began to exert pressure on the glands in its mouth, preparing to expel poison. It shook free of the young bull that had it, but it was still surrounded. The creature moved slowly, trying not to panic the lesser beasts, but its eyes darted from one to the other, trying to determine which was the weakest, which could be explosively assaulted, ripping a hole in the circle, and affording a portal of escape. However, the surrounding beasts looked fit and strong.

A dominant male made an utterance, and the rhythmic noise stopped. This male approached the creature, but made no aggressive motions. It peered into the hunters face, and seemed to study it with its dull inferior eyes. It made its typical herd beast noises, and in response, similar vocalizations came from others of the group. All the while it foolishly looked at the creature's face. It did not watch at all what the rest of the creature's body was doing nor even note the actions of its own comrades, save for an occasional glance at one of them after making some of its sounds. The stalker was braced for the fight that it knew would erupt in a moment. Violence was the only currency of intercourse the creature knew to exist between its type and the herd. All its long life, and all of the traditions of its kind affirmed this. The creature and its brethren hunted, killed and ate members of this species. They drank their blood. In this manner the stupid nurtured them. The members of the herd, while capable of resistance, were usually no match for the hunters, but with the current odds, who knew how things might go. There was no knowledge, no concept, of non-violent encounters between the two species. The creature wished not to provoke the battle at this moment, however, because of the current terrible disadvantage in numbers and deployment. Nevertheless, it knew a death struggle was inevitable. There would be violence if the hunter made an escape. There would be violence if it did not. It was the way it had always been, and the way it would always be. It was not good or bad, just the way of the world.

The dominant bull gently touched the creature with one of its forelimbs in an investigatory manner, and the creature's pulse quickened. Was this the start? It was confused by a second touch. Then a female slowly and carefully looked at its face. The group began to guide the stalker along the passage. They were not frightened nor were they agitated. The dominant male began to lead the group, and would from time to time turn to look back at the hunter, occasionally making its nonsense noises.

In this manner they moved along the passageway. They came to a point where the passage ended, and new passages extended to the right and to the left. On the wall directly ahead were odd markings, the meanings of which were completely unintelligible to the creature: CLARK 3.

7

Janis Michaels and Mark Smith stood as though transfixed for a moment. Neither dared to move. On the ceiling along the sidewall of the cubicle, just inside its entrance the girl was hanging from the ceiling. She was upside down; no bonds held her. Somehow her feet had gained purchase enough to support her weight. Her shoulders were hunched sharply pointing to the floor, and her forearms were crossed over her chest. It was not possible to tell if her eyes were opened or closed.

"She looks like a bat," Smith whispered. Janis was not sure if he was addressing her, and she ignored him.

"What are you doing," she asked the girl quietly, trying to keep her voice calm. There was no response, and the girl did not move.

How is she doing that? Janis queried silently.

"Can you hear me?" she questioned. "Are you okay?"

The girl made no response.

Sharon was groaning piteously beyond the curtain that closed them off from the rest of the E.D., and there seemed to be quite a commotion out there.

"What's she hanging from?" Smith asked, again to no one.

"I have no idea," Janis said, answering him any way this time.

Fragments of Sharon's drama could be discerned through the din that had arisen: "Get her into Trauma Room A."…"Chaou call ophtho"…"On call surgical resident for the E.D."…"Dr. Skorian"… "Come on, let's move it"…"Where the hell's the gurney?"

Someone had mentioned Philip Skorian. That's right, Janis thought. He's on call for the E.D. today. She knew there would be no sailing trip with him today. But they were going to be seeing each other today, that was for sure.

Janis reached for the girl hanging from the ceiling. As she did, she said, "Come on, honey. I don't know what you're doing or how you're doing it, but you're safe. Come down."

As she reached for her Smith, alarmed, barked, "Janis, don't do that."

At the sharp tone in his voice the girl's eyes flicked open wide, and she dropped to the floor, somersaulting as she did so, and landing on her feet.

An athlete, Janis thought, but her thoughts froze when the patient looked directly at Smith and opened her mouth widely. The teenager's teeth were all pointed fangs, and Janis could have sworn their edges looked serrated. The girl spit directly at Smith, hitting him on the right cheek and right side of his neck. Smith yelped and jumped back. The teen looked quickly at Janis, her mouth now shut, once again a burgundy slash. She crouched, and leaped through the curtain, which flapped out of her way. Janis rushed to the door, and peered out in time to see the girl making long, quick, arcing leaps across the E.D. corridor. An elderly couple was coming through the door at the end of the hall. The girl rushed by them and in an instant was gone.

Janis turned when Smith groaned, and saw him clutching his face with both hands and leaning against the cubicle wall.

"Mark, you okay?"

"She spit at me. It burns like hell." He was talking through clenched teeth.

Janis had no idea why he would feel burning, but the doctor part of her propelled her to his side, and she gently placed her hands on his, carefully removing them from his face. She gasped slightly in surprise and confusion as she looked at the skin where he had been struck just a moment before. It had already reddened, and small blisters were forming.

"Damn," she said. "What did this little bitch do?"

"Did you see her friggin' teeth?

"Yeah. She must have had them filed down. Some punk thing probably. This looks like you've been burned."

"I feelth like ith too."

Janis felt cold in the pit of her stomach. Was he slurring his words?

"Are you having trouble speaking?"

"I feel therible." He IS slurring his words, she thought. What the hell's going on here? Was he allergic to some component in the patient's saliva?

Had she eaten some sort of food he was allergic to? These didn't seem very likely given the near instantaneous response, but they were the best she could muster at the moment.

"Are you allergic to anything," she asked. Smith shook his now drooping head.

There was a small stool on wheels in the cubicle. Smith reached for it, pulled it over, and sat down.

"I'll be right back," Janis told him. She stepped out of the cubicle, and told a tech to go in and stay with Smith. The tech obeyed.

"Where did they take Sharon Calder?" She called to another tech, her eyes noting the blood on the floor, not yet cleaned up.

"Trauma Room A."

Janis, at a slow run, headed toward the corridor that led to the small operating room. Halfway there she was halted by a cry for help from room 7. She did a quick about face, and ran back to the room. Throwing the curtain out of the way she entered, and found the tech kneeling on the floor by a collapsed Mark Smith, the stool on wheels having scooted a few feet away when he fell.

"Mark?" Her eyes moved to the tech. "What happened?"

"I don't know. He just rolled off the stool."

She knelt beside him. "Mark, can you hear me?" She gently tapped his cheek with her flat hand, and to her surprise his head lolled over on his neck without tone. He moved his arms feebly and meaninglessly, and said nothing.

"Help me get him on the stretcher," she said to the tech, and together they lifted him onto it. Janis placed her stethoscope on his chest, moved it and moved it again.

"He's not breathing. Hit the code button." The tech reached for the bright red button above the head of the bed, and hit it hard a couple of times. Then the tech hurried to the opening of the cubicle, and cried out "Code Blue room 7! Over here!" Once again, everyone's attention in the Emergency Department was focused, training galvanizing them for the intense act of resuscitation.

"His heart's still beating, but he's not breathing," Janis said calmly but intently to the first arrivals. "He could move his limbs a little, and I think he's had some sort of toxic or allergic reaction. Any rate, we've got a respiratory arrest here, and my bet is some rapid onset paralysis." She heard the rumble of the crash cart approaching, and quickly it was shoved into the room. Quick nursing hands cracked the seal, and opened a set of drawers. From behind Janis came hands that slapped monitor leads on the fallen doctor.

"Ambu bag here, doctor," and someone placed the breathing bag with the face piece into Janis' hands. She moved quickly to the head of the bed, and positioned Smith's head to extend his neck, thereby making his airway straighter. She placed the mask over his nose and mouth holding it in place with the fingers of her left hand, and squeezed the bag with her right.

A familiar voice at the entrance of the cubicle: "Janis, you need my help?" It was Philip Skorian, who upon arriving at the E.D, had assumed that the commotion he saw in front of room 7 indicated where he had been paged to assist.

Janis looked up, and smiled grimly at him. "No, Phil, I've got this one covered. There's an injured nurse in Trauma Room A for you...one of ours."

"What happened?"

"We're not...or at least I'm not...sure yet. It looked to be some sort of face injury. A patient did it."

"A patient?"

"Yup. Some wacko punk kid...who, by the way, must be a gymnast, and has run off into the hospital somewhere."

Phil's eyes widened, "Is that Mark Smith you're working on?"

"Yes."

"Same attacker?" Janis nodded, and Phil shook his head as if to clear his disbelief. "See you in a while, Janis." She looked up, but he was gone already.

"Somebody give me a laryngoscope and a tube please," Janis said. Again fast hands moved at the cart. "We'll need an I.V. and start D5W at KVO." K.V.O was the standard slang for keep vein open, and meant that the I.V. was to maintain access to Smith's blood for the administration of medicines should they become necessary.

Someone proffered the scope and tube to Janis. The tip of the tube was already lubricated.

"Hold on to that for one second," she said, and gave several full squeezes on the ambu bag to hyperventilate Smith. It would give him extra oxygen for the moments he would not be receiving any while Janis placed the tube into his trachea.

"Okay," she said, now taking the instruments. She deftly placed the tube and secured its position with tape. Then she listened with her stethoscope to make sure both lungs were receiving air. She detached the facemask from the ambu bag, and attached the bag to the end of the tube.

"Take over the breathing," she said to one of the nurses. Janis lifted and released each of Smith's arms, and each one dropped flaccidly to the stretcher with a thump when she let go. He's completely paralyzed, she thought, realizing he had not gagged or struggled when she had placed the tube.

"Dr. Michaels, can we be of any help here?" Janis looked again at the entrance of the cubicle where now stood Savita Reddy and Tom Piano. They had answered the Code Blue page.

"Hi guys." Her voice was somber. "Actually, you can. I want to go to Trauma Room A for a minute. Can you take over here?" They nodded.

"First, I need to talk to you." She motioned to a nurse to take over her role for the moment. Then she made her way to the entrance of the cubicle, and guided them outside the room, where she briefly explained what had happened. Both junior doctors registered shock when they learned that it was Doctor Smith who had had the respiratory arrest, but they rallied instantly, and were soon in the room continuing the resuscitation.

Once freed, Janis hurried to Trauma Room A. She peered through the glass of the door, but did not enter, as she was not wearing scrubs. A nurse inside looked up, and saw Janis, who beckoned to her. The nurse went to an intercom, and pressed a button.

"Can I help you?"

"Yes, I was with this patient just before she got hurt. Could you please tell me the extent of her injuries?"

"Who are you?" Janis did not know this nurse. She was miffed at this question given the fact that she was wearing a white coat, a doctor's nametag and had a stethoscope in her pocket. But it was protocol.

"I'm Dr. Michaels. I'm one of the cardiology fellows."

The nurse glanced at Philip who was hard at work doing an initial assessment of the wounds, but he looked up, having heard the exchange, and nodded his approbation.

"She has a series of deep scratches, like claw marks really, on both sides of her head tracking to her eyes. The worst part is what happened to the eyes. They're gone, gouged out, basically."

Blind! Janis felt sick. She liked Sharon Calder.

"I've got to get back," the nurse said, nodding her masked and capped head in the direction of the trauma table.

Janis held her right hand palm up in a brief gesture of thanks, and looked away. Claws? She thought about the repugnant fingernails she had noted on the patient. What was happening here?

She walked back to the nursing station where Chaou was sitting, pale and wide-eyed. Matt Collins had arrived a bit latter than the other residents, and was now standing at the entrance to room 7. He noticed that Janis was back, and quickly made his way to where she stood.

"Has anyone called the cops?" he asked. Reddy and Piano had told him what had transpired.

"I don't know."

"Smith is acting chief in the E.D. while Delebar's on vacation. He's down and obviously can't make the decision. Chief of Surgery's in the O.R. with a 'horrendioma' so we probably ought to call your father to get the okay."

Janis nodded.

"I'll do it," he said, sensing her severe discomfiture.

He reached for the phone in front of him on the counter, and dialed 4453. The phone rang twice.

"Dr. Michael's office," came Melinda's voice.

"Hi Melinda. It's Matt Collins. I need to speak to the boss stat."

"He's on a conference call, Matt. Can I tell him what it's about?"

"We're having a problem in the E.D. and I want his okay to call the cops."

"What happened?" There was concern in her voice

"Let me talk to him, Melinda. I'll fill you in later."

"Just a moment."

Matt was not kept waiting long. Dr. William Michaels had spent most of his career at this hospital, and the last five years of it had been as Chief of Medicine. He had been influential in the choice of Dr. Collins as the Chief Medical Resident, and he respected him. If Matt wanted to speak to him stat, then everything else would wait.

"Hello, Matt."

"Hello, Dr Michaels," and the chief resident quickly briefed the senior physician as to what had just transpired. When he was finished there was a brief silence, then Michaels asked, "Where is this kid now?"

"We don't know. She bolted out of the Emergency Department."

"Do we know if she's still in the hospital?"

"No, but I doubt it. My guess is she's out of here. Probably planning her next hit of PCP or whatever the hell else she was on."

"Did they get a tox screen?"

"They didn't get anything, but this kid had to be on something. Nobody would do this if they were straight."

"Well, to answer your question, yes, call the police. Get them over here ASAP. I'm coming over to the E.D. I'll talk to you soon." Uncharacteristically he hung up without farewell pleasantries, but that was absolutely understandable in Matt's book, given the circumstances.

Five minute later William Michaels entered the E.D. He wore a long white coat, and the usually kind eyes, behind his rimless glasses were serious and penetrating. He quickly took in the scene he had walked into. Most of the staff were going about their assigned duties, but all wore faces stiffened with tension. One nurse stood behind the first nursing station, staring at the central corridor with reddened eyes, tears in single glistening strips down each cheek. The police had responded quickly and three of them stood at the other end of the corridor talking to another nurse, a tech and Dr. Michaels' daughter.

The senior doctor's expression was focused and calm, but behind that interface with the outside world, his mind was in fifth gear. There were several issues he wanted to deal with immediately: The theories of his chief resident aside, was the criminal still in the hospital? What would be the best way to investigate this without causing panic? What was the full extent of the nurse's injuries? How was Smith doing? And most important, was Janis unharmed?

He walked in steady cadence down the corridor. He was a tall man with rangy shoulders, and muscular physique despite his age. He usually seemed to dominate a room when he entered it, but that did not happen now. He was eclipsed by the lugubrious mist of shock that permeated the whole department.

"Hey, Dad," Janis greeted him as he approached.

"Hi, Jan," he said with still serious eyes and a half smile. He wanted to put his arms around her, but he didn't.

The three officers looked at him as the nurse and tech nodded tight lipped in greeting. He nodded back, then turned to the policemen.

"I'm Dr. Michaels. I'm Chief of Medicine, and I've heard what happened here. Can you gentlemen tell me what you know?"

They did not know much. What they did have were a good deal of questions. They were imposing by design, and they took charge of the conversation that ensued. When they were done with them the nurse and the tech went off in different directions, and the older Dr. Michaels asked his daughter to wait a moment. He stepped quickly to Room 7, and looked in. Smith was still being breathed for by means of the ambu bag, and he, his I.V. and all the other equipment being used to monitor and sustain his vital signs were being prepared for transport to the Intensive Care Unit.

Michaels went back to Janis, and gently took her by the elbow.

"I need to talk to you," he said, and he guided her towards the waiting area where the friends and families of the newly sick and dying were sequestered every day from the force of the Emergency Department. They sat down as far as they could from the others in the room, facing each other at right angles from easy chairs positioned in a corner.

"Jan," he began. "When we were speaking to the cops a minute ago you said something about seeing that kid hanging upside down from the ceiling like a bat."

His daughter nodded.

"They didn't believe you."

"I know. I don't think I would have believed the same story if someone else were telling it to me. But I know what I saw, Dad, and I saw that kid do that."

"Then flip over to the floor and spit something toxic at Smith?"

"Umhm," Janis nodded, eyes fixed on her father's eyes.

"But how did she hang from the ceiling? It's solid. And what could she have spit at him to have made him so sick?"

"I don't know."

"Pointed teeth?"

She nodded again. He sat back in his chair, breathed out slowly, heavily, and folded his arms across his chest. In tune with each other, they said nothing for a moment.

8

The creature bounded down the corridor of the E.D feeling something it rarely knew...fear. The herd had been too organized and too aggressive here, and now the beasts would be moved to passion. The creature could sense a unity among those who had been near. It had clawed the face of the one who had tried to touch its throat with two of her fingers. The harsh sound from one of the bulls in close proximity had surprised it into expelling its poison. Now the hunter would be hunted.

The creature's species had a sense that compensated for its sparseness in numbers. Its members could feel the mood and, in higher forms, sometimes even the very thoughts, of others creatures. This was a wonderful tool, useful in hunting but also in defense. The prey would try to harm it now... try to kill it. There was fear in the herd; there was fear in the creature; the atmosphere was electric, and the stalker would hide.

When it darted into the corridor, it had no idea which way led to safety, so it made an impulsive decision. It would return to the site where its strong sense of smell had told it food could be found. It would return to Clark 3. It shook off the jonnie and then in spurts it used its speed and ability to blend into its environment. The first corridor outside of the E.D.had been clear, and the creature bounded full speed, reaching the other end in seconds. Before pushing through the double doors, it heard foot falls on the other side that would have been inaudible to any human ear. It leaped to the ceiling in a single movement, scuttled a few feet to a corner dark in shadow nearly above the doors, and maintained its grip, inverted, motionless, barely daring to breath. The ceiling was high enough for the creature to be above the line of sight of the four males now passing through the doors below. They wore white garments, and were chattering their bovine, stupid

---

sounds with animation. Its special sense told the creature that they were intent on assisting a sick member of the herd. Stupid, thought the hunter. Stupid of them to waste meat and blood.

The group passed, and the creature unfolded its lithe form, somersaulting silently to the floor. Staying low, it pushed the two doors slightly, peered through the central breach, and darted through. Quickly and silently it slid its way under and behind an unobtrusively stashed gurney. It paused a moment and then was off again.

Eventually it found its way to the unfinished environs of Clark 3. The dirty, white painted cinderblock walls rarely greeted the eyes of the public or the gray suited hospital administrators who walked the main corridors and smiled their political smiles at those they thought important.

The ceiling on this level was painted black in the hopes that the contrast with the walls would cause its unfinished essence to be ignored by those beneath it. It was effective and had been inexpensive, enhancing the budget of Grounds and Buildings some time in the remote history of the institution.

The creature noticed all this. It saw that running back and forth across the ceiling was a complex array of thick, black, painted dusty pipes and cables. The tops of the pipes were invisible from the ground. This was the perfect portal into dark invisibility. The stalker leaped up, and with its right hand caught a pipe. The other hand caught on, and the creature swung up in an arc, flattening itself lengthwise as it reached the zenith of its movement to avoid collision with the ceiling, and landed crouched on its knees atop one of the thicker tubes. It backed up a little, and hunkered down in the darkest shadow it could find. It bent its arms and legs to fit the shelter, and it became very still. Here was where it would wait. Those who would pursue it would eventually give up, assuming the hunter was no longer in the hive. That would not take long, and then the feeding would begin.

Jimmy was a deiner in the pathology department. As such it was his responsibility to assist the pathologists as they performed autopsies. This was not suggested in the job title specially created for him, which was Pathology Aid, nor was it the sole extent of his duties, which included tending to the orderliness and cleanliness of the morgue and autopsy rooms, running errands for the department and any other simple tasks that might be necessary.

Jimmy's favorite part of his job was helping at the autopsies. It made him feel powerful; it made him feel like the doctors must feel. The prosector and the deiner were in total control. It was decisive, important work. It was to find out what had made people sick, and it made Jimmy feel smart.

Jimmy was in his forties. Born of a schizophrenic mother abandoned by her husband, he came into the world in the infirmary of a state-run institution. He had acquired the equivalent of a fifth-grade education, and while he did all he could to deny it, he knew in the darkest, most locked up part of his spiritual attic that he was not very bright. Yet he did his best to keep the door to that room closed, and went about his uncomplicated life with a benevolent optimism that was never destined to flower. The Pathology Department loved him. His broad grin, upbeat attitude, the seriousness with which he performed his duties and his great attendance record had earned him a secure position. The secretaries always smiled at him and said hello when he passed by, and the doctors were nice. Jimmy felt at home in the hospital, and in that home Jimmy's hearth was the warmth he felt in his department.

Jimmy was alone in the morgue now. He was mopping the tile floor, pushing a pail of dark, soapy water along with his foot, and humming a tune he remembered but for which he could not recall the words. He swirled the mop on the floor, happy and at peace with destiny. When he came to a stain, he would push on the pole to apply more pressure, and move the mop back and forth a few inches until the mark was gone. This room was his responsibility, and he took pride in carrying out his duties. This was his work.

Jimmy was expecting an arrival. A deceased patient was to be delivered to the morgue, and upstairs had notified him that the body would be arriving shortly. Jimmy's role would be to take the body, on its gurney, into the freezer room, and place it into one of the storage drawers. He would carefully shut the drawer, and be sure when he left, that the door to the freezer room was locked. Jimmy had done this important job many times.

He extended the mop to swish it over another part of the floor, but froze in mid-swab. He had heard something faint and near by. He didn't move, but stood, listening carefully. He was concerned because there was nothing else here to make a noise. An unwanted visitor might be a problem, but a rat would be a lot worse. Jimmy hated rats. He'd known them as a child. Maybe it was a rat, and the thought made him a little nervous. He strained to hear it again, but could not. He wasn't even totally sure, really, that he had heard anything in the first place, but he sensed that something was nearby. He knew it, and he knew it was menacing. The hairs on his arms tingled.

I'm just imagining it, he lied to himself, but he placed the mop upright in the pail, and left it there. He looked under the tables, doing it slowly so as not to come upon anything suddenly. He found nothing. Cautiously he walked to the freezer room, and grabbed the chrome handle of the door. He pulled it so that the bottom moved outward toward him with a click, and then he carefully opened it. He could look directly down his line of sight through the opened door to the far wall of the cold room. He saw nothing troublesome. He opened the door fully and leaned his torso in. His neck craned first to the left, and his eyes saw nothing. Then he looked to the right…again nothing. He brought his head out of the freezer.

That's weird, he thought, frowning; then shrugged, and ambled back to the pail. With his big hands he reached behind himself, and tucked some of his wrinkled shirt back into his pants. He tugged on his worn leather belt to hitch his drooping denims up a bit. Then he took the mop handle in both hands, but paused one more time, listening. Nothing. Pursing his lips, he shook his head slightly, and pulled the wet mop out of the pail, and plopped it sloppy wet on the floor. He sloshed it around, but he wasn't humming anymore.

The thumping on the door slammed his heart into turbo drive, and with widened eyes he turned toward where the sound had come. A second flurry of thumping, and Jimmy wanted to run, but as the vacuum sensation in his chest began to abate he realized the sound for what it was. Someone was knocking on the door.

The new dead person, he thought. Someone's delivering it. Time for me to put it into the freezer as nice as I can. He was always very respectful of his patients.

Jimmy walked to the morgue door, and reached for the handle, but stopped before he touched it, uncertain if he was being wise.

Stupid, he thought. Anybody else in the department would chuckle to see him worried like this. No rat was knocking to say, "Hi there," and there was nothing to be scared of. Jimmy didn't like it when others chuckled at him unless he was trying to be funny. He grabbed the doorknob, and turned the handle.

He could feel the breeze from the big door moving as he pulled it in quickly and with some force. Then he sighed.

"Hi," he said to the two young adult male attendants who stood at the front and back of a stretcher in their white wrinkled uniforms.

"Hey, Jimmy. How you doin' man," said the front one. Jimmy smiled at him, and nodded. He knew him, and he was okay. He eyed the man at the foot of the stretcher, and Jimmy didn't know this one. He felt a little reserved as he always did with new people, but he nodded to be polite. The man nodded back.

"You got the papers for me?" Jimmy asked in a soft voice, his eyes running over the stretcher on top of which lay a mounded, unmoving lump covered by a clean white sheet. The front attendant proffered a clipboard with several attached papers on it.

"Got 'em right here,"

Jimmy accepted the clipboard, and pretended to read the first page. Then he reached into his shirt pocked to retrieve a pen, fingers trolling for it as his eyes returned to the clipboard. The top form looked like what he usually received so he felt it must be in order. He flipped the other pages, concluding summarily the same thing for the whole packet. Then he signed his name, and returned the papers to the man who had given them to him.

Jimmy remembered to check the decedent's thin hospital I.D. bracelet, and read the name, saying it softly, "Mary Logan."

Next he helped the two men wheel the body into the center of the morgue, where they left it, stretcher and all.

After the two attendants left Jimmy went back into the freezer room, without thinking closing the door behind him as he always did, and pulled out a preselected drawer.

The creature did not leave its obscure shelter for a long time. Eventually, however, its sense told it that the search for it had halted, at least for now. Like a shadow passing over the pipe it slipped around it, and dropped silently to the floor. Crouching, it listened, then sprinted toward the source of the scent of carrion. There was the smell of many dead, most faded with time, but it knew that this was a place where the dead were stored. There was another moveable fragment of wall to pass through. It had been left ajar, and the creature smoothly, snake-like unflexed its arm and applied its left palm to the door pushing slowly and firmly. The door gave way without noise. Cool, but unhealthy air washed over the predator, its nostrils flaring, saliva flowing. It crouched again, readying itself to enter the room. Its eyes darted around quickly, then it bounded toward the stretcher in the center of the morgue. It did not see the human in the freezer room, and could not hear him as the room's insulated door was clicked shut. The predator stood straight up at the side of the stretcher, and with its right hand, short dark claws digging in, it gripped the sheet, and threw it off the body.

Jimmy was thunder struck. He stood inside the freezer room looking out through the door's narrow, vertical, wire mesh window. He had never seen a real naked woman before. Pictures, yes, but not a real live one. And there she was, right in the center of his morgue, standing by the stretcher, and not a stitch of clothing on. Her short brown hair was wild, and she was filthy, but still…a naked girl in his morgue. Jimmy had no idea what he should do. His hand reached for the interior door handle, but it froze on the way. What was she doing? She had ripped the sheet off the dead body, and thrown it on the floor. Then he gasped, sucking in air, and cutting it off as his throat closed. What was happening could not be. He felt his vision graying out, and fought not to faint.

The creature looked at the form on the stretcher for only the instant it took to scan it for problems. There were none. It retracted its dark lips revealing its sharp serrated fangs, its mouth stretched wide as if it were unhinging, and the creature's face plunged forward over Mrs. Logan's abdomen. The teeth bit deeply into the flesh, which tented up as the creature's head pulled away from the body. Its head tugged hard to the left and the right then broke free with its prize. The hunter raised its head further, face looking towards the ceiling, and the large mass of skin, fat, and muscle dropped into its throat.

Jimmy, though his vision was dimmed, could see a moving bulge as the glutinous mouthful descended in the creature's throat. Jimmy thought he would die when the girl looked directly at the window where he was watching. His heart seemed to seize up, and his sphincters slackened. Then he remembered that the glass was mirrored. He could see out, but this monster could not see in.

While he did not know that he was doing it, his hand was in his trousers pocket fiercely gripping his ancient, nearly worn-out rabbit's foot. It had been given to him by the only relative he had ever known. When he was ten, an uncle, curious to see who he was, came to visit him in the State Home For Boys in which he grew up. The man had spent an afternoon with him, and had taken him to an amusement park, and bought him candy and the rabbit's foot. That day had forever after been the zenith of Jimmy's childhood memories, and the rabbit's foot was his lucky comforter. The uncle never returned for another visit.

Though a grown man, it was the hand of a child that now held the talisman. The creature's mouth opened again, but Jimmy's eyes were closed, and he turned away, his back to the door, and he let himself slide down it to a squatting position on the floor. He didn't move. He barely breathed. He was cold.

9

To say it had been a miserable day would not come close to describing it, Janis thought as she stood in front of the full-length mirror on the back of her bedroom door. She was numbed by what had happened to Sharon and Smith. On top of that nightmare there had still been the rest of her work to complete. The day had ground on with unrelenting slowness, precluding an early escape from the hospital to go sailing. Now, at least, she and Phil were going to have dinner. She needed to talk. She hoped Phil was in a frame of mind to do that. He could alternate between taciturn absence without going anywhere, and empathic interest in what she felt. She hoped for the latter.

Janis raised her arms, and ran her fingers through her hair, then shook her head lightly to loosen it. She looked at herself critically in the mirror, and applied her favorite shade of lipstick.

"Okay," she said softly to her reflection, and moved briskly out of her room, down the short hallway of her apartment and into tiny foyer before the door. She felt something brush against her leg.

"Hey there little guy. How you are doing?" She smiled at the cat flirting with her for a little affection before she left. She bent down, rubbed his head, and scratched his back. Her hand moved to his ears, caressing them gently. Then she moved her fingers to his throat, and she could feel the rich vibrations of his purring.

"You stay out of trouble while I'm gone. No parties, and don't play my music too loudly." She smiled again, and as if he had understood her, the cat rubbed his head into her hand in loving appreciation.

"I won't be out late, Elvis," and Janis scratched his head one more time.

The restaurant was small and dark, and well known for its Italian cuisine. Janis and Philip were in a corner booth; she had been doing most of the talking. Ordinarily it might have been the start of a romantic evening, well deserved after an extreme day, but this was not to be a romantic night for Janis.

Phil looked tired, and his tone of voice confirmed it, "Janis, it's been a long day, could we talk about something else?" Janis knew which of his personae he would embody tonight. Still, she resisted.

"There was no chance to salvage the eyes?"

"There were no eyes. Just debridement. That was all we could do."

"I heard Smith is beginning to move a little." Phil nodded in response. Janis continued, "That hanging upside down was unbelievable. I have no idea how she…"

"The operative word here is 'unbelievable,' Janis." His voice was low and hardened. "I've heard you tell that hysterical tale too many times today."

Janis could feel her cheeks flush in a wash of insulted disbelief at his words and his tone.

"I don't know what you really saw, but it wasn't some human bat. I do know that one of the best nurses in the hospital was disabled today, and a doctor I've shared a lot of cases with is down with God knows what. It's hard enough to process all that without having to imagine this gothic nonsense."

Janis said nothing. She wanted to say something, but she couldn't think of proper words. One thing she knew she was not was hysterical…ever. Philip looked at his food, and avoided her face. The silence was tangible. When she finally opened her mouth to speak, her cell phone rang.

Janis opened her purse, and without fumbling removed the little phone, placing it to her ear.

"Hello?…Hi Dad."

Phil looked up.

A brief silence as she listened, then…"You're kidding." Her tone was measured. "Where do they want to meet?…Are you serious. What happened?…Who?…Okay, sure…I'll be right there…See you in a bit." She stood up.

"What was that all about?" Phil asked.

"My father," her words blunt in tenor. "There's been another incident at the hospital. It looks like my imaginary friend has struck again."

"I didn't say you imagined her."

"I have to go. I'll take a cab." Before he could respond she turned, and walked away quickly.

By the time the cab left her off at the hospital Janis was barely thinking of Phil. Her father had said that there had been an attack in the morgue by someone matching the description of the strange patient in the E.D. The police wanted to talk to everyone who had encountered her.

Mrs. Logan was dead. What kind of person attacks the dead?

Janis went directly to Clark 3 and the morgue. The place was alive with police, and a crackling sense of energy. She made her way to her father, still in his long white coat, where he stood near the door of the freezer room. In front of her father stood a detective and a uniformed policeman, and behind him, to the side, sat Jimmy, a blanket draped around him as he shivered on a stool. Janis knew Jimmy from his many travels in the hospital. Mildly challenged, dedicated to his job and engagingly friendly, many people, including the younger Dr. Michaels, knew and liked him. Jimmy looked terrible now.

"Hi, Jimmy," she greeted him solicitously. "You okay?"

In response he looked up at her miserably, his face pale, his lower lip trembling, saying nothing.

Janis turned to her father, who smiled at her tight lipped as he nodded a greeting. He was glad that she was there.

"This is my daughter," he announced to the two policemen with him. "She's a cardiology fellow here, and got a good look at the person Jimmy was describing."

The two policemen turned to Janis, and she was reminded of the double-barreled big guns of a battleship turning on a new target.

"Tell us about her, Dr. Michaels," the detective said.

For the next few minutes Janis delivered a descriptive soliloquy of her encounter in the Emergency Department. She described the girl physically in great detail, then related the events that transpired after the exam as best she could. Neither of the policemen, nor her father interrupted her, their faces intent.

"What happened to Mrs. Logan exactly?" Janis asked them when she had finished her tale and waited a moment for a response that didn't come right away.

"Okay, you're a doctor," said the detective shrugging. He pointed to the stretcher now pushed into a corner of the room, the sheet replaced over the body. "Take a look for yourself,"

Janis walked over to it. Seeing some bloodstains on the sheet, she walked to a counter against a near wall, and pulled two examining gloves out of a printed cardboard box. The bleeding had only been an ooze, as the patient had been dead at the time of the attack, and there had been no heartbeat to drive a pressured pulse. Nonetheless, like all doctors of her time, Janis had had it ingrained in her to use gloves if there was any chance of contamination with body fluids.

She grabbed the sheet with the thumbs and forefingers of both gloved hands at what appeared to be the head under the cover, then lifted and pulled it back toward the feet. A fetid, butcher shop smell assaulted her, blending with the sight of wet carnage, and created a wave of nausea that rose from deep in her belly, flowing upwards through her body, to engulf and squeeze her brain.

"Oh, my God," she whispered. Mrs. Logan's throat was gone down to the vertebrae. Her abdomen was gutted, its contents missing. Much of the muscle mass and fat of her upper arms and thighs was gnawed away, the remnant beds of tissue left ragged.

As she scanned the body, trying not very successfully to suppress her emotions, Janis noted markings on the lady's flanks where skin remained. They were clearly bite marks where the flesh had not been torn away. Whatever had done this horror had had many sharp teeth, and Janis could not explain something.

"Dad, look at this," she asked her father, not turning her eyes toward him. He came to her side, and peered where she pointed.

"They don't look like human bite marks, do they," he said softly.

"The girl had, like I said, apparently filed her teeth into points, but this is weird. There are too many teeth. Look at this."

There were too many tooth marks to have been inflicted by a human.

"The only thing I can think of," offered the senior Dr. Michaels, "is that she was wearing some sort of oral prosthesis…maybe some sort of dentures or overlay."

Janis, frowning, nodded. Dentures in a teenager was a reach. Maybe they were some sort of overlay appliance, if such a thing existed. This whole day had taken on a dreamlike surrealism that she found disorienting.

"How did Jimmy witness this and survive," Janis asked the detective who had joined them by the body.

He shrugged again. "We couldn't get a whole hell of a lot out of him. As you can see he's pretty shook up."

Janis walked over the still shivering man, knelt in front of him, and placed her right hand on his left shoulder.

"Jimmy," she said gently, scrunching her head down to better see his face. "Jimmy, how come the girl didn't attack you?"

He looked at her miserably, and pointed toward the freezer room. "I was in there. The door was closed. She was here." He pointed to the center of the morgue. "I never saw a naked...She was pale and dirty...She didn't see me."

"How did she get into the room?"

"I don't know. I didn't hear nothin'. I was going to go out of the freezer, and saw her through the window. I couldn't believe what...I couldn't believe what she did."

Janis patted him on the shoulder before removing her hand, and stood up.

"What has this lunatic got against clothing?" she asked of anyone who cared to answer.

"I don't know," the detective replied, but I'll tell you one thing...We'll know a whole hell of a lot more in a little while. We're combing this place. We have the doors sealed off, and in case she got out we're going door-to-door outside as well. We got a lot of uniforms on this one." Then he added, "Would you be willing to work with a police artist, Dr. Michaels?" Janis nodded her assent. The detective asked, turning towards Jimmy, "How about you sir. Would you try to describe this woman to an artist?"

"Sure," but from the look of him, the detective had his doubts as to whether Jimmy would be of much use to them.

Janis was tired when she finished with the artist. Her father had waited for her, and now that she was done she looked at him carefully.

"You eat any dinner yet?" she asked, knowing the answer.

"No," he replied, shaking his head slightly.

"Well, come on. What do you say we go over to my place, and I'll make us up some pasta?"

Her father looked at her. "I thought you and Philip had plans tonight."

"We did, but it fizzled."

"What happened?"

"Nothing. You want to come for dinner?"

"Sure."

When they got to Janis's apartment she offered him a seat at the table in the little kitchen that opened off the small foyer. The senior Dr.

Michaels remembered the humble apartment he had lived in during his years of training, and smiled. He could not identify if the smile had been one of sympathy or nostalgia. He ignored the invitation to sit, and stood, arms folded, leaning against a counter.

"Give me a job," he asked his daughter.

"Janis shook her head, smiling, "No job. Just relax. I'll have everything ready in a moment." And she did. Much of this dinner and others had been premade and frozen against the times when she would have to prepare and gobble up food quickly. Emergencies were unpredictable in her life.

As they sat at the dinner table, generous bowls of spaghetti with marinara sauce, French bread and salads in front of them, her father looked up at Janis, and asked, "So tell me, what are your thoughts about what happened at the hospital today?"

How different her father was, she thought, from the mercurial Philip Skorian.

"The whole thing is just too weird," she answered. "We have a sociopathic, naked, late adolescent cannibal running around the hospital. That's so absurd."

"Correction…we have a sociopathic, naked, late adolescent cannibal that spits some sort of toxic substance." The slight smile on his face had nothing to do with humor.

Janis smiled too. "You could read something like this in the tabloids, but this stuff is going to be national news just because it's so bizarre."

Her father nodded. "I wonder if the police here have a profiler. I would love to understand the psychopathology of this better.

"Do you have any idea what the toxic substance could be?" Janis asked.

He looked down at the table, and shook his head. "No. It was obviously very caustic, and it seemed to be a neurotoxic substance of some sort, but I have no idea of what it was specifically. She must have had some sort of container in her mouth with who knows what kind of delivery system. But that's just guessing."

"Her mouth didn't seem full of anything," Janis offered. "I would think a poison delivery system or killer fang teeth from hell would be bulky. Also, who would make dentures like that? You'd also have to assume that she was missing all her natural teeth. That means that they were removed or were congenitally absent…both unlikely."

Bill Michaels nodded again, and both of them were quiet for a few moments.

"Jimmy looked pretty bad, didn't he?" Janis asked.

"Ummhumm. I think they were going to take him over to the E.D. to get checked out. Does he live alone?

"He lives in a house in the community for challenged but functional people."

"Good. He shouldn't be alone for a while."

"Dad, what do you think happened to this girl? How do you think she got this crazy?"

"I would bet that her life has been full of terrible abuse. The nudity must have something to do with sexuality. The rage is obvious. She seems so far off the chart that she probably isn't rehabilitatable. There might even be some genetic abnormalities at work here."

"You know, she's probably publishable in some psych journal. I've never read or heard of anything like this before. Anyway, I just hope she's out of the hospital."

"My bet, Honey, is that she's long gone," but he wasn't sure.

10

After feeding in the morgue the creature retreated to where it had sought refuge before, among the ceiling pipes and cables on Clark 3. Its belly full, it felt comfortable and satiated. It insinuated itself along the tops of two intersecting pipes, its form gracefully draped about them, clinging like shadows, unnoticeable to anyone who might pass below.

It felt the lethargy now of its own physiology resonating with the lunar cycle. The three days comprising the period just before, during and after the full moon, the time of hunting, had passed. The feeding time was over. The creature would now spend the next few weeks in a twilight state between slumber and wakefulness. The mating time was still to come. It would grow stronger, its body preparing itself for the ordeal of reproduction.

It knew that it was going to be hunted now. Entering the hive where the prey kept its sick and dying, had ruled out its usual style of anonymous killing. After most of the hunts in its long centuries of existence it had been able to retreat without pursuit, disposing of the remains of its kill in ways that prevented detection. However, there had been occasional times of pursuit. Its intelligence, strength and speed, its ability to make itself unseen and the sense that made it aware of the minds of others had always given it the survival advantage it needed to elude those who would kill it.

As it lay in repose, swept away by the oceanic dreamy state of another of its cyclic quiet periods, its mind moved back to other times. It remembered, long before it had crossed the great water hiding in the two masted sailboat long ago, one of the times in the old world when it had been hunted.

It had been a time of crisis for the herd. A pestilence was ravaging it, and many were dying, their bodies marked by the dark lesions that distinguished this illness. The feeding, in general, had been good, but one night the creature, stalking yet another kill, burst from fields of hay into a cluster of dwellings in which dwelt many families of the hunted. The sky was clear, and the full moon was high in the heavens. The world was suffused in shades of blue and silver. Clear, cool autumn air mingled with the smell of many hearths, and while the streets were empty, the majority of the herd had not bedded down for the night. The windows of their dwellings were shuttered closed, and their doors were shut against the vapors of the night that carried plague, but from the cracks came light heralding activity within.

It was into one of these dwellings the fleeing prey had fled. It had been a female, young, but mature. The struggle would have ended quickly, but the hunter had underestimated the speed and intelligence of this one. It had darted into a thicket, and from there dived into a small pond. The hunter eschewed water other than for sustenance. It was not a good swimmer, and its skills were diminished in that medium.

As the intended victim swam across the pond the hunter tried to run around it to intercept her on the far shore, but there were dense obstructions, and the woman was out of the water and running through a wheat field, toward her village as quickly as she could before she could be taken down. The wheat slowed the creature down just enough for the young woman to make it to her dwelling as the hunter emerged from the field at the edge of the village. The girl pounded frantically on a door which opened only long enough for her to dart in. In the still of the village the hunter could hear muffled frightened and angry voices from within the dwelling.

The heavy door flew open, and a large male stood in the doorway. In his hand was a crossbow. He had taken it from the grasp of one of the many dead soldiers recently found in a nearby field following a skirmish. The small battle had been fought as part of the great war that had been dancing with the plague across the land, a sweeping, whirling dance that swept over and trampled those who found themselves attending this grand ball of death.

"No John!" wailed a female voice in the tongue of that time from within the cottage. "Please. Don't go." But the man took another step forward, and pulled the door closed.

"Bar the door," was all he said. He stood on the lone granite step of his house, a threshold now possibly leading him to dark oblivion. John was a large man, in the prime of his fighting manhood. He wore a cloak of coarse wool with a hood that hid his long hair. His bearded face was clear to see in the moonlight, moonlight that washed over him, transforming him into a hulking specter, the guardian spirit of his village, yet mortal.

John knew the creature. He had witnessed its work at each of the two previous full moons. The first victim had been a child of ten. A boy, his nephew. After driving off the attacker, John had forbidden the boy's mother, his gentle sister, to view the body, but he had seen it. It had fallen to him, his weeping brother-in-law and an old woman who healed the sick to prepare the body for burial. All three of them had seen the bite marks that had the arch and size of a human bites, but the tooth marks had been too numerous and all had been sharp, cutting deeper than any human bite could. It was the form of a girl that had been driven off, but it had been no human that had mangled the boy. It had to have been a beast by the markings, and if that were so, then it was a beast of terrible evil, perhaps a demon, for, though not witnessed, it must have been able to change its form. No normal bear or wolf they knew of left marks quite like these, and so this seemed the most reasonable answer. It could transform, but it had betrayed its real identity with its bite marks.

This theory was reinforced a month later. Again, it was the time of the full moon. A farmer of the village, late at night had gone to the communal well for water to help cool the fever that racked his wife. As he prepared to lower the bucket into the well he glanced to the right, and startled terror ran through him like an ague. He saw a huge bat hanging from the eves of a building. An old man was sitting on a step directly under the beast, and before the farmer could cry out a warning to the old man, the bat flipped over and landed on the elder. The two figures struggled, fighting between a barn and a large haystack. The farmer, too frightened to help watched. He recognized the victim as one of the villagers who had grown simple with time, and often wandered about at odd hours. The other now seemed to be a young female person of slight build who now had her face deep in the old man's neck, seemingly drinking from the great veins there. The old man fought as best he could, but quickly fell to his knees. The farmer at the well, finally gathering his wits, let out loud cries of alarm again and again. The attacker, the bat like person turned human, turned her face to him, made a hissing noise, and fled in quick, loping strides.

The old man died before help could come to him, and again John had had the opportunity to view the work of the full moon stalker. Again, he saw the marks of the demon. He shuddered at the sight of it, knowing this was something beyond his ken. This was a dark danger, mysterious, foreign to men. This was evil come to ravage the land where disease and war had not completed the task.

The villagers held a meeting the next day. They would send a messenger to the Baron down the river. He was a strong warrior who ruled the village and many miles of the surrounding terrain. The messenger would relate what had happened, and ask for help. In the meantime, the men of the village would stand ready should there be another attack. Each family would keep whatever it could muster as a weapon inside the door of their houses, and each man would be prepared to fight. It was forbidden for peasants in this kingdom to carry arms unless ordered to do so in by the Baron, but each home had something that could be used. The handle of a hoe, fitted with an improvised iron piece could serve as a temporary pike. A scythe could be used to bring down more than wheat, and rarely when a peasant fell upon the remains of a fallen soldier, the dead man's weapons had a way of disappearing by the time porters arrived to dispose of the body.

Now John, in a great voice, called the men of the village into action. In moments they were streaming out of their cottages and huts, each with a weapon of some sort in his hand. A few had been designated to stand watch for the village as the others gave pursuit, and, except for these, all the men, following John, ran in pursuit of the creature.

When the creature had abandoned the chase of its intended prey it had retreated into the wheat field, but in so doing it trampled a path, which the villagers now followed. The hunter could hear and smell them approaching. More than that, its special sense let it read their hearts, and they were resolute. They would not be frightened back, and there were too many of them to be confronted directly.

The stalker ran back to the same pond that had confounded its hunt moments ago, and hurried as best it could through the thick scrub growth and fallen trees that had impeded its attack. The creature was toned and lithe, and could make its way through the tangles with greater facility than its pursuers. It would gain time and distance.

When it made it to the far side of the pond, it backtracked. It could hear the clamor of the humans as they pressed on, and when it found the right place it bounded up the trunk of a great tree and flattened itself out on one of its lower branches. In a moment John and his band were passing directly beneath it. They moved on, and as the creature had hoped, they had strung out a bit. The last human of the troop was breathing hard, and had a large belly and short legs. As he passed under the tree the creature silently, with the liquidity of a dark shadow moving along dark objects, rose up and dropped, feet first, onto the man's back. The man would have cried out, but the creature clapped one hand tightly over the man's neck. The victim thrashed about, still standing, but the creature, perched in a crouch on his back, was quickly drawing blood from his jugular, swallowing it in deep gulps. The victim was soon drained, and the corpse was left fallen in the brush. The creature paused, crouching on the ground, the shadows of trees striping it in the moonlight. It looked with its squinted eyes in the direction the militia had gone, and knew it could, if it wished, be the hunter of its pursuers. This would be a dangerous and unnecessary game. At this moment it was well fed, though not on meat, and it was satiated. An alternative was to fade off in a direction away from the humans, who had not yet discovered that they had been outsmarted. There was really no reason to pursue them. The stalker would find a safe place to doze and digest what it had taken in. It could hunt again soon enough.

John and his men never found the creature that night. Eventually their battle rage ebbed into fatigue, and after a day and a half they retired back to their village, and on their way found the remains of their fallen neighbor. Although they were not able to bring in the monster, they told their story often to any who would listen, and the tale spread throughout the kingdom. The monster did not return, but fear of it remained. The Baron, an intelligent man, though illiterate, as were most people of his day, was known for the consideration he gave to the well-being of his subjects. As he heard the story told repeatedly he came to believe that magic was needed to ward off a return of this evil. There was a monk he had heard of reputed to have such magic skills, who lived in a monastery in the northeast section of the Baron's domain. The Baron decided that he would personally seek out the monk, and in the brilliance of a clear autumnal noon, set off on horseback with two armed retainers to bring the man to his fortress.

They arrived at the monastery at dusk, their horses frothed from the final impatient push to reach their goal before dark. Immediately they asked an attendant to fetch the abbot, who greeted them, and ushered them into an atrium at the center of the building. The atrium was comfortably appointed with chairs and a table. Fruit and wine were brought, and when the travelers had refreshed themselves, the Baron directed the conversation to the subject that had brought him there.

"I have heard the tale of the beast that has been seen as a girl," the abbot said, his hospitable, jovial tone becoming dark and serious. "There is no question you have touched upon the work of demons, and the task at hand is extremely dangerous."

The Baron nodded, his clear dark eyes watching the abbot closely.

"The monk you have requested," the abbot continued, "has, regrettably, passed on. The plague took him. Though we cannot supply you with the magic you request, we can, if you wish, use our abilities as scribes to record the events as you might be able to relate them to us. Certainly your account would be the most accurate, and once recorded perhaps other advantages can be found."

The Baron was disappointed and fearful for his people as well as for himself and his family, but there was no better alternative, and he agreed to work with the scribes. Two monks served the purpose of writing the words. Each wrote them exactly as the Baron related them, producing two identical documents in an effort to assure that the story would survive.

In time the archbishop learned of the documents, and asked that they be brought to him. He placed them in his great library for review, but died the next night clutching his chest and falling into the arms of a friend. His library was famous in an era when the written word in Europe was not prevalent, and for many years its contents were used by those few in the region who could read.

The creature languished in its hidden sanctuary on Clark 3. Memories slid in and out of its consciousness, as did occasional ideas and concepts and dreams. It was mildly concerned for its safety if, as it believed, it was to be hunted again. Its need for a secure food supply was imperative given the approaching time of mating, and where it now found itself promised an easy bounty of both fresh food and carrion. But it needed an advantage, extra security, for while the members of the herd were not particularly intelligent there were many of them in this place, and the danger of accidentally being over run was real.

In time an idea took form in the hunter's mind, and its simplicity was pleasing. It would use its special sense to identify a prominent member of the herd, and through it read the thoughts of its pursuers and manipulate their actions. This more than casual use of its sense would be tiring, but it had worked in other contexts in past times, and the creature had no doubt that it could be employed successfully here.

As it scanned the thoughts of various beasts in the herd, it found an older male who served in many ways as a leader. The male was respected by many, envied by a few, and knew much of the lore of the hive. This leader also had a female offspring, and the emotional bond between these two was unusually strong. The creature had encountered the female before; she had been the one accompanying the male it had attacked with the mouth poison most recently.

The plan continued to take form. Control the beloved offspring, and there would be control of the leader. In his concern for his child the dominant bull would leave his own thoughts unguarded. He would be less likely to detect the probing mental fingers of the creature's special sense crawling through his mind to learn the plans of the prey, and he would be easily manipulated. Or he could be turned to whatever course was desired simply by twisting the daughter. This was a good plan, and the stalker felt satisfied. The next hunt would be a good one.

11

Janis looked up, and could see that the impending late afternoon thunderstorm was coming on fast. The air was still, and smelled of ozone. A lone crow called mournfully in the distance, and then went quiet. All the earth seemed silent save for the sound of the river at her feet, and the surrealism of it all made the hairs on the back of Janis' neck prickle. This long trek in the country had been, up to now, just what she had needed to unwind. Earlier the sky had been cloudless and the air clear, but gradually, with stealth, a new front had slipped in and brought with it a disconcerting sense of otherworldliness. It was menacing, and, though she knew it was a throw back to silly, formless childhood fears, she felt on edge. She bent down, and grabbed a few pebbles from the narrow riverbank, and idly began to toss them one by one into the river. The erstwhile pristine blue water, with shades of white tracing wakes in the current by the glacial boulders that pierced its surface, had now gone slate gray, dull, and somehow, in a way she could not describe, looked old.

The storm would be heavy, and she had no rain gear. This didn't bother her. The weather was warm, and she liked the idea of being doused and refreshed by what the heavens were about to pour forth.

From somewhere far away on the other side of the river lightening breached the sky. Janis counted the seconds, and shortly a prolonged baso profundo thunderclap rolled towards her. A few large drops of rain began to mark the surface of the river, and in a moment Janis felt them too.

She continued her casual hike along the riverbank. The rain came on a little heavier now, but still without much force. The wind began to pick up, and it, like the rain, forced the river to acknowledge its presence with a change of surface texture. It blew Janis' honey brown hair about, and stroked her face like an old banshee caressing the face of one upon whom a spell had just been cast. Janis felt a slight rush of anxiety, but dismissed it as the thrill of being in the approach of a thunderstorm, but somehow, deep inside her, there was an awareness. This was different. This was more than just a storm. There was great misery on the land, and it was coming towards her.

Nonsense, she told herself, turning her face into the wind to feel it, to affirm that she and nature were part of the same great cycle. She breathed deeply, but the smell of ozone was stronger now, and the air was wet and fecund. There was more thunder, coming now from a different direction, from below the horizon somewhere in the netherworld of storms. Again thunder, startlingly loud this time, and from a third quarter. Janis thought of how game must feel when hunters on horse back with beaters in the bush would begin to close their surrounding circle, preparing for slaughter

There was another noise. It was high pitched, hissing, and near by. Or was it nothing, just the wind shuffling a scattered deck of leaves nearby. Once again she felt prickling on the back of her neck. While the sound was surely nothing of importance, Janis gave in to an impulse, and broke into a jogging stride. Better to set some distance between her and this spot, silly though it might be.

A large, dazzling flash of lightening in front of her was followed almost immediately by blast of thunder that reverberated through her lungs. She startled, darting reflexly off her course a few paces, and stopped. That had been very close. Too close.

Janis' peripheral vision detected motion. She turned toward it, but there was nothing. Nonetheless, she sensed a presence. Something was nearby, something spawned by the storm, and something that wished her ill.

Stupid, she told herself, and then jumped at the sound of another soft quick hiss, this time beside her in deep grass. Her heart lurched. What was that? She had seen and heard nothing definitive, but she felt unsafe and vulnerable. Her eyes scanned the grass, but detected nothing of concern.

The rain had grown heavy, and rivulets of water ran down her bare legs. She stood motionless, and then she felt it. A small, strong hand closed around her ankle. A tiny sound escaped her throat, and she pulled her leg back violently. She looked down, and saw waxy white fingers grasping to regain purchase, and then the hand and forearm retreated into the high grass. Whoever belonged to it must have been lying or crouching in the wild growth.

It didn't matter. This was enough. Janis began to run.

She ran with abandon, her drive primal. Something awful was near, and it wanted her. The rain was dense now, and the wind had become harsh. Visibility was impaired; the world seemed to melt in the inundation. She could hear something behind her. Maybe it was a confluence of storm noises and her imagination, but she believed that she heard footsteps running behind her. She wanted to look back, but dared not.

Several bursts of white light exploded in the gloom, and vollies of thunder resonated around her. She continued to run, and so did whatever was chasing her. After a while her breath began to come in rasping gasps, and she feared she would not be able to maintain her pace for long. As her air hunger grew, she became aware of a new sound. It was the sound of rushing water, and she knew that at the end of a brief stretch of rapids lay a waterfall. In short order her run played out, and she stood motionless on the edge of a great drop. The rain was so dense that she could not clearly make out the bottom. For some reason the sound of her pursuer had ceased, but that gave her no solace. She sensed, she knew, it was creeping up on her, measuring her and planning a final rush. Janis looked around her again, and another round of cannonade shook the air. Panic swarmed her, shutting down her mind. Her body frozen, she was without plan. But the time was now. Something was moving. The only option was to jump, and that was a bad option. But, still, she needed to…

"Oh my God," Janis gasped. She looked down on the pavement three stories below her. She was standing by the railing of the little porch off her living room. Rubbing her ankles with his flanks was Elvis. Was it he who had brought her back? Janis was not sure, but she was thoroughly unnerved as she realized that again she had been sleep walking, only this time it had taken her to the edge of catastrophe. She remembered her dream clearly. Would she have acted it out? Would she have leaped from the summit of the waterfall in her dream, and died in reality, broken beneath her balcony. People would have assumed suicide.

Janis' legs felt weak, and she began to tremble as she backed away from the railing. The night was dry, there was no rain, there was no lightning, and there was no malevolent entity after her. She bent down, and picked Elvis up.

"Come here, buddy," she said to the cat as she nestled him close to her. "Did you wake me?" Her voice was soft, loving. "Did you save me? Are you my hero?" She lightly scratched his fury face, his eyes shutting slowly in pleasure.

This was the third time in three weeks that she had experienced somnambulism. Never before in her entire life had she experienced this problem. She had asked her father, after the first episode, and he could not recollect her ever having done this as a child. It had been disconcerting, but now it had taken a dangerous twist. This was going to require some sort of professional evaluation. But that would be something to deal with tomorrow. Right now she just wanted to stop shaking. As she walked back to her bedroom, she looked behind her, and her breath stuck. In the light of the three quarters moon coming in through the now closed glass door that led to the porch she could see she had left wet footprints. Wet footprints, but there had been no water.

She ran to the light switch on the wall, flipped it on, and squinted, eyes unaccustomed to the light. She walked back to where she had reentered the room, but now there were no wet tracks. Everything was dry. Had she emerged from her dream more gradually than she had thought? She went back to the light switch, and flipped the light off again, then returned yet again to examine her path. No footprints, no illusion with the moon light playing off irregularities in the floor. Leaving the room in darkness, she made her way to her sofa, and sat down.

Janis knew that she was too agitated to sleep. On an impulse she picked up the phone on the coffee table, and dialed Phil's number. She glanced at her watch, three o'clock in the morning. So what. She wanted a human voice. The phone rang, and on the third ring, she heard the receiver at the other end being lifted, and there was a slight delay before Phil's sleep laced voice spoke.

"Hello?"

"Hi Phil. It's Janis."

"Hey, what's up?" She could sense him trying to clear his head.

"I'm sorry to call you at this hour, but I just had a pretty scary experience, and I...I needed to talk to someone."

Phil's voice became instantly alert and solicitous. "What happened?"

"Do you know anything about sleep walking?"

Phil breathed a smiling sound into the receiver. "Have you forgotten? I'm a surgeon, not a shrink." His voice became serious again. "Were you sleep walking?"

"Yes."

"And?"

"I almost jumped off my porch."

"What!"

"I almost..."

"I heard what you said. You mean while you were sleeping?"

"Yes."

"That's no joke, Jan. Let me come over, and we'll talk, and maybe plan how to make things safer for you. Don't go back to sleep until I see you."

"Would you mind? I don't want to trouble you."

"I don't mind at all. I'll be right there." She did not protest, and in a few moments she went back to her bedroom to fetch her robe.

Phil's concern for her was genuine. He cared about her. He liked the fact that she had called him. She was usually so self reliant that she never played to his hidden need to be in control, to be a dominant male. He had never basked in the role of protector with her, although to have done so would have been a great pleasure for him. Janis was beautiful, but not vulnerable, and in some primitive way that had bothered him. He had always enjoyed feeling superior to his women, and perhaps it was this flaw in Janis that had prevented him from being as close to her as he would have expected at this point in their relationship. Philip's good looks, athletic appearance, breeding and casual manner had made him irresistible to many women over his life, and he had begun to wonder lately if his time spent with Janis had been well spent. In his heart he knew it was she, not he, who offered resistance to their relationship flowering further. He should have bedded her long ago, and perhaps tonight's little crisis would prove to be the turning point, in what had begun to look like a frustrating dead end.

Janis made her way to her kitchen, and began to make coffee. Years of being on call had made this the elixir of conversation, and it was habit that prompted her now. She was not sure she had made the right decision to call Phil. Lately she had begun to tire of his unobtrusive but constantly present self-absorption, and although he could be fun and was very intelligent, she had her doubts as to where their relationship would lead. It was his intelligence now that she sought...and the hope that he would be in an understanding frame of mind. She needed that now, and the thought that she needed it irritated her.

Less than fifteen minutes after they had finished their phone conversation the buzzer in Janis' apartment sounded.

She pressed the button on the wall in her foyer. "Hello?"

"Hi Jan, it's me. Buzz me in." Janis pressed the button that unlocked the front door to her building, and a few moments later there was a crisp set of two knocks on the door to her apartment. She peered through the tiny lensed window in her door, recognized Phil, then unchained and opened the door.

"Are you okay?" His voice was gentle.

"Yes." She smiled. "Come in. I made some coffee." She led him to the kitchen table, where he sat down, and waited as she poured coffee for each of them, then placed milk and sugar on the table with two spoons and napkins. There was silence briefly as they stirred their drinks.

"Tell me what happened," Phil prodded her.

"I had a sleep walking experience, like I told you. I've had two others recently, but this one was the worst."

"The porch."

She nodded. "Yeah. The dream itself was heavy, very frightening. I dreamt it was a beautiful day, but a bad thunderstorm came in, and it was violent. There was something following me…chasing me. A pale hand belonging to something hidden in high grass grabbed me. I'm sure that part came from that lunatic kid at the hospital a few weeks ago."

Phil's mouth tightened. The police had not captured that wacko yet, and the hospital staff still remained tense.

"Anyway, the chase continued until I got to a waterfall, and I was going to have to jump to escape whatever was after me. Then I woke up, but I was at the edge of my porch against the railing." She paused, looking down as if debating whether or not to continue. "When I went back into the apartment I turned back, and saw wet footprints. Mine. I saw them. But it had not been raining; just in my dream. When I flipped on the lights they were gone, and when I checked with the lights off there was no illusion from the moonlight. I either hallucinated them or else something really weird is going on."

Phil, though genuinely sympathetic to her discomfort, and concerned about her near accident, began to feel irritated. Her gaze was self-possessed, and her voice analytical in tone. There was no panic, and no need for a strong male shoulder to cry on. He wanted to wipe away tears. He wanted to comfort a frightened girl emerged from a grown woman in a moment of stress. He wanted to hold her, to comfort her, to kiss her and finally to seduce her.

"Nothing weird is happening," he answered. "The footprints were probably left-over parts of the sleep state. The dream…well, that whole mess with that psycho in the hospital, Smith, Sharon and that elderly patient, what's her name was enough to give any of us nightmares. Obviously, the sleepwalking is another sign of stress. I think it wouldn't be a bad idea to talk to someone in the…"

Janis wasn't listening anymore. 'That patient, what's her name.' Her name had been Mary Logan. She had been a widow and was still missing her deceased and still beloved husband. She was an intellectual. She was a mother, and her son had been planning to visit her. She had been a real and engaging person.

Janis knew there really was no good reason why Phil, who never knew her, should have remembered her name, but it had suddenly just seemed so typically Phil. She wasn't being fair, but she didn't care. That was the way it was.

Phil, finished, was waiting for her to respond. She debated bringing up the next thing on her mind, then decided to say it anyway. It would be cathartic to do so, and maybe that would help.

"There's something else, too. Lately I feel like I'm being watched. It's probably paranoia over the violence recently at the hospital, but it feels so real. Nothing in particular triggers it. I just randomly get a strong creepy feeling that something is watching me. The funny thing is the feeling comes and goes abruptly; in between there's nothing there."

"It probably is paranoia. I really doubt you're being stalked, but given the fact that that kid at the hospital got a clear look at you, maybe you ought to tell the police. Maybe you're making subliminal observations, and that gives you this feeling…but I doubt it."

"I doubt it too. I mean, I can get this feeling when I'm here at home, the blinds are drawn and I'm alone. No subliminal observations there. I think it's got to be the jitters, but who knows."

Janis unintentionally brushed her napkin onto the floor. Still seated, she bent to pick it up, and as she did so her loosely bound robe and the front of her thin underlying night garment fell away from her, briefly revealing much of her full, well shaped breasts. This did not go unnoticed by her guest, who felt a surge in his want for her.

After a little more talk he said, "Come on Jan. Let's go into the other room and relax a bit. Maybe a little music will help you", and he rose from the kitchen table to walk her to her couch in the living room. She felt this to be off target and slightly odd given what they had been discussing.

I don't want to relax she thought; I want to deal with these things… and a little music? That's stupid.

She needed to talk, to share her discomfort, and now she had a growing sense that having called Phil may have been a mistake.

Phil turned on her radio. It was pretuned to a station he particularly liked, and he went to the couch to join her. He sat down close to her, and put his arm around her shoulder. Ordinarily Janis would have liked this from him, but she was too disconcerted now.

"Have you heard anything more about the investigation of the girl? Who she is, where she's from, that sort of stuff?" Janis asked.

"Shhhh," he replied, and to Janis' disbelief he began to lean towards her, eyes half shut, obviously intent on kissing her. This was, of course, nothing out of the ordinary for them, but it was not at all what Janis wished for at this moment.

Janis' cheeks flushed with annoyance at this ill-timed advance, and before she could turn her head to end it, something happened for which she had no explanation. Her right hand rose of its own accord, quickly, fingers bent like claws, and leveled off in front of his eyes. She could feel her muscles tensing to strike, and, startled and afraid, she forced them to stop. She returned her hand to her lap, but was stunned. She hardly felt Philip's lips meet hers, and made no response to his gesture.

How had that happened? The hand had risen, and poised itself to attack in some beastlike fashion independent of her will. She had stopped it, of course, but she had not initiated it. The whole event had quickly transpired in the time it took Phil to lean towards her, but that little speck of time had dazed her. Somehow she knew that anger had moved the hand, but had it had been her anger? She was dissociating, this was crazy, and her heart was pounding.

Philip breathed in soft exasperation. "What's going on, Jan? I mean…"

"I don't know what's going on, Phil. I do know that right now the last thing I want is to get physical. I need to sort all this other stuff out." She didn't think he had noticed the errant hand, and she did not tell him about it.

"There's not that much to sort out. I think you just have a severe case of nerves, and that's it." Janis could discern the annoyance in his voice, although he tried to hide it. She knew why it was there, and that, plus his trivializing of her feelings, made her angry.

"Look, I'm not some ditz having an hysterical fit. This stuff is serious to me, and, who knows, it could have consequences. I'm trying to deal with it, and you want to do what?...wisk me off into some romantic rapture, and somehow save me from my fears. With the arms of the big strong surgeon around me I'll feel safe and secure?...Give me a break." Her tone was not kind, and Phil felt it.

After a few minutes of uncomfortable and profitless small talk Phil suggested that he ought to go home, it was getting late, she was safe now; and Janis did nothing to deter him. After he was gone she turned on every light in the house, and reviewed the events that had transpired. The dream, in and of itself, had been harmless. The sleepwalking had not been harmless given where it had led her. And that business with her hand...that was perhaps the most frightening thing of all. What exactly had happened there? Had she developed some kind of bizarre seizure disorder? It was certainly no simple twitch. The gesture had been one of insane violence. What might have happened? Would she have attacked him like that patient had attacked Sharon Calder? She felt a deep chill run up the center core of her soul. Something was seriously wrong.

12

The creature moved its limbs, and arched its back in a slow feline stretch. It was satisfied. In past times when it had intently used its special sense to study the thoughts of prey or enemies for prolonged periods of time, it had been able, with effort, to do just that: know what they were thinking. But now it had tried an experiment. Stimulated by the female's annoyance it had tried to see if it could control the movements of the simple beast, and it had worked! Maybe the creature's talent was ripening with the centuries, or maybe it had, unknowingly, possessed this quality all along. That was not important. What was important was that it had actually made the female move her hand. It had almost been able to make it strike, but was overridden by the host's own alarm. Nevertheless, this was a great discovery that could have huge value in future hunts. Could prey be made to assist in the predation of themselves or others? Could pursuers be misled or even turned against each other with this tool? It was much too early to know, but further experimentation and practice would be imperative.

For now the creature was content just to know that its power extended beyond what it had known before. There was plenty of time to work with it in the future.

It had also done something else while it had mentally crawled through the interstices of Janis' mind. It had learned her language. The creature had done this before on rare occasions with other herds. Like those of other herds, this language was composed of combinations of simple throat, palatal and tongue sounds. It was dull sounding and limited, as were the other languages, but all animals of this type did seem to have the ability to communicate vocally with each other.

Given the fact that it was now known to be in their midst, and that further pursuit was inevitable, the hunter had decided that being able to communicate with them might prove useful. It had learned the name of its mental host, Janis. The sound was displeasing, reminding the creature of serpentine noises.

As it lay in its perch it whispered the sounds to itself, trying to master the phonetics. It experimented with combinations it thought might be of utility, and assumed a tone of innocence to reduce alarm in those it might encounter. It practiced to develop a proper timber, learning from Janis' memory, and it chose the sounds of a nearly adult female of the herd.

"Please, could you help me? I'm frightened"…"I don't want to hurt anybody."…"I'm scared."…"Would you please come closer? I can't hear you."

In its own way the hunter smiled. Then it stretched again, and slept.

13

In the clarity of the next morning Janis felt less alarmed, but nonetheless, looked for her father in the hospital cafeteria for breakfast. She knew that whatever she told him, he would not minimize it, and would give her his sincere best advise.

After listening to her tell him what had transpired with the sleepwalking he said, "My suggestion, Honey, would ordinarily be to give this a little time, and see what happens. The timing with the recent troubles here is probably significant; everyone is upset, and maybe time is all you need for this to go away." He sipped his coffee, and looked at her over the cup. "However, this balcony thing is a bit worrisome. It wouldn't hurt to check with the sleep lab here, and see what one of those gurus think." He smiled at her warmly, and waited for her to reply.

"I don't know, Dad. I don't want some big work up for this...At least at this point. I think you're right. This is all going to go away. I think what I'm going to do is lock the apartment doors before I go to bed, and put the key in some hard to reach place. Then we'll see. If this doesn't all clear up soon, I'll see the Sleep Unit people."

Quite a girl, his daughter, thought Bill Michaels. Intelligent and calm, she was going to make a great cardiologist. From the day she was born he had been proud of her. It was odd, he thought. She would, in some ways always be his little girl with pig tails sitting in his lap as he read to her, but she would also forever be his brilliant daughter, who never shirked challenge, who questioned everything, and who had an over riding desire to be a good person. He was very lucky.

Janis looked carefully at the older man opposite her at their table in the cafeteria. Kind, driven and sharp as a tack, she had always admired him. Sometimes she thought much of him was imprinted on her, but she never let that outshine her own individuality. She looked at his influence as complementary to her development, but never as the development itself. No matter what, her Dad had always been there for her, and she loved him without reservation. As she looked at him now, having patiently listened to her story, his strong craggy face attentive and sympathetic, she felt again that warm, special tenderness that always lived in her heart for him.

She paused, then, "Dad, there's something else. I wasn't going to mention it...but here goes."

He cocked his head slightly, turning it as he did so, revealing his increased attention.

She went on, "Lately I feel like something's watching me. It's weird. It feels like something malevolent, unhuman, and yet I can't tell what it is."

He smiled gently, "Don't you think that could just be an after shock to the recent violence here? I mean they haven't caught that girl yet, and if you're nervous it wouldn't be such a stretch to feel like someone's after you."

"Not someone, Dad. Something. And it doesn't feel like it's after me or looking at me from a distance. It feels like it's actually in my head. Not physically but mentally."

Her father frowned slightly. "Jan, do you hear your own words? If a patient were saying this how would you respond?"

She looked down at her hands folded with interlaced fingers on the table, knuckles slightly whitened from tension. She made them relax, and sighed.

"I know it sounds nutty. If I heard this coming from someone else, I would look for some psychological reason too, but this is different. It's too real. And there is something else."

She told him how she had almost struck Phil.

"Are you sure it wasn't just some strange spasm. You know... terror in the night, nerves on edge. You could have just been hypercharged, and maybe had some sort of nervous reaction."

Janis shook her head. "It wasn't like that. There was an emotion...not mine, that drove it. I think if there really was something reading my mind, then I was, in a way reading its mind. It felt like I could feel its emotions for an instant." She took a sip of her coffee, and avoided her father's gaze. He said nothing.

"Dad, I'm serious. I know what this sounds like, but I can't deny what I've experienced. I know people believe their delusions, but I've never had anything close to psych problems, and I've certainly seen my share of blood and mayhem in my career without being rattled into decompensation. I just can't dismiss this. The more I think about it the more it feels like I'm right."

The senior Dr. Michaels leaned forward, his back straightened, face serious, concerned. "Honey, I hear what you're saying. I believe it feels real to you, but the scientist in me, the physician, can't accept this at face value. This has to have a psychological basis, and your other symptoms support this. New sleep walking, nightmares, paranoid feelings." He looked like the chief of medicine he was. "Would you consider seeing one of our folks in psych?"

Janis felt deflated. She did sound crazy…well not crazy, but certainly symptomatic in some way.

"Okay, Dad, I'll tell you what. Let's just put this on hold for a little while also, and see how it plays out. I won't rule out seeing someone in psych in the future, but you try to think out of the box and hold out a possibility, no matter how little, that I might be right."

He said nothing for a moment, and then he looked her straight in the eyes. "Here's what I think. You have always been a realist, and you're right, you have never shown even a trace of psychiatric problems. However, as a clinician I think my explanation is the most reasonable, but as your father, because you want it, I will agree to consider all possibilities."

Janis could feel her muscles relax. Then she stood up, leaned across the table, and kissed him on the cheek.

"Thanks, Dad," she said, and he could hear the gratitude in her voice.

The next few days passed without incident. Janis and her father went about their tasks as they had before the problems occurred. There were no more nightmares, nor was there any more sleep walking. There were no more attacks, and the general tension in the hospital seemed to have eased a bit. Janis saw patients in consultation, presented them to Dr. O'Brien, who was still the teaching attending physician for her service, and began work on a talk she was going to give to medical students on the hemodynamic monitoring of patients in the intensive care unit.

Two days before the moon was to be full Tom Piano appeared on the ward in the morning to join Janis.

Janis was pleased. Tom was beginning a month rotation on cardiology, and she welcomed the help. She enjoyed teaching, and liked him, and, therefore, she anticipated a pleasant month ahead.

"So, you going to teach me everything you know about cardiology," he asked her, smiling.

"Ah, so you don't want to know too much," she joked, returning his smile.

Tom found her very attractive, and this, combined with her sharp mind and ease with people, made her seem almost illusory to him. He had never been particularly athletic, and his looks were only average at best; this and his working-class origins had, unfortunately, left him feeling that women like Janis were beyond his reach. Still, he liked her, and knew she liked him. It was just never going to go any further than that, though he wished it different.

"We have a couple of patients that I haven't seen yet this morning, and then I have a cardiac catheterization to do. You can come watch that if you want," she said to him.

"Sure. I know the patient you're doing. I admitted him yesterday."

"Good, then you can tell me if I missed any of the history when we discuss him later."

"I thought he was going to rule out for sure," he said, referring to a negative work up for a heart attack. "But his enzymes were up, and his EKG evolved. When he had the post infarction angina I knew you guys were going to want to cath him for sure today."

"He's young, with risk factors. I bet we find something to fix. Anyway, let's go see the rest of the patients." She smiled at him, and he smiled back, but looked down at his feet as he did so. Then they went off to make rounds.

The cardiac catheterization was over, and Janis stood with Tom and Dr. O'Brien in the viewing room.

"Okay, let's start with you, Tom. Tell me what you see on this film," O'Brien said, pointing to one of the several x-rays on the view box. "We've already viewed the cine so this shouldn't be too hard."

Tom moved closer to the fluorescent-lit box. The room was dark, and the transilluminated black, white and gray films had an ethereal quality that was not altogether pleasant. He looked closely, letting his right index finger move over the film as he quickly made his observations.

"I think this is the anterior descending artery," he said thoughtfully, his finger indicating one of the delineated blood vessels, "and this is its first marginal branch," his finger moving a little. "So this is a pre stent film. The stenosis is here," his finger now pointing to a narrowing in the vessel."

"Not bad," O'Brien said pleasantly, standing next to and slightly behind Tom. His hands rested, one holding the other, draped over the front of his buttoned long white lab coat that stretched to cover his expansive abdomen. "Okay, now let's take a look at the post stent film. His hands now moved to the keyboard in front of him. He typed quickly then rolled the wheel on the mouse next to the keyboard.

"So, here we are," O'Brien continued. "The stent is in position," and now it was his turn to point, demonstrating the mesh tube spreading the interior of the artery open, correcting the narrowing that had caused an inadequate amount of oxygen to reach a large segment of the patient's heart.

"Cool," Piano said softly.

"Janis, you did a good job. I think this man is going to do quite well now." O'Brien was smiling.

"Thank you," she said.

"Okay, that raps things up here for now. Are you people going to see that consult on Clark 7" O'Brien asked.

"Tom is going up there now. He and I will go over it, and we'll be ready for afternoon rounds with you."

O'Brien nodded, made a slight wave goodbye with his hand, and left the room.

Janis looked at her resident. "So, why don't you go now to see the consult, and page me when you're done so we can go over it together."

"Okay, sure. I'll give you a call when I'm ready for you." He couldn't help letting his eyes run over her as he spoke, and he smiled self consciously, hoping she hadn't noticed, then he left to see the patient.

For the moment, Janis had nothing pressing to do, and decided she would go to the library. Her back ached a bit from leaning over the catheterization table for so long. She would go to the hospital library, find a comfortable chair, and read a journal.

Taking the elevator down to the first floor of the hospital she drifted into her own thoughts. She paid little or no attention to the people who got on and who got off the elevator as it descended. Tomorrow there would be two and possibly three caths to do. Two of the patients she had met before in O'Brien's office, but one she had never met, and had been told that his hospital record was missing. This irritated her. If they could get it early enough she could begin by…

The elevator stopped at the first floor. The doors opened, and she got out. As she was exiting, she looked up into the open face of Jimmy, as he was about to enter the elevator.

"Hi, Dr. Michaels," he said, a certain innocence in his voice.

"Hi Jimmy."

He stopped, and let the elevator doors close without getting on board.

"How are you feeling, Jimmy? That incident in the morgue was pretty tough on you."

Jimmy's eyes looked haunted for a moment, then he looked away. "Yes, Dr. Michaels, it was pretty tough on me." His simple countenance became tense and pinched. "I still get dreams about it."

"I know what you mean. Has there been anything unusual about those dreams for you. Have you had any strange feelings since that stuff happened?"

"No. The dreams aren't good, but I don't remember much about them. The only 'strange' feeling I get is that I'm scarred more."

Janis nodded.

Then Jimmy's face brightened, and he fished his right hand into one of the pockets in his trousers.

"Here it is," he smiled. He held up for her his badly worn rabbit's foot. "This gives me good luck. I keep it with me all the time. When I get feeling bad I just hold on to it. You look a little upset, yourself, Dr. Michaels. Would you like to keep it for a little while?" He proffered his beloved talismanic possession to her.

Janis' heart warmed. "No thank you Jimmy. You hang on to it. But maybe when you hold it sometimes you could think some of the good luck over to me."

"I will. I got to go now. Nice seeing you."

"Nice seeing you too Jimmy. Have a good day," and Janis smiled at him kindly. Jimmy turned, and headed toward the stairwell, not wanting to wait for the elevator's return.

Janis liked the quiet of the hospital library. The few hushed sounds that occasionally floated in the air always made her think of the peace she loved in museums. She went to the rack where the medical journals were, and scanned them. She removed two cardiology journals, found a comfortable chair, and flopped down into it. One journal she put on the floor, and the other she opened, holding it in her lap. She turned to the table of contents, and chose four articles of interest.

"Janis." The voice was sibilant, but clear.

Her head snapped up to attention. She had heard her name, but had not heard it. It had been a thought, clear as if a spoken word, but a thought nonetheless...but not her thought. Her heart began to race. She didn't move, her eyes scanning the library in front of her, her mind seeking clues.

"Janis, I am with you."

"Who are you," she whispered very softly.

"Janis, I won't hurt you, because I know you, and I need you, but you will help me, or I will end your father."

"What are you talking about? Where are you?"

"I am with you, and now I'm gone" And it was gone.

Her hands were shaking, and she could feel a film of moisture breaking out on the skin of her forehead and the small of her back. Her pulse still raced, and she could feel her heart banging at the inside wall of her chest.

Am I hearing voices, she thought? No, she had heard nothing, but the perception had been real, the thought vivid and foreign. The physician in her knew the psychiatric ramifications this could have were it to root in her, but this had definitely not felt anything else but real.

Isn't that what all psychotic people think, she wondered? Impossible! I'm not crazy. Then what had it been? She closed her eyes, and listened. The only real sounds she heard were the muted library sounds of a computer terminal keyboard being used, and the fluttering of some pages being turned rapidly. She set her mind free to search, but she sensed nothing. There was no alien source, there was no explainable reason for what she had just experienced.

I'm having some sort of seizure variant; she thought. That could explain it, and I wouldn't be crazy.

She considered calling one of her friends in the neurology department.

Only if it happens again, she thought. It would be embarrassing. We'll see. It must just be my imagination. I mean, think of what happened here a few weeks ago. I was in the middle of it, and maybe it got to me more than I realized.

The initial surge of panic dimmed a little, but she remained shaken. Nightmares, sleepwalking, paranoia and now this.

She wanted to refresh herself, wash her face, maybe, with cold water, get up and move, though she had just sat down. She rose, and placed the journal she had been about to read on her seat. The restrooms were located in the hall outside the library. She walked slowly, trying to look as calm as she possibly could, self-conscious that her sense of inner trembling might betray her fear and confusion to others.

Janis put her right palm on the metal plate of the door and pushed. It was heavy but balanced, and moved inward without much resistance. There was another woman just leaving the restroom, and Janis made herself smile, albeit weakly, at her. Alone now, she walked to one of the sinks, turned on the cold water, and let it run over her hands. It felt good. Turning her hands over, she cupped them together and bent over, carefully scooping the collected water to her face. Refreshing. She repeated the ritual, and reached for the paper towels. Gathering a bunch in her hand, she applied them to her face, wiping off the water. Then brought them to her eyes, and pressed gently as she rubbed them over her closed lids.

Janis straightened up, moved the towels down from her face, and looked in the mirror. For an instant her mind rejected what transpired. On their own her eyes squinted, and her lips drew back in a rictus, a snarl totally foreign to her, revealing her parted teeth. A hissing sound emanated from her throat, and she sensed again, a thought as though heard, a young woman's voice, rich in sibilance.

"Do you see me, Janis? Do you believe in me now? You are not insane. Look at me reflected in your own face. We are together."

Janis again felt her heart slamming in her chest at a frightening pace. She tore her gaze from the mirror, and turned her head away, the muscles in her face returning to her control. Her eyes opened wide, and her lips relaxed, closing over her teeth again.

"Look at me, Janis!"

"No. What are you?" Janis kept her voice, though tremulous, low, a whisper, not wanting it to magnify in the echoes of the rest room.

"I am ancient, Janis. I am hungry, and I will be satisfied. You will use your father and his power to mislead my pursuers. I will grow stronger, until and for the mating to come, and then, maybe, if you do all I ask, I will leave you in peace.

"I think...I think I recognize the face in the mirror. Are you the girl from the Emergency Department who attacked my colleagues?"

"No girl, Janis. I am nothing you could comprehend, and if you did you would not believe your own conclusions."

Silently Janis fought tears and a choking sensation. She was crazy. Her life was teetering. She would allow herself to be admitted to the hospital, and would undoubtedly be treated aggressively by others who would try to save her sanity. She would carry a diagnosis with grave implications, and she would never be trusted…would never even trust herself…to care for the critically ill. Her career would collapse. Even if it did not go so badly, she was in for a long, uncomfortable coarse of treatment.

"You are not crazy!"

"You don't exist." There was a surge of anger that Janis felt, but it was detached from her; it came from another.

"You will help me, and to be sure you do I will prove to you I exist. I am elsewhere, and I will give you this proof: On the night before the full moon I will rise. I will take my first victim of the new cycle on the floor of the hive you call Clark 3."

"Hive?"

"What is your word? Ah yes, 'hospital.' This death will occur in such a way as to not attract attention, but I will leave you a clue. Then you will know that I do not live only in your head. You are only my implement. We are not one."

It was gone. It did not take its leave, or explain. It was simply out of Janis' head, but she knew that it could return at will.

Her knees were weak, her hands trembled, and nausea welled up in her. She would be sick. Leaning over the sink, she retched again and again. Finally, finished, still shaking and weak, sweating from the effort, she turned away from the sink and the mirror that might reveal more horror to her. Janis did not dare leave the bathroom for the moment fearing her appearance would attract attention. She moved to the wall, and leaned her back against it, and slowly let herself slide to the floor. She prayed no one would enter the room, see her like this and start asking solicitous questions. The would-be cardiologist, by nature usually calm and pragmatic, buried her face in her hands, completely at a loss as to what to do next. This sort of thing did not happen. She had had no preparation for it in her entire life, and she wondered now if anyone had. And if someone did have a history of this type of experience, Janis was sure of one thing: no one else believed it. She forced herself to breath slowly, with control as she noticed her fingers becoming numb.

I'm hyperventilating. Focus. Don't let yourself panic. Think! How can I think? I don't know what this is. So what! Focus.

Her heart seemed to skip a beat. Her father! It had threatened her father. Was she the real danger? Was she crazy, and a threat to her father? No. The entity had not been of her psyche. It had felt too real. She would ignore the clinician in her, and obey her heart. The voice had not come from within her, and it had threatened her father. She had to go to him. She had to protect him.

He will never believe me. He will be clinical; he'll be afraid for me. But it can't be allowed to matter; I'll make him believe. I will make him believe!

She was not sure her legs would support her, but with one hand leaning on the wall she managed to get herself standing again. She started to turn towards the mirror, then stopped herself, and without looking at it she neatened her clothing and her white coat. She ran her fingers through her hair, straightening it and pulling it off her face.

Through the door she went, and back into the main life flow of the hospital, now turned surreal to her. It seemed misted, dream like. Maybe it was a dream. Wishing it to be so she tried to wake herself, but that was in vain. She was awake. She pushed on.

William Michaels sat at the circular table in the small conference room that was part of his office suite. Arranged before him were the pages of a document he was studying with some frustration. It was the third draft of a grant proposal to study the effects of topical cotinine, a metabolic product of nicotine. He and his research team wanted to study its affect on tissue sodium channels when applied directly to the mucosal lining of in-vitro live mouse aorta. He did not like the r-value of the major curve in the preliminary data that was to serve as the pivotal point in the large proposal. Its statistical significance was borderline. Should the experiments be repeated? No, not necessary, and the delay would give advantage to the competing group in Philadelphia.

Recalculation...maybe, but his statistician was not likely to have made a mistake. The computation was most likely fine. It was statistically significant after all, but...

He leaned back in his chair wearily, lacing his fingers behind his head. He closed his eyes, and welcomed the darkness that enveloped him behind his lids. How many times had he been at such a juncture in the span of his academic career? It usually worked out. This was a good project, and the preliminary data was compelling.

"Melinda," he called through the open door of the room. "Have you got the statistics file for this damned thing?"

"Just a moment." A few seconds later Melinda stood in his doorway holding the file, but her pleasant middle-aged brow was furled into a frown.

"What's the matter?"

"Your daughter just came in, Bill. She doesn't look very good."

Now it was his turn to frown. "What's wrong?" She shook her head, and shrugged. "Send her in please."

Melinda stepped away, and in a moment was replaced by Janis, who crossed the threshold, closed the door and sat down at the table opposite him. Melinda had been right; she didn't look good. Her face was pale. It glistened with a thin patina of sweat. Her lips were held tightly, and her hands trembled slightly.

"What's wrong, Honey?" his voice reflecting his rising concern.

She did not meet his gaze, but held a hand up to indicate she needed a moment to compose herself. Then she sat back in her chair, sighed and folded her hands on the table.

"Dad, I need to talk to you, and I have to ask you to trust me on faith. I am not crazy, but this is going to sound like I am. I want you to listen to what I say not as a doctor, not even as a practical person. I want you to listen to me, trust me and on blind faith believe in your daughter based on everything you've ever known of me."

Bill's heart sank. Foreboding stole over him like the shadow of the rising axe passing over the condemned on a scaffold. He was pretty sure he knew what the subject of this was going to be, but it was the adrenaline soaked nature of his daughter's demeanor that caused him the most pain.

His words were measured. "Jan, we've always been able to talk about anything. Nothing's changed. I'll try to listen like you want me too. Whatever you have to say, I'm listening." He tried to smile encouragingly, but was not certain how it came off. "Is this a continuation of our discussion from a few days ago?" She knew what he meant, and nodded. "It's okay, tell me." His voice was gentle.

She told him all that had just transpired, her eyes sometimes filling with tears. She struggled to keep her voice even, but her anxiety was evident, and Bill's concern for her grew deeper.

When she was done he spoke slowly, with deliberation, "I said I would try to look at it from your point of view the other day, and I won't go back on what I said, but I'm worried you're still thinking this way, so you have to meet me half way. If a few days go by and nothing backs up your ideas and you still believe in them strongly, then you have to agree to be evaluated by someone from our psych department." He didn't want to corner her, but he didn't want to be irresponsible either. He feared she might think he was patronizing her, paying lip service to her request.

"Thank you." She paused, then asked, "When is the next full moon?"

"I heard it on the radio coming into work today. The weatherman said something about tomorrow night being really beautiful because of the clear air and the full moon."

"That's what I thought. That means she, or whatever the hell it is, is going to kill tonight; to prove her existence to me like I told you."

"Jan..." He didn't finish, but looked away.

"I know what you're thinking, but you promised."

"Okay. And do you promise me also?"

She nodded. "Yes, that's fair."

Bill felt some relief. Chances were nothing bad would come by waiting a few days for her to get some attention for these aberrant thoughts. And she had made a commitment he planned to hold her to.

And if she's right a part of his mind asked? He shook his head nearly imperceptibly, and answered himself silently. God forbid.

"We need to prevent a disaster from happening tonight," Janet said, looking at her hands still folded on the table.

"Okay. If you're right about this stuff, then that is definitely our priority. Here's what I think we should do. Obviously, if you tell your whole story, uncensored, to the police they will never take anything you have to say seriously again. I suggest we tell them we've both heard a rumor that there is going to be a problem tonight. We can stretch the truth a little and say we both heard it separately. If they ask us who told us, it's just going around the hospital. We don't remember who told us. I'm the chief of medicine, and you're also a physician, so I suspect they'll believe us when we say we've heard something. Maybe then they'll send some people over, and that should be helpful."

"I was thinking the same thing," Janis said, her affect becoming a little more animated. "Maybe I can contact this...this thing again, and learn more about what it's planning."

"No. Don't do that. If we, for now, go by your assumptions, then that would be potentially very dangerous. The best thing is for you to avoid contact with it as best you can. Again, if your ideas are right, which I really doubt, then we are dealing with frank telepathy, something we know nothing about. How would you even know if it causes brain damage, never mind what it might try to make you do?"

Janis said nothing in response, but nodded assent. There had been the threat to harm her father, and she had taken that threat very seriously, even if her father obviously did not. Whatever it was that had contacted her wanted her help. She would need to be very careful. She would need to think very clearly, and her eyes became more focused, her hands no longer tremulous.

14

The sun was setting, and the creature stirred. Its dream had been sweet and pure. In it there had been a hunt, the game healthy, strong members of the herd. There had been much blood and much meat, moonlight spilling over the scene like blue gray phosphorescent ink. The creature had drunk deeply, and eaten its full, and was now strong, stronger, in fact, than it had ever been before, and if the rutting were to start now, it might very well kill its mate as coitus ended, simply by the power it brought to the act if not for the simple joy of it.

The creature opened its eyes. The dream was gone, but hope bounded up in its place. It was time for the hunt to resume. Three day and night cycles of feeding. The hunt would become gluttony as the hunter's body prepared itself for the stress of breeding. Ordinarily, its intellect and its instinct would have compelled to be very secretive about the killings. Its kind was few in number, and avoidance of detection had been pivotal to its survival for such a long era. It would have concealed the gore and the carcasses to help prevent the detection of its presence. The herd would have found its own reasons, as it always did, for why some of its members had left its ranks. The herd would have been, as it always was, wrong. Now, however, circumstances were different from usual. The herd knew of the creature's existence. The herd would try to find it, capture it, kill it. In a strange way, this was liberating. There would be no need for secrecy here. The hunt could be enjoyed more freely, with more passion. Plans could be bolder. Strategy could be more flamboyant. This hunt would be, without doubt, exhilarating, in a way that most others were not.

Of course, this particular hunt had also brought the creature's detailed awareness of Janet. Curiously it had found her interesting. While Janet

---

was certainly low, a member of the species of prey, with all its bovine stupidity and its inability to perceive the world in the rich, full fashion of the creature's sort, she had some features that made her stand out. She was more intelligent than most of her species. Her analytical skills were relatively good, and her mind was adaptable. The hunter knew that Janis' detection of its probing her had shocked her, but she had not been completely cowed by it as would have been expected from past experience. She had maintained an element of defiance that the creature could not help but note. Janis' mind contained a language base superior to most of the others in the herd around her, and this, plus her other memories, had been most informative and useful. Janis would be a tool for the creature, to be used somewhat differently than had originally been planned. By studying Janis' knowledge it would continue to learn better the ways of the herd. Given her advantaged position among her peers the creature would gain information to use in polishing the finesse of future hunts. The creature would not hurt Janis for several reasons, and to its surprise the most salient was that Janis was...interesting.

The first kill would need to bring forth its promise to Janis, including leaving her a clue. She would accept its existence then. The hunter stretched its back slowly and self indulgently as it thought of ways it might accomplish this. As promised, the kill would occur on Clark 3, and that was, of course, where the hunter had languished among the pipes above the corridor. The pipes had been warm, giving comfort to the killer as it had rested. They had afforded cover from detection from below, and now they would supply the vantage point from which it would choose and kill its next victim.

Its body froze as it heard a sound rise from the low steady drone of noises distinctive of the hospital. Janis' mind had taught it that the sound was humming, a recreational noise. The sound was female, and approaching from far up the corridor. No human ear could have heard it at this distance, but the stalker had, and it tensed itself for what was to come. From the shadows it could see a fat female with short hair and a thick vacuous face. The creature assessed her carefully for the task at hand. Its vast, newly acquired knowledge told it that the woman was pushing a pail of water with a mop and that she wore the maroon uniform of a 'maintenance worker.' She was of middle age, and given her body habitus the amount of nutritious muscle would not comprise a large proportion of her weight. Its bulk would make it difficult to conceal the carcass, and might even interfere with the efficiency of the kill. Such efficiency was important, as accidents could befall hunters, and the creature could be hurt. No, this would not be its choice for this particularly significant kill.

Slowly, silently, the creature moved up the corridor, its body adherent to one of the larger pipes. It was a primordial shadow on a branch, moving as though to the rhythm of a quickened solar orb.

It paused, ears twitching, listening. It sniffed the air, and caught the scent of something familiar. It could not place where it had encountered this complicated smell before, but it had been after it had entered this... hospital. The creature slowed its breathing, concentrating, nostrils flared, and other senses on high alert. In part it was the smell of something living, of something...What was the herd vocalization for this?...human. This human was drawing closer, but the smell was more complex.

Now the hunter could identify it more completely. It was a mixture of the scents of the chemicals that had been present in the room with the carrion from the last feeding cycle, and the odor of a person who had not bathed recently. Janis had known this person, but the creature could not remember his identification word, his name. It would wait now, and when the moment came it would posture itself correctly.

Jimmy had been tired. The day had been long, with lots of errands. He had never lost the feeling of oppressed apprehension that had clung to him since he had seen that crazy girl in the morgue, and the weight of this had made every day since more tiring. He was going home soon, and that would be good. He would go his room in the house for 'special people' in which he lived. He would take his shoes and socks off, turn on his little T.V., and lay on his bed. It would be good to do that, and he liked the shows that would be on tonight.

The others who lived in the house were nice. There were three other men and two women, who, like him, were special, but they had other problems, and Jimmy knew he was the smartest of them. There was also the kind young man with the big smile who cared for them. This one was full of energy, and liked Jimmy and his friends. He would talk to them. He always made sure they had food and supplies, stayed with them at night and took them to appointments. Jimmy didn't need help with the later. He could use the bus, and cherished his independence. He was one of the "upper level" people, and sometimes he would help the man with the smile. The others in the house, as a result, looked up to Jimmy, and he liked that. But tonight he hoped everyone would leave him alone. He wanted to rest and watch T.V.

The secretary on Clark 9, a busy surgical floor, signed the receipt for what he had delivered, and he tucked it into his pocket.

"Hello, Jimmy," came a male voice from behind him. Jimmy turned, and there stood Philip Skorian smiling at him.

"Hello Dr. Skorian. How are you?" Despite his fatigue Jimmy smiled back. He liked the handsome surgical resident, and besides, people said he was the boyfriend of Dr. Janis Michaels, and Jimmy liked her a lot. Jimmy knew Phil from many places in the hospital, but had originally met him when he would run specimens from the O.R. to pathology for frozen section review.

Philip was dressed in surgical scrubs and a white coat. He held a folder under his left arm.

"I'm fine. You're working late tonight, huh?"

"Yup. But I'm going home now. Are you seeing a patient?"

"Yes, I just finished a consult, and I was going to visit Sharon Calder."

Jimmy frowned. "The nurse who got hurt?"

Phil nodded. Jimmy continued, "I don't know her, but it's awful what happened to her. You know, I saw that crazy person who hurt her. She was very scary."

Phil nodded again. "I know."

"How is Dr. Michaels?"

"She's good. I'm going to see her tomorrow night if I ever get out of here."

Jimmy smiled, "You have a date."

Phil smiled back, "Yes, I guess you could call it that; although I hope I can stay awake. It's been pretty tough lately."

"I know what you mean. It's been really tough."

"Jimmy, you know it's actually lucky I met you. I know you keep your stuff at the morgue on Clark 3. Are you going back down there before you go home?"

Jimmy shook his head. "I was going to just leave, but I don't mind going down there if you need me too."

"Good, thanks. That'll save me some time. The guys in Security... their office is on that floor... are going to give me a problem tomorrow about my parking in the wrong place. Will you slip a note under the door there for me?"

"Sure."

Phil asked the unit secretary for some paper, and leaning on the counter in front of her, he quickly scribbled his note. He stood up, folded it, and handed it to Jimmy.

"I appreciate it, thanks. I have to go. I'll probably see you tomorrow." He lightly touched the man's shoulder.

"Bye, Dr. Skorian." He watched for a moment as the resident walked quickly down the corridor.

Another errand, Jimmy sighed. Oh well, Dr. Skorian is a doctor, and this note must be important. Besides, maybe this will help Dr. Michaels too. They could get out earlier for their date. Jimmy liked the idea of helping two people at the same time. Home could wait a few more minutes.

Now Jimmy was walking down the corridor on Clark 3. There were a few windows in the narrow, Spartan corridor used mainly by hospital personnel, and delivery people. The corridor did not serve the general public, and lacked the tastefully framed prints and warm color schemes of the main thoroughfares. The night glowed silver as he looked out the first window he passed after leaving the elevator. He saw his own face reflect back at him, and he felt a mild pang. He had never thought himself even close to handsome, and he envied people like Phil Skorian. It must be nice to have girls look at you the way they did him. He walked on. The corridor was empty, and he could hear his own footfalls, his shoes squeaking slightly as his feet flexed to his cadence.

Unexpectedly, Jimmy felt a presence. He could not tell if he heard something or not, but he felt as though he were not alone. Pausing for a moment, and looking down the corridor behind him, he saw no one. The corridor was empty, or so his eyes told him, yet there was something nearby. He began walking again, but he was moving slower, more cautiously.

This is stupid, Jimmy thought. I hate it when I get the creeps like this. There's nobody here.

"You're wrong."

What the hell was that? Jimmy came to a complete halt, and the hair on the back of his neck and on his forearms rose. He had not heard those words really, but they had come to him as a thought. It had been a clear, distinct thought, but it was not from his head.

"Who's there," he whispered. Silence. "Is anyone there?" Nothing again. Jimmy blinked, and resumed walking. This time he walked faster, wanting to leave Dr. Skorian's note at Security, and be rid of the corridor as quickly as he could.

It had been nothing. Just nerves in the long empty corridor at night. It was just...

"Are you afraid?" The tone was ironic, and if it had been a true voice it would have issued from someone with suppressed amusement. Jimmy, placed his hands to his ears for a moment, shook his head, and said nothing. He turned three hundred and sixty degrees scanning all he could with his eyes, but there was no one there.

"You didn't answer me."

"Where are you?" Jimmy said in a hushed voice, bottle-necked with dammed up intensity. He would have liked to scream, but he did not.

"I am here. I have been waiting for you."

"Are you going to hurt me?"

"Yes." It was playing with him, enjoying his vulnerability as a cat would that of a trapped field mouse.

"Nooo," Jimmy groaned. Fear grew in his belly, feeling hot and empty. His throat felt choked, and he wanted to cry. More than that, he wanted to run, but he was afraid of what that might bring about. The idea of an all-out chase seemed terrifying, and yet what was here to chase him? He could see no one else in the hall. He heard no real sounds of note. This was like a dream. Maybe it was...was...what was that word the smiling man at the group home used when the people there were afraid of the dark or a storm? "Imagination". That was when you think there is something, but there isn't.

"Would you like to see me?" the voice that wasn't really there asked.

"No. Stay away. You're my imagination."

"That's not true." The voice seemed on the verge of laughter, but it was not convivial. Rather, it was the tone one might hear from a dark spirited child as he or she pulled the wings off a fly.

This was too much for the gentle, simple man so loved by all who knew him. His mind shut down, and he began to run. It was an all-out stampede of a run. His arms pumped, and his legs flew. He was not very well coordinated, and so he did not move with the speed he wanted. Jimmy felt as though he had entered another plane of existence. A world of nightmares. The kind you wake up from screaming. The kind where you don't dare go back to sleep for a while. The kind where you want your mother...if you had one.

He tripped, one of his own feet hitting the other. He went sprawling forward, nearly spread eagle, his arms breaking his fall, and slid a couple of feet on his stomach. His panic intensified. His thoughts were broken shards clattering incoherently as they rattled in his head. Stumbling, he scrambled to his feet, and incredibly slipped, nearly loosing his footing again. On his feet finally, he was running, vaguely aware that his wrists hurt.

"Stop now!" the nonexistent voice commanded. The imperative was irresistible for Jimmy and he froze. His eyes were wide, rolling wildly from side to side. He could not gather enough air in his lungs.

It was here. It was right here, but where?

He looked up, and what instinct had intended to be a scream left his mouth as a strangled squeak.

Above him was the adolescent girl from the morgue. Impossibly, she hung upside down by her feet from a pipe, toes somehow adherent and holding her. Her arms were folded over her chest, and her shoulders were hunched like those of a giant bat. Jimmy shuddered as he noted her nakedness, her dirt smeared pasty, ivory white skin, contrasting sharply with her thin burgundy-colored lips. The lips retracted, and the poor man looking up at her moaned at the sight of the many sharp teeth.

The bat like girl's facial muscles were moving, working her cheeks, and suddenly her mouth expelled a liquid that hit Jimmy squarely in the face. His jaw had gone slack, and some of the fluid entered his mouth. Some of it also hit his widened eyes. The contact with these delicate tissues allowed the toxin quick access to his blood stream, and almost instantly he could feel his strength leaving him. He reached for the only help available to him, and desperately pulled his rabbit's foot from his pocket. His fear hit a crescendo, the panic unbearable; but as he began to fall to the floor his terror left him, dissipated like dense smoke in a quickening wind. He knew what was going to happen. He would, very shortly now, be going home.

Janis had never seen the case that Tom Piano had gone off to evaluate. Too upset to be clinically effective, she had had the good sense, after leaving her father's office, to call Dr. O'Brien, and ask if she could go home, feigning illness. He had agreed, and she had left the hospital. She went home, determined to calm herself, and regain her analytic edge. She changed her clothing, and went to the gym where she worked out as if the devil were chasing her, and smiled grimly thinking that maybe he was. Earlier in the day, before the misery began, she had agreed to see Phil the next evening, but she wondered about the wisdom of that. She needed to talk about what was happening to her, and she knew he was far from being the optimal person to listen.

After a hot bath, she fell asleep listening to music, and awoke early the next day, refreshed. She felt no relief from her concern over recent events. Her risk, while hard to estimate, was, nonetheless, great, but her mind was clear now, and her panic gone. If there were to be another encounter with the mental intruder, she would be calmer and more deliberate. It would no longer be a shock.

She had obtained her father's indulgence, but she knew he would not be able to sustain it for long without progress in putting forth her case. There was now a brief window of opportunity to prove what appeared to be the impossible; but how do you prove the obviously unreal to be real? What do you do when you discover that you are the only person in the world to know that two and two does not always, after all, equal four? Maybe she really was crazy. She even hoped so, because then she could fight her way back to the solid rules of the world she had always taken for granted. Unfortunately, she was growing more and more convinced that she was totally sane, and that she had experienced what astronomers and physicists might call a singularity: an unexplainable occurrence that simply had to be acknowledged despite the fact that to do so was counterintuitive, because that was just the way it was.

She went to the public library, wishing to do something proactive, and retrieved books on telepathy, scanning selected sections. She spent a couple of hours scouring the Internet. Not surprised, she found nothing that seemed scientifically sound in all this material. There were plenty of anecdotal reports, and, she had to confess, some were quite interesting. There were many experiments that had been done, but to her way of thinking most of the results had been subjectively interpreted. Some experiments gave results that seemed measurable, but could not be reproduced by others, or were the products of poorly designed studies.

She sat back in her chair by the computer terminal she had been using, and covered her eyes with her hands, pressing them gently. This was fruitless. Had she found anything impressive she would have called the investigator or author, and told him or her what had happened to her. It would have been a risk, because her story sounded so wild, but she would have tried it, for the attempt might have proved to be the oracle through which might have been found explanations for, what seemed to her, the yawning mouth of Hell. However, there was no such person for her to contact. She was on her own, and she distinctly felt the vulnerability that status gave her.

Okay, what now, she thought? Then a cold idea seemed to pierce her mind: what if this thing or person who could contact her mentally could monitor her at will? Was she being observed even now? Would any strategy be open to inspection and therefore rendered useless?

No. There had been a feeling. It was an awareness that the other was intruding. What was it that it had said? "Janis, I am with you." The feeling was not here now, and they were not together now. Janis believed the presence would return, and wondered if she could shield her thoughts from the interloper when that happened.

"Enough of this," she sighed. "I'm going home."

She pushed back her chair, rose, and walked through the common reading room to the granite exit of the library, then descended the stairs quickly. Her car was parked just a few yards away by the curb. She unlocked it, got in, buckled her seat belt, put the key in the ignition and engaged it. The car's engine came to life, and so did the radio. The news was on, and as she listened, she again felt as though her heart had stopped beating in her chest.

"The body found in the hospital," the newscaster was saying, "was apparently that of an employee, whose name is being withheld for now pending location of next of kin. This gruesome murder follows on the heels of other recent episodes of violence that have rocked the hospital recently. While this is the first apparent killing there, the other events are felt to be connected. Reporting live this is…"

Janis didn't hear the signoff. It had happened. The intruder had done what it had promised to do.

Both Janis and her father had followed through with their plan to notify the police. The policeman on the phone had promised there would be some uniformed officers in the building. Where the hell had they been? Janis knew she was being unfair. There was no way that the police could monitor all areas of the hospital at the same time. Still, she was frustrated, and felt guilty. Who had it been? Did she know the victim? God, I hope not, she thought.

She drove her car away from the curb and into traffic. She knew where she was going to go. She had to touch base with her father. While this was not proof, it certainly was good circumstantial, corroborating evidence to support the encounters with the intruder she had reported to him.

She walked into the anteroom of the senior Dr. Michaels' office.

"Hello Melinda," she said, as the secretary looked up from her computer screen.

"Hello, Dr. Michaels. Are you here to see your father?"

Janis nodded, and Melinda picked up the receiver of her phone, and pressed a button.

"Your daughter is here. Okay." She smiled up at Janis, and said, "Go right on in."

Janis forced a smile, nodded and went to the door of her father's inner office. He greeted her by opening the door from within for her.

"Hi, Honey. What's up? Come on in." He smiled, and gestured with an arm for her to enter. "Would you like some coffee?" She nodded, and he went to coffee brewer and cups that stood on the top of a low bookcase. He poured two cups, and gave her one. They both took their coffee black.

"So to what do I owe the pleasure of your company," he asked, smiling again.

"Did you hear the local news?" He did not respond. "Someone was killed here last night."

"What?"

"I just heard it on the radio. They're linking it to the other violent stuff that happened here.

"Remember? I told you she, or whatever it was, said she was going to kill again; that it would be last night. She threatened you, Dad, if I don't help her, and now I'm really asking you: Do you believe me? Will you work with me on this, and most of all will you please be very careful?"

His smile was gone, and in its place was a frown and a look of intense concentration. When he spoke, he did so slowly, his voice a bit lower than usual, and his words carefully chosen.

"Jan, I admit this is very weird, but I have to be honest with you: I don't believe that there are telepathic psychopaths, but I did promise to go along with you for a little while, and I will keep my promise.

Who was killed?"

"I don't know. They didn't say."

"Well, I can find out. Just a second; I'll call security."

He picked up the phone, dialed a four-digit extension, and waited a moment.

"Yes, hi, this is Dr. Michaels. I heard there was some trouble here last night. Is that true? Thanks." There was a brief moment of silence in which the secretary on the other end of the line went to get the chief of security.

"Hi this is Dr. Michaels. Fine thanks, and you?...Listen, did something bad happen here last night?" There was a long pause now, and Bill's face darkened as the voice on the other line spoke. Finally, he said, "That's terrible. It's horrendous. I can't believe it. The poor guy. Yes. Fine. Thank you very much. Bye."

He put the receiver back on its cradle, and sat back in his chair, his eyes on his daughter.

"Well?" she asked.

"You were right. There was a death here...a murder, and it was grizzly like the other incidents. It was Jimmy, the fellow who works in pathology."

Janis gasped. Her father went on. "Do you want to know the details?" She nodded. "They found him on Clark 3. His neck had been bitten into, and much of his body had been eaten! This is disgusting. What kind of person does this sort of thing? He appeared to be virtually bloodless. What the hell?" He looked away from her.

"Poor Jimmy." Janis' eyes filled with tears.

He nodded. "The police..." There was a knock on his door. "Come in." Melinda stepped into the office.

"I forgot to give this to you when you came in, Dr. Michaels," she said, looking at Janis, and offering her a large envelope. "I found it propped up against the outer office door when I came in this morning." Janis rose from her chair to accept it.

"Thank you, Melinda. What is it?" The secretary shrugged, and left the room, closing the door after her.

Janis held the envelope in both hands. Across the front was written very simply "Janis Michaels," the letters penned in rough block letters, much like what one would expect from a child just learning to write. She tore it open, and reached inside. Her fingers closed on something she could not immediately identify, but when she pulled it out she knew right away what it was, a small cry escaping her throat.

"What's the matter Jan? What is it?"

She looked at him, with sorrow and worry rapidly chasing each other across her face.

"Proof," she said. It was Jimmy's rabbit's foot.

15

The creature was satisfied. The kill had been successful. A full belly right at the beginning of a lunar feeding cycle was always welcome. It would have removed the carcass for the sake of secrecy, but its preternaturally acute hearing had warned of approaching danger. The humans who wore blue "uniforms" were near by and they were a threat. It knew they would oppose the feeding, and try to protect the herd. It knew this from its exploratory forays into Janis' mind. No one at this hour should be coming down the corridor with the commanding cadence the creature now heard, and fearing it was one of the uniformed ones, the hunter bolted away, loping down the corridor, then leaping up into the pipes, and slinking into the darkest shadows. The approaching human was, in fact, one of the herd protectors, and the hunter watched now for his reaction as he spotted the remains of the kill. The man froze as he fully realized what he was seeing, his eyes wide and unbelieving. His right hand quickly moved to his side, and removed something, the word for which the creature could not remember, but which it knew was a powerful weapon. Over the centuries the creature had never truly feared the weapons of the herd. Its recuperative powers were quick, very quick by human standards. Except for certain crucial wounds most injuries a human could inflict would heal within moments. That was not the case if another of its kind inflicted wounds with claws or teeth. The creature had no way of knowing this was due to a certain microorganism indigenous only to the surface of beings of its type. Despite its great powers of rejuvenation, it currently wished no contact with any member of the herd that had any significant chance of injuring it. If, by accident, a vulnerable site were to be injured, its ability to reproduce during the coming season of rutting might be compromised.

Because of the infrequency of this biological imperative, eons of evolution had honed a reproductive drive that was essentially impossible for it to resist. It would not be deterred.

The human in blue garments held his weapon, and assumed a defensive posture. His eyes moved quickly, scanning the hall for any threat. He moved rapidly to the carcass to examine it, and immediately realized it was devoid of life. He turned his face toward an object he wore just below his color bone, and, pressing a button on it, spoke in nervous staccato bursts.

"Alex, this is Ben. I've got a victim here. I'm on Clark 3, weapon drawn, and I need back up ASAP."

Words came back from the apparatus. "Got you, Ben. I'm on my way, and calling in more cavalry. What is the status of the victim?"

"Dead. You're not going to believe this bloody mess. That psycho's got to be back."

"Or never left. I'll be right there. Be careful. Over."

The man with the weapon moved to position himself with his back against one of the corridor walls. His eyes never stopped scanning, and when the creature listened very carefully, it could hear the man's heart pounding. The stalker considered the possibilities. It could try to use its cunning to bring down this large male. That might render more food, but not without serious risk. It knew the man's friend was coming, and there was also the man's weapon to consider. Despite its sense of torpor after having eaten well, the hunter decided to move, not to attack but to leave Clark 3, and seek refuge elsewhere in the "hospital." It knew that it could leave the hospital and its congestion thereby minimizing the risk of discovery and injury, but game was very plentiful here, not to mention vulnerable.

And now there was something else. It wanted to be close to Janis. It had perused the depths of her mind enough to have grown fond of her. It was not the fondness that exists between equals. It carried no sense of commitment or respect. Emotions of this sort had no place among the killer's type. Janis was part of an inferior species, and the creature regarded her as Janis herself might have felt about a pet calf: an animal with some endearing qualities, but in the end expendable with little provocation. But more than fondness, the creature was curious. It simply wanted to know more about this complicated female, with her advanced sense of commitment, and her refusal to crumble in the face of fear. It would remain in the hospital. It would linger in shadows, moving unseen, feeding, and learning.

From Janis' mind it had learned much about the hospital. It was pleased when it found a particular switch-backing stair well located where it had sensed it would be. It was in this manner that it found its way to Clark 4, and the treasure that it would yield, though the creature found it hard to believe that such a find really existed.

16

Janis was convinced that the rabbit's foot was offered as proof, and as promised, that the person or thing that had spoken to her in thought existed. Oddly this gave her relief. It was her doubt that had made her indecisive, but now she believed her experience to be founded in reality. It was not simply the vaporous phantoms of her mind, but a living entity that had spoken, or rather communicated with her. That meant that, like all living things, it had weaknesses among its assets that could be exploited, and Janis galvanized her determination to discover them.

She and her father spoke at length about all this. He had Melinda cancel his next two appointments, and the two physicians talked and drank coffee. He remained the skeptic, and she the impassioned believer. Still, they spoke with respect, each letting the other put his or her case forward. They considered the possibility of telepathy being something real. They discussed theories as to why these events were occurring. Of course, most of what they talked about remained without definitive answers, but one important thing was affirmed. Despite the different ways they each considered the total body of problems they were facing, they agreed, that at least for a while, they would treat all of it, including the telepathy, as events to be considered explainable, and both agreed to follow this course until the issues were resolved or they were shown to be wrong.

It had always been like that, the two of them communicating openly. It had been her Daddy who had tucked her into bed almost every night, when she was little, reading short stories to her, and telling her about the world. It had been her father with whom she had discussed her first concepts of ambition, eternity and God. The bond was good, and it held now.

"Okay, Sweat Heart," he was saying. "Each of us has our own ideas about this stuff, but we'll proceed like we just agreed. I think this is very dangerous, and I don't want to act independently of the police, but like I said before, if we tell them about the communications you've had I think we will loose..." Bill's phone buzzed with its unique sound that indicated there was someone on the intercom. He rose from his chair, walked to his desk, and picked up the receiver.

Melinda spoke to him from the anteroom, "Phil Skorian and Matt Collins are here to see you."

"Okay. Thanks. Send them in please."

"Whose here," his daughter asked, annoyed at the intrusion

"Phil and Matt Collins want to meet with me. You can stay." Her annoyance played across her face, and he added, "Let's just see what they want, and we'll get back to all of this in a minute." He smiled at her, and walked to the door of his inner office and greeted the two men.

"Hello, come in. What can I do for you both?"

"Sorry to bother you, sir," Phil, as the more senior of the two began. "We heard about what happened last night, and we...well...Matt and I have been talking about the effect the other incidents had had on Janis... the sleep walking and stuff, and we were worried about what effect this new attack might have on her."

Janis had been sitting out of their line of sight, but she could hear them plainly. She rose from her chair, and walked towards them. Both physicians shifted uneasily at her presence.

"You were worried about me?" Her eyes flashed from one to the other. "And you were going to my father to discuss it? What is this, old time male chauvinism? I think you can talk to me directly about all this, and I certainly don't mind if my father hears what we have to say. But I am not going to be treated like some child."

Phil held up his hands, smiling, though uncomfortably. "Okay. Sorry. We meant well."

"And you discussed with Matt here about what I had told you in confidence?" Her face flushed slightly as her gaze focused only on him now.

"He's chief resident, smart and he's your friend. Yes, I did discuss it with him, but out of concern and nothing else."

Janis' lips were pressed together, and she hesitated, not certain whether to continue berating him or to back off given his good, if misguided, intentions.

Bill spoke first. "Let's all of us sit down for a moment and talk. Phil, Matt..." His right hand gestured to some chairs, then, placed on the small of his daughter's back, it gently guided her in the direction of another chair. When he too was seated there began a second round of consideration of all that had come to pass. The elder Dr. Michaels described his decision to suspend his skepticism about Janis' personal experiences with the killer. He told how he was doing this in respect for her, and because, in the short run it would do no harm. But there was an agreed upon provision that this would not be endless if future events showed this to be ill founded. They all shared their thoughts, argued and listened to each other, and in the end they all agreed to adopt the senior doctor's point of view...for the time being.

This concluded, the discussion moved to what they thought would be the next best step, and in so doing they formed an alliance against the threat to the hospital.

"As far as I'm concerned," Janis said, her face turning toward each of them as she spoke, "I think, at this point, I need to tell the police what I've experienced. I know that risks their shutting me out as a crank, but cops have used psychics sometimes."

"You're not a psychic, Janis." Matt countered.

"I know, but still. Maybe I can communicate with this person...or thing. I've thought of initiating a...can you call it a conversation?...with her, but to be honest I've been too scared to try."

"I don't blame you," Matt said.

"What if I can learn something from her about what makes her tick. Maybe there's a weakness, something that could be used to end this mess. At any rate, the police might be interested in this angle. And if they decide I'm just a nut, well...nothing is the worse for that."

"Unless you come across something concrete in the future, and they don't believe you because of it," Phil said reflectively. Janis nodded, but said nothing in return.

Her father spoke now. "It's your reputation, Jan. Given what you are trying to do with your life, you need to consider that too."

Phil added, "I don't know if you guys have seen this morning's local newspaper, but the press is beginning to get all stirred up."

Janis looked at him. "I heard the news on the radio. This is not going to get easier."

"Well, anyway, Jan, you have to consider the ripple effects of your decisions here." Her father's eyes reflected his sympathy and his worry. "Once you step forward, you'll no longer be just someone who was present when all this started. You'll be one of the players people will be paying attention to.

"And did you think of this? If this killer is communicating with you, then, there is by definition, some sort of relationship it has with you. If it perceives you have turned against her, then what? She might go after you somehow. If she has access to your mind, who knows what she could do?"

Phil shook his head. "I don't like this, Jan. The whole thing is too out there, and if this really is as we have agreed to consider it for the time being, then we are on totally unfamiliar turf, and you're considering being the point person. We wouldn't even know how to begin to protect you."

Janis considered telling him what she thought of his wanting to protect her, but decided against it. "This telepath already knows I'm against it. I didn't exactly welcome it into my brain, and if she can read minds then she knows I am totally against her."

Her father looked her directly in the eyes. "That's true, Jan, but passively hating something is different than actively taking up against it. If this, what ever it is, senses that you are a threat, who knows, maybe it could force you to act against yourself? You say it made you nearly strike Phil, and it made you grimace at the mirror." Phil looked up startled.

"When did you almost hit me? And what about the sleep walking?" Phil asked. "Remember the porch?"

"That's true. I don't know. I just can't stand by and do nothing. I guess it just comes down to sometimes you just have to take a risk." This evoked a flurry of negation from the little group. Janis let her nearly having struck Phil pass.

"I really hate this," Bill said slowly, with suppressed emotion.

"I know you do, Dad. I'm sorry. I don't think I have a choice, really. You know what I mean, though, don't you?"

"It's different. I love you. I want us to find another way."

Janis shrugged, "You guys aren't considering that what I'm going to do isn't really all that dangerous to the telepath. I don't know where she is, why she's doing these things or anything else that would help the police get her. All I can really say is that I've had some sort of mental contact with her."

Matt spoke, "Janis, it sounds to me like you've made your decision. My only suggestion would be to think about it a little more. But whatever you decide, I'm in this too. I don't know what we should do ourselves. We should leave most of all this to the authorities, but I do know that I'm a doctor, and I'm going to do whatever it is I have to do to help. The police catch crooks, and it seems to me that at this point the best I can do is help you. If this were someone else other than you, I don't know how I would react, but I know you, and if you want to take this route then I can go along for a while. You have a possible strange opportunity here, so who knows."

Janis smiled at him gratefully. "Thank you, Matt." Then she added, "I think you're all going to hate this, but I want to try something. I think it would be best for me to try this with all of you present in case something goes wrong." Her father cleared his throat and looked away. Matt and Phil looked directly at her.

"I am no natural telepath, assuming such a thing exists, but I have been able to receive telepathic communication from this person." She frowned. "I can't even believe I'm saying this stuff, it sounds so bogus, but this problem came to me, not the other way around. Anyway, right here and now I want to make a test. I don't want to think it over, because I might chicken out, and right now I have the momentum to try."

"What do you want to do?" Bill asked her, but he thought he knew what her response would be before he even asked the question.

"I want to make a telepathy test. I want to first see if I can contact any of you; you know…do I have any hidden talent. I doubt I do, because there has never been even a glimmer of this in my whole life.

"Then I want to try to contact the telepath. It made contact with me more than once, and maybe that triggered synapses in my brain or something that would allow me to contact it."

"Why the hell would you want to do that?" Phil asked, sounding irritated.

"Because I might be able to learn something about it. I wouldn't necessarily be confined to mental discussions. Maybe I could feel its feelings, learn its hidden thoughts…"

"Get yourself killed," Phil finished her sentence. "This thing is malevolent. It isn't going to passively let you enter its mind and look around. It's going to try to stop you, and there are many ways it could do that. Just tell the police what you know, and leave it at that."

"No."

"Look, Jan, I care about you. You are not just skating on thin ice here, you're stomping across a deep lake with a very thin layer of ice and neon lights flashing 'danger'."

Janis smiled, and laughed slightly through closed lips. "Very poetic. I appreciate your concern. I really do, but I need to try this."

Bill knew her tone of voice. "Okay," he said, "If you're going to do this at least you're doing it with all of us present. Let's get it over with."

"I hope my logic is correct," Phil added, nodding his head slightly. "I hope this is all bull."

Janis ignored the comment. "Okay, all of you be very quiet, and sit very still. I'm going to try to think something to each of you, first as a group and then one at a time, in case there is a difference."

Her father pursed his lips, noting silently to himself how, no matter what, when faced with a challenge she always moved with a clear systematic attack. She had been like this since she had been a child.

All agreed, albeit without enthusiasm, and the experiment began. Janis closed her eyes, and two thin vertical little lines of concentration formed between her brows. A few minutes passed, and no one said a word. Finally, Janis opened her eyes.

"Anything?" she asked. Bill shook his head. Phil and Matt both said, 'no.'

"Great," Janis mumbled. "Okay, here goes the big one. I'm sure I'll feel silly if this doesn't work, but bear with me. I'm going to try to contact the telepath."

"I think this IS silly," Phil complained. Janis wondered how they were possibly going to go out together tonight if he didn't stop the attitude. She frowned at him, then looked straight ahead and closed her eyes.

"Jan, I think it would…" Phil was stopped mid-sentence when she briskly held up her hand to silence him. Then Janis returned her hand to her lap, and she became motionless save for her regular breathing. The furrows returned between her brows. Nothing happened. A full minute passed, then another. Still nothing happened.

17

The creature had found Clark 4 to be of a different nature than the floor below it. Unlike the previous floor, which was utilitarian and not meant for public foot traffic, the fourth floor was painted in pleasant colors, and colorful pictures were hung on the walls. It was, the creature had learned from Janis, the home of the registration area where "outpatients" went through the ritual of "registering" for entry into the hospital. It was also where the "laboratory" was located, as well as the "blood bank."

When it reached the floor it used its prodigious skill at blending in with the environment to camouflage its presence and avoid detection. There were not many people about at the moment, and the task was not too difficult. It was able to use its new language skills to read the markings to the side of each door, and was gratified to learn that what it had learned from Janis about this floor had been correct. This day and night was the time of the full moon. After the following night the feeding cycle would be over for another lunar cycle, and the mating time would be even closer. It was imperative that it escalate its ingestion of nutrients, and it was still incredulous about the existence of a blood bank, a storage room for herd blood. If true, this would be a bonanza unlike any it had ever encountered.

It would be important not to be rash. The herd could and would close in on it if it acted prematurely or without care. It decided that the wisest course of action would be to find another safe place to hide, and emerge at night, when detection would be much less likely. It was annoyed that the ceiling here was not like that of Clark 3. It had no idea that the drop ceiling was easily penetrable, and that beyond it were the same types of pipes that had offered it a safe perch on the other floor. To the hunter the ceiling looked solid and impenetrable. Therefore, hugging shadows and darting forth when human eyes were not looking, it made its way to a dark deep little alcove that held two wheelchairs and a gurney, and in front of which had been placed a screen. It would slither its way under the gurney to hide in the darkness beneath it. Its keenly sensitive eyes could discern the pattern and amount of dust in the alcove, and it knew that it had not been disturbed for a long time. It would be safe there.

The hunter darted behind the screen, and hunkered down, crouching behind it, listening before it went under the gurney to be sure it had avoided detection. It was then that the unforeseen struck. There was a lightning flash of dazzling light, and a pain in its head such as it had never before experienced. Its body went rigid, its back arched violently and painfully, and, immobilized, it fell over on its side, still hidden by the screen.

It could barely breathe, its chest heavy, and it perceived faint sounds that were not real sounds at all but reverberations in its mind. They were the sounds of beasts from the herd communicating, but it could not discern the words, even with its new vocabulary. The creature felt terror more intensely than ever before in the millennia of its life. It was helpless, immersed in a void of dark space and scrambled sounds, none of which leant itself to orientation. It could detect hostility around it, but could identify nothing definitive. Was this death? And if so, how?

It could not be death. Its body felt pain from the tetanic contractions of its muscles, and this would not be so if it no longer lived. No, this was something real and awful and unanticipated. The hunter was working hard now to make itself draw air, and the growing sensation of suffocation augmented its horror.

What was this? How to escape? To where had it been transported? The pain! The pain was becoming unbearable.

And then it was back, returned safely to its hiding place. Lying on its side, on the floor behind the screen, its muscles were unknotting, and the pain dissipating. It gasped greedily for air, and it was completely exhausted. Its terror eased, but fear still gripped it. Had it been magic, some evil thing the herd had somehow concocted unbeknownst to it in some desperate grasp for defense. Doubtful. Still, despite the mystery, there had been something familiar about it, as if the creature had been there before. But just where, exactly, had it just been?

18

No one expected Janis' convulsion. One moment she was sitting in quiet repose in her father's office, and then, in an instant she began making a low, ominous growling sound, then lurched backward into the chair, her back arched, the veins in her neck bulging and her face turning an unhealthy deep red. The three men bolted from their chairs, and rushed to her.

"My God," gasped Bill.

"Jan?" Phil called out.

For an instant all three were frozen, then Bill place two fingers on her carotid pulse and his ear to her chest.

"She's moving air without obstruction and there's a heartbeat," his voice wavered.

"Has she ever had a seizure before?" Matt asked.

"No."

All of her muscles were rigid except those needed for respiration. She did not twitch, nor did she thrash about, and although her father knew this could still be a convulsion, something in him doubted it. This feeling was not from his rational self, it came from somewhere vague and deep in his mind. He didn't just feel it, he knew this was not a convulsion, but he did not know why he knew it. This was something else, though he had no idea what it was.

Janis' eyes did not role back, but stared straight ahead of her as if focused on something.

"We should protect her airway," Phil said forcefully.

"She's breathing fine," Matt said. "Give her a moment, and just let's not let her fall. This might resolve quickly."

Bill thought how strange it was that, although her back was arched and her body rigid, she had not fallen over, but maintained her posture, awkward though it was.

For her part, Janis remained fully conscious. She could not understand the sounds that the men in the room with her were making. She was barely aware that they were present, but she felt comforted by the sense that her father was near. It felt as though she had been transported. Her mind was elsewhere and with her at the same time, and it was in a milieu totally foreign to her. It was an environment that did not move by the rules of logic she was accustomed to. It was a dangerous place, full of suspicion, aggression and hunger. It seemed familiar, and yet it was not. She had never experienced anything like this in her life.

And then she knew. She had made contact. It was a bad fit, her nervous system not totally compatible with the foreign host's mind, but it had happened, nonetheless. She had done it. Although not physically connected, she had entered the killer's mind in a virtual sense. It was exhilarating, and it was horrible. She felt nuances of emotion she had never experienced. There were, aggressive, fearful, twisted feelings, and she realized that her very emotions and those of the wild adolescent with whom she was communicating had now intertwined, each modifying the other. But was this person really an adolescent at all? There was a distinct feeling that maybe she was not. In fact, there was the distinct feeling that this entity was not even human, though Janis knew that this could not be.

Then fear. What if she could not extricate her mind to her own total control? What if she could be made a prisoner in the mind of this hostile entity? It had exerted a degree of control before. She pictured her body mindless, institutionalized, alive but in limbo, living out decades in nothingness. The fear became panic. She pulled her mind back. She needed to return to herself. Could she be blended with this thing? Could she disappear as the individual she had been?

This is beyond endurance. I have to get back…Now!

Mentally she pulled away as hard as she could. No change. She tried shutting off all thought, hoping that this would break the connection. It failed. She tried again, this time trying to maintain it as long as possible, and this time she was successful. There was a total nauseating confusion of all her senses. Briefly she was disoriented, and then there was a sudden sweet awareness of normalcy.

She was back.

In her chair, her body went limp. A healthy color returned to her face, and her breathing became easier. She could see the room and its welcome details; better, she could see her father's face as he bent over her, his tension obvious.

"Hey, Dad," her voice wavered.

"Hi, Jan. Are you okay? How do you feel?"

"Everything hurts, but I think I'm okay." She tried not to let him see how scared she had been, and in fact, still was. "It worked. I made contact."

"Are you sure?"

"Yes,"

She noticed Phil and Matt, and smiled.

"Hi, guys. How long was I away?"

"Maybe a minute," Phil answered. "You had a convulsion."

Janis sat up better in her chair, groaning slightly as she did so. She ran her fingers through her hair, then shook her head.

"It wasn't a convulsion, but I sure feel like it was."

"It was a convulsion Jan, and I think you should go to the E.D., get checked out by neuro and get a C.T. scan."

"What are you talking about?" she asked, an edge to her tone.

Phil's voice grew more forceful as he spoke. "Look, you've been experiencing changes lately. Nightmares, sleepwalking, the perception of some sort of mental telepathy and now a seizure. You're a doctor. Use your brain, damn it. This could all easily be explained by some sort of brain disorder. I think…"

"Phil you are out of your mind if you think…"

"Hold on, Jan," her father gently interrupted her. "He's got a point. Just because this all feels real to you does not mean that it is. If you encountered a patient with your experiences, you would be saying the same thing too."

"Dad, I know what I know. Something strange…No strange is too mild a word for it…something really different is happening. We have to be open minded and think…"

The senior Dr. Michaels placed his hand on her shoulder. "Tell you what. Meet us halfway. You go to the Emergency Department, and get evaluated, and if nothing turns up, we take up where we left off. If, on the other hand, God forbid, we find something neurologically that could explain all this then we…change tack."

Janis looked at all of them one by one: her father's concerned earnest face, Phil's expression of exasperation, and Matt nodding agreement with what the other two men had just said. She would totally loose their tenuous support if she did not acquiesce.

She nodded without enthusiasm. "Okay, but the work up has to be done stat. If I'm right, then we will be wasting time, and I want that minimized at least."

While nodding his assent, Bill Michaels was already walking to his desk, to take the phone and call the duty doctor in the E.D.

Wishing to please his daughter, Bill placed the full weight of his position into the balance. He called the Emergency Department, and personally spoke to the doctor there. Then he called the chairman of the department of neurology, and called in a favor. He did the same with radiology. The end result was that within three hours, a possible hospital record Janis thought privately, she had been examined by both the emergency physician and the chief of neurology. She had had an electroencephalogram and a CAT scan of her brain. The exams and both tests had all been negative, and she beamed as she announced to her father that now he was to keep his word.

"Back on track again, right, Dad?"

"Okay, Honey," he spoke slowly. "For the time being, anyway. Thank God there's no brain lesion giving you symptoms, but we haven't eliminated some psychological cause. But, I promised you, so I'll go along for a bit more."

She hugged him, then added with obvious misgiving, "I feel duty-bound to tell the police what I know. I'm sure they are going to look at me like I'm crazy, but I would be remiss if I didn't give it a shot." She smiled again, "Who knows, maybe I'll find someone who'll take me seriously. I'll bat my eye lashes at him." She chuckled, turned and walked away. "See you soon. Thank you," and she waved over her shoulder.

Finding a policeman was not difficult. They were in the hospital in force, and they were all business. They were interviewing people, taking notes, walking briskly down corridors towards destinations only they knew, reassuring visitors who asked if everything was under control, and Janis had heard that there were several crime scene investigators on Clark 3 and that a profiler had been called into the case as well. Janis noticed that not only were the local police present, there were some state troopers as well. She had made her way to the front lobby of the hospital, and now approached two officers who were animatedly talking to each other, each referring to his own set of notes.

"Officers, could you please tell me who on site is in charge of this investigation." They looked at her, taking into account her white coat, nametag and stethoscope, then one of them pointed.

"That fellow in the sport coat at the end of the hall, talking to that nurse. That's Chief Paltini." The other one nodded without facial expression.

Janis knew the name, but little about him except that he was local. She thanked the policemen, and marched right toward the man they had indicated, taking up a position next to but slightly behind him, saying nothing, waiting for him to finish with the nurse.

He turned to her, "Can I help you." He sounded annoyed at her uninvited presence.

"When you're ready, I have some information that might be useful."

He nodded, turned to the nurse, and asked her if she could think of anything else that might be of use. She told him about two people she had seen the day before that she thought looked particularly unsavory, and although the police chief nodded as she spoke, he did not make any notes.

The nurse walked off, and Paltini turned toward Janis. He was short, darkly complected and had eyes that bespoke intelligence and focus. Janis' enthusiasm sustained itself, and she returned his gaze.

"What's on your mind?" he asked her. He eyed her nametag. "Dr. Michaels is it?"

"I'm Dr. Janis Michaels. I'm a cardiology fellow here, and I have a strange story to tell you."

He smiled dryly, and nodded. "I'd be glad to hear what you have to say. Could we sit down? They found two comfortable chairs close to each other, and after they were seated, he leaned forward, resting his elbows on his knees.

"Okay, Doc, I'm ready. Tell me your strange story."

Janis told him all that had occurred relating her to the girl who now terrorized the hospital. Despite misgivings, she included the parts about almost going off her balcony, and the bodily control that had seemed telepathically inflicted on her. She also made sure she told him that she had just been cleared of any brain tumor or other structural lesion that could have altered her mind.

When she was done, the police chief looked at her, and she was pleased so see that there was no contempt or annoyance in his gaze. Maybe he got it on her first try.

"Doctor, you're right, that is a pretty strange story. But you know what? I have a brother who is a cop in a big city, and he's used a psychic more than once in solving some cases. He's no dummy either, and he swears she really helped. So I'm not going to toss out anything that might be helpful. Would you write your name and phone number down for me?" He proffered a pen and index card after retrieving them from the breast pocket of his sports jacket. When she had complied he put the card and pen back in his pocket, and smile at her without emotion.

"I appreciate your time." He stood up. "What I would like you to do is just be aware. If you get any indications of where this kid is or what she might be up to please call me." He produced a packet of business cards from his shirt pocket, and gave her one. "You can call me any time. Thanks very much for your time." He shook her hand, nodded and moved on.

That's it, she thought? No dismissal of what she had to say as hysterical ramblings, but no enthusiasm of what might be the only direct contact with the killer outside of what had occurred in the Emergency Department. Basically, nothing positive or negative? He had not indicated pleasure or displeasure with the information.

Well, at least I did my duty, Janis thought, frustrated. Maybe the guy is just very poker faced. At any rate, I'm not going to dwell on it, and I can always call him if I have questions or more information, so I guess it was worth the effort.

With that she put the interview out of her mind.

19

Before the pain from the muscle spasms had subsided, the creature had twisted its way under the gurney. It lay in the alcove, behind the screen, sunken in shadows beneath the stretcher. It would not be detected here. The resolution of its discomfort escalated its confusion and sense of disorientation. For many minutes its thoughts remained disjointed, shocked, and it could not make itself focus its intelligence on the problem. What had just happened? After a while, as its mind raced back and forth considering the experience, it realized that throughout the entire episode there had been something familiar. It had not been tangible. It was not the memory of a specific place or event, but there was a "flavor" to it, like the scents that females of the herd sometimes used, just on the edge of one's awareness, and when present, created near subliminal memories in those nearby. Yet it was not the memory of a smell. It was…The creature's mind reached, and then revelation. It was familiar terrain. Janis. Somehow Janis was involved. The hunter remembered hints of a sense of presence. Without being there in actuality, Janis had been all around, almost imperceptible, weaving in and out with varying degrees of faint intensity, a phantom. All around…The hunter had been in her presence. That was, of coarse, impossible unless Janis had done something unprecedented. Her mind did not naturally contain the special sense the creature possessed, but her mind, while still of the herd, and therefore fundamentally primitive, was more impressive than most of her kind. Janis had reached out to the hunter! It had not worked properly because her mind was not of a type to initiate such an action, but, nonetheless, contact had been made. Perhaps the previous contacts the hunter had made had changed her somehow, resetting her abilities. The creature was only sure that the ability had not been there when it first entered her mind.

Incredible! The creature's breathing was fast and anxious, and it struggled to control its emotions. A serious threat had now appeared. At the very least, incapacity could be inflicted, and who knew if Janis's primitive ability could be refined. Janis would have to be dealt with.

The creature did not want her dead. That would be easy enough to accomplish, but foolish. Janis could still be used as a tool to the hunter's purposes. It would be far better to control Janis; to stop her from ever using her warped power again.

Always, the creature had found one of its finest tools to be fear. The herd felt fear in many exquisite ways, and the hunter had often found that this could be shaped and guided to bend the prey to its will. It had become a master craftsman with the aid of this tool, and it knew how it would apply its art to Janis, who was, without a doubt, an unusually interesting and challenging specimen. It was going to be interesting to see how this would play out.

That night, after Phil left her at her apartment, Janis gathered Elvis into her arms, sat down on her couch, and drew her feet up under her. This had been a bad day. The news about Jimmy had been dreadful, the convulsive episode had been painful and inexplicable, the neurological exam had been unnecessary and, finally, her evening with Phil had been a bust.

They had chosen a nice restaurant they had visited before, but both of them were paged enough times to be irritatingly disruptive. Then there had been the re-emergence of the discussion regarding the believability of Janis' experiences. Phil just could not let it go. He was a man strong in his opinions, and not reticent in voicing them. Tonight had been no exception. Perhaps he had tried to suppress his need to argue the point, but in the end he certainly failed. It was patronizing to be talked to in that way. His affect had been solicitous rather than confrontational, but somehow that had been even more annoying. If only he could have respected what had been decided before: just suspend, for the time being, clinical explanations for what had happened to her. In the end that is essentially what he did, but the price had been a debate, temper flares, and basically a ruined evening.

When she had first met Phil, Janis had found him attractive and charming. He was funny and charismatic, and it had been fun to be with him. As time passed, however, and as he grew more comfortable with her, the charm diminished. To be sure, he did nothing purposefully noxious, and was always polite, and he cared about her, but that special luster he had presented himself with had not proved to be durable.

The truth was Janis had begun to realize he was falling short of what she hoped to find in a partner. Now she was freshly irritated with him, and she doubted their relationship was going to last much longer.

"You know, Elvis," she murmured to the cat. "I'm ready to drop. I'm not going to make any relationship decisions feeling like this. What I am going to do is draw a hot bath, soak and go to bed. What do you think, baby?" She stroked his throat with her index finger, and he started his low throaty purring.

"Why can't I find a man like you?" she smiled. "Easy to please, unopinionated, and likes to cuddle." She chuckled, and scratched behind his ears. He lifted his head, closing his eyes in pleasure.

After a while Janis gently placed him on the couch, and stood up.

"See you later baby," she said, and she turned to go draw her bath.

As the water poured into the tub Janis poured in a small quantity of scented oil, and could smell its sweet subtle fragrance. She tested the water, and was satisfied with the warm, almost hot, temperature. She disrobed, letting her clothes fall carelessly on the bathroom floor; it felt good not to be neat.

As she eased herself into the water, Janis sighed, waiting for the heat to relax her muscles and soothe her spirit. She let herself sink up to her neck, and closed her eyes as the moist warm air rising from the tub embraced her face.

This was good. The day may have been tough, but this was good. She had largely been able to avoid clinical responsibilities today, thanks to the help of one of the other cardiology fellows. Considering what she had had to deal with, that had been the right thing to do. Tomorrow, however, would be different. She would have a heavy clinical load, but she looked forward to it. Throwing herself into her work with its mandatory mental focus would be a balm, after the surrealistic scattered chaos she had been wandering through.

She slid deeper into the bath, letting the water cover her head, then pushed herself up again, her hair clinging warmly to her ears and neck. Her mind drifted. A warm bath was just what she needed.

Languidly she reached for her large sponge and a bar of soap. She lathered the sponge liberally, holding it in her right hand and extending her left arm. She ran the soapy sponge down one side of her arm then up the other side. She moved the sponge to the other hand and slowly washed her right arm. As she continued to clean herself, she felt a deepening drowsiness. The warmth of the water permeated her skin, and seemed to mix with her essence, calming her further, releasing her tension. This was heavenly. She closed her eyes, and the darkness behind her lids seemed to envelope her in a gentle, almost tender vortex of sleepiness. She became less aware of the room, and aware that she was beginning to doze, she let her head lean back on the tub so she would not be likely to slide down and startle herself choking. She would only allow herself to sleep for a few moments. She did not want to awaken in cooled water.

The bathroom drifted away. Phil left her mind, and the darkness seemed to become her world, a wonderful world probably not unlike that of a baby in its mother's womb, warm, safe, nurturing.

She could hear a voice. At first it was indistinct, but unmistakably it was that of a young woman. Janis would not have minded this, but she knew this voice. She prayed she was dreaming.

"Janis."

Had she heard her name?

"Janis, we are together again."

Janis clenched her teeth, and her sense of peace was gone, instantly, as if vaporized like a drop of water hitting a hot pan.

"We are not together," she answered. "I'm having a dream, and that's all you are. You're not...I don't even know what to call you, but you are not for real."

"I have had many names in many tongues during my life."

"You seem to be mastering my "tongue" pretty quickly." There was no admiration in her voice.

"I have been studying you Janis. I have entered your mind even when you have not been aware of it. The simple sounds and concepts your kind uses to communicate, your languages, are very simple and easy for my kind to learn, especially studied from within."

"I doubt that. You're arrogant, aren't you."

The voice chuckled. "I don't think you can call it arrogance when one species is truly superior to another."

"Another species?"

"Of course. You don't think that you and I are really alike, do you?"

"It doesn't matter. This is a dream. Go away."

"You are not really dreaming, Janis. How do you think it was that you drifted so easily into your current state? No, what you are experiencing is real. You caused me a problem earlier, and I want you to know that you must never to do that again."

The young voice was a bit at odds with the diction and the threat, but Janis was paying close attention, regardless.

"What do you mean?"

"You tried to enter MY mind. It didn't work, but it did cause me discomfort, and I plan to repay you, and show you that you are not to do that again."

Janis felt her physical and mental stress ratchet up.

This is a dream. I'll be damned if I am going to let this go on, she thought, yet she could not make the voice go away, and she could not make herself wake up.

"And what do you plan to do?" she asked.

"I am going to...what would be a good way to say it...take you with me on an adventure tonight."

"No. You are not going to take me anywhere." Her tone was defiant, but her mood was fearful...and the creature knew it.

"You do not need to be afraid, Janis. I am going to take you with me in our minds. You will be safe, and you will see through my eyes, but you will see directly what I am capable of."

"That's ridicul..." Her words were strangled off by her shock. She was "seeing" Clark 4. The image was in her field of vision, but she could not change it by moving her eyes or turning her head. She felt a chill despite the warm water around her as she realized she was, in fact, seeing through the creature's eyes.

"Ah, so you are seeing with me. Good." Janis did not respond. She was a passenger, and she was very scared.

The creature moved in its usual way along the corridor. From shadow to shadow, insinuating itself along the contours of less noticed areas, it moved swiftly, silently and efficiently. It was not clear to Janis what its destination was, but it was clearly moving in goal directed fashion.

A door. A quick image of signage next to it, and the virtually instantaneous comprehension of its meaning: Blood Bank.

The creature looked down as its pale delicate fingers with the long, dark, thickened nails grasped the door handle, turned it, and pushed inward. The door moved, and the stalker slipped in, swiftly, crouching deeply as it did so. Stealthily it moved sideways, silently, as soon as it was past the threshold. It was in shadow, but the room in general was well lit with fluorescent overhead lighting. In front, to the right was a blacktopped counter with a rack of test tubes. Next to the rack, also on the table, was a centrifuge, the top of which lay flapped open.

To the front and left was the end of a refrigeration unit. Diagonally, through the creature's eyes, Janis could see its glass doored front. Straight ahead was a desk cluttered with books, papers, a coffee mug and a few three ring binders.

The creature scanned the room rapidly with its eyes, but kept its head and body totally still. Suddenly, still crouching, it moved towards the front of the large refrigerator. It paused for a moment, looking through the glass doors at its contents. There were many plastic bags containing blood and organized by blood type. There was a separate section for autologous donation, blood to be retransfused back into the donors at the time of future surgery if the need arose. There was also a section for "blood products," consisting of bags of platelets and white cells. Next to the glassed-in unit stood a smaller stainless steel refrigerator with no window. The creature opened it, and saw many bags of frozen plasma. It reached out with the fingers of its right hand, and touched one of them. It was cold and hard. It would not have time to consume these, and it closed the door. Furtively the creature looked around, first to the left and then to the right, its vision tracking each time to beyond its mid back position. The visual panning caused a mild sense of nausea in Janis. She swallowed, and waited to see what would happen next, while she continued to hope she would awaken from this nightmare.

The hunter reached for the handle on the glass front of the large cooling unit, hesitated a moment, then opened the door with a hard tug. Cold air poured from the unit, and stroked the creatures face. Janis did not feel this, but somehow knew it was happening, and knew it pleased her host.

Greedily the stalker reached in, and retrieved a bag of type A blood. Holding it in its hand, it brought a corner to its mouth, and bit into it. Quickly shifting the bag to ensure none of the red nectar was lost, it let the liquid pour into its mouth, swallowing glutinously. The creature took the bag in both hands, and squeezed it to make the blood flow faster.

"Stop it," Janis said softly, not daring to speak loudly. "Stop it. This is disgusting. People need that."

"I need it, Janis."

"Why?"

"I am a predator. You and those like you are prey. Your blood is your essence, the most rich and prized part of you. Its value to me is enormous."

"Let me go. I don't want to watch this. Is there anything that will make you go away? Is there anything that will satisfy you without causing destruction?"

"That is why I like you Janis. Unlike most of the herd…your species… you don't cower in my presence. You have courage.

"No, to answer your question, there is nothing that will make me go away until I am done. Your hospital is a great source of potential nutrition for me, and, especially now, that is very much needed."

"Why?"

"Ah, you have so many questions. But I can answer you because your kind does not have the courage or ability to believe you if you tell them what I will reveal to you. They only believe in me as they die at my hand."

Her use of the language is not that of an adolescent, Janis thought. Who…what…is she?

"One question at a time, Janis." It was reading her every thought now. "You asked me why the special need now. The answer is that I am preparing. My kind mate rarely, but such a time is coming soon for me. I must be in a condition most favorable for this."

It's going to mate! I really want to wake up, Janis thought. This is hell. I want this to end.

"It will," came the voice in her head again, contemplatively this time.

The hunter grabbed a second bag of blood. Again, it tore a corner with its teeth, and consumed its contents. It rested for a moment, licking its lips slowly, then reached for yet another bag.

The hand froze mid-reach. The creature cocked its head, nostrils flaring and ears moving in twitches. Someone was coming. With electric speed it withdrew its hand, closed the refrigerator door, and bounded back into the shadow near the door where it had entered. There was a clattering noise and a thud. The door swung open, and a heavyset woman in a housekeeping uniform lumbered into the room, pushing a large wheeled trash barrel with her.

She was fat, and would probably make a messy kill. There was plenty of food here to be had without struggle, and the noise of bringing her down could bring problems. The creature decided to wait. If the female saw it, then it would dispatch her quickly, otherwise it would let her go.

Janis was not privy to these thoughts. She saw the woman, and her heart ran wild.

"Don't kill her," she pleaded. "You have all that blood. You don't need to kill her."

"Janis, I am not going to kill her, unless she sees me." These words, though only thoughts originating in the hunter's head and arriving in Janis' mind, carried a tone of patronizing impatience.

The woman lumbered to the desk straight ahead, bent with a grunt, and pulled a plastic bag from the wastebasket there. Holding it by the open end with one hand, she twisted the bag with the other, knotted it, and tossed it into her barrel. She cast a dull look around the room, and turned to go.

It appeared to both Janis and the creature that the woman's gaze lighted on the hunter. Adrenaline hit the creature, and Janis felt it. She almost screamed. The hunter's muscles flexed, ready to leap and rip the life from this cow.

The woman's eyes moved on. She had seen nothing out of the ordinary. The creature believed she was too stupid to feign this so seamlessly. Its exquisite vision detected no dilatation of the woman's pupils. Her complexion neither blushed nor blanched. The hunter's muscles relaxed, and Janis felt the adrenaline ebb.

The housekeeper left the blood bank, and both Janis and her host relaxed.

"Thank God," Janis said softly.

"God had nothing to do with it, Janis. If she had seen me she would have died." There was a pause, then the creature continued. "I am going to resume feeding now Janis, and you will watch. When I am done, I will release you, but I want you to be certain of why I took you on this little journey. You will not ever try to contact me through my mind again. It caused me discomfort. I have chosen not to kill you unless I must, but you have been with me now in a way more intimate than you have ever been with anything. You know what I can do. You have had a glimpse at my heart. Are we clear on this point?"

"Yes," the response carried all the fear the creature had hoped for.

Janis was suddenly released. The creature had finished its glutinous meal, more than satiated. It needed no more nourishment this cycle, and would retire until just before the next full moon.

The water in the tub was no longer hot. It was outright cold. Janis had no idea how that had happened, as she doubted she had been in the bath long enough for it to occur naturally. Maybe it had to do with the energy expended in her bizarre, vicarious sortie into the blood bank. She did not ponder the thought, but focused instantly only on leaving the chilling water.

When she tried to rise her joints were stiff and she felt weak. Nevertheless, she exited the tub quickly, and wrapped herself in a towel as rapidly as she could. She was shivering.

How was that temperature possible, she wondered? The energy drain must have been huge. It had been consumed in a manner in which she was not at all familiar, but there was so much lately with which she was not familiar!

Once dried off she got into her comfortable bulky terrycloth robe, and grabbed her hair dryer. She welcomed the warm air it produced, and as it flowed, lifting her hair in small waves, she tried to process what had just happened. She wanted to discuss it with someone. Phil was out of the question. Her father was already indulging her, and she knew he was struggling to do so. He was conflicted by his desire to be protective of her mental health and at the same time to be respectful of her autonomy of thought, no matter how "out of the box" it might be. Her heart warmed thinking of this. How very "Dad" of him to be in this quandary. However, if she could reach him, before the disaster in the blood bank was discovered she would go a long way to proving her point about her telepathic contact. On the other hand, she thought, if word of her knowledge leaked to the police she might be seen, not as an involuntary telepathic "voyeur," but rather as an accomplice. It would be so much easier for them to think this and that she had concocted the telepathy story. How else would she know what had happened so quickly? Would her father think the same thing? He might if he thought she was suffering a psychosis perhaps induced by the stress of what had happened in the E.D. Could he think such a thing? Could she take a chance like that? The pain he would feel if he came to believe this would be unspeakable.

Janis came to a decision. She would tell no one what had just happened. She would let the authorities follow their course of discovery and reaction. It was the safest path to follow. But she had learned something, and it was a big thing. She could cause the creature misery...enough misery to have prompted this most recent contact. To use this as a weapon would be tremendously risky, but it could be done. Precautions would have to be taken, but she could definitely strike if she needed to.

A new fear gripped her as she watched her hair flowing with the hot air from the dryer in the mirror. The creature had said it had entered her mind, and studied her when she was not aware of it. It had even polished its English this way! It was chilling, and Janis felt violated. It was intolerable. It could not be that such an overt invasion had been imperceptible. It must have been that she had missed the cues. They had probably been subtle, but she would be vigilant now, and if she felt anything to suggest the creature's presence, she would conceal her thoughts as best she could. This was particularly important now that she knew she could take an offensive posture. The very fact that she was considering an attack stance was a shift for her, and she knew that she would try to form strategy. After all, there might be other things she could do. She had drifted into combat mode, and were the creature to detect this she would lose a great advantage.

How does one totally hide one's thoughts? Such a capacity was probably unprecedented. She had found nothing in her search that indicated anything to the contrary. Perhaps there were unrecorded incidents, but how could she tap into this?

As if in answer, a thought came to her. The Internet; not the scholarly side of the net, but some chat room on telepathy. Somewhere in the vague, ill-defined mass of crackpots and eccentrics that reveled in such terrain, she thought, maybe there was someone who had truly experienced telepathy. Maybe such a person might know how to shield thoughts. She smiled wanly, realizing how ridiculous she would have seemed to herself not so not so long ago when the world had normal dimensions and a sense of order.

Twenty minutes later Janis sat in front of her computer, typing her first inquiry into a chat room she had found dedicated to telepathic experience. Almost immediately she found someone who wanted to "talk" to her.

"I'm Jade," the words scrolled onto her screen.

Janis hesitated. She was embarrassed, and decided on total anonymity. "My name is Michael," she typed, feeling slightly guilty.

"Cool, a guy. You said you wanted to talk about telepathie?"

Janis sagged at the type-o. The intelligence of her new acquaintance was in doubt, especially since Janis had just spelled the word correctly.

"Yes."

"Well?"

"I need to talk to someone who has some experience with it. Someone who has actually used it."

"Well, that's not me. I just think it's fun to think about it. Rhonda has done it though."

"How do I find her?"

"I'm right here." Apparently, Rhonda was in the chat room too.

"Rhonda?"

"Yup."

"You know about telepathy?"

"I don't know much about it, but I can do it."

"Are you serious?"

"Yup."

Janis had her doubts. This was ridiculous. These two are idiots, and I am too for talking with them. She was going to quit this, but she would try one more question.

"Okay Rhonda, tell me the most impressive thing you've done with it."

"Helped catch a crook."

Janis lurched toward her computer monitor. "What?"

"That's right. It was way cool, but I got to help the cops out. A little kid got snatched, and I found the kidnapper, gave him a read, and told the cops where to find the kid."

"You're kidding, right?"

"No, I'm not. It was weird though because I've had problems with cops myself before."

"Where are you now?"

"England. U?"

"U.S.A."

"GTG."

"What's GTG?"

"Got to go."

"No, please, this is important. I need to talk to you."

"GTG, but I'll give you my email if you want."

"Yes."

Janis carefully wrote down the address, and tried to thank Rhonda, but she was already gone. She switched to her email to write her inquiry.

She did not reveal anything about the serious nature of her circumstances. All she asked for was a way to block intrusion. After tapping the 'send' button she sat back in her chair. That was enough. If this worked, fine, but she very much doubted anything would come of it. The kid (assuming it was a kid) in England was probably just an hysteric with a frothing imagination. Janis found she had lost her enthusiasm for pursuing chat rooms.

20

When two days passed with no response from Rhonda, Janis gave up on her. She would simply try to be alert to any signs of intrusion, and hope for the best. This left her anxious and frightened, but there was nothing else she could do. She decided to throw herself into her work. It would be a distraction and keep her brain filled with material that would not tip her hand to the person, or perhaps thing, that had so badly disrupted her life.

It was morning, and Janis had just arrived at the hospital. She was beginning her rounds, and as she picked up the vital signs chart on her first patient, she heard the page operator on the public address system.

"Code Blue I.C.U.... Code Blue I.C.U. Dr. Collins, Dr. Reddy, Dr. Michaels I.C.U. stat...Dr. Collins, Dr. Reddy, Dr. Michaels I.C.U. stat."

Janis quickly put her chart down, and ran for the stair well. There would be no waiting for the elevator.

When she reached the I.C.U. she saw a huddled group around the bed of the patient in cubicle 7.

"Let me by," she said firmly to the respiratory therapist who blocked her approach to the bedside.

The therapist turned toward her. "Sorry Dr. Michaels," and he stepped aside. Janis came to the side of the patient's bed, but could not see the patient's face; the nurse assisting Savita Reddy as she intubated the patient blocked her.

Janis, looked up at the monitor, and quickly noted the regular, rapid rhythm with the abnormally widened complexes.

"We have V. tach here," she announced. "Does this patient have a pulse?" Savita held the newly placed endotracheal tube in place as she listened with her stethoscope to both sides of the patient's chest, checking to see if both sides were being aerated. The nurse who had been helping her reached forward, and felt for a carotid pulse.

"No pulse."

"Okay, let's try shock. Are we charged up?"

"Yup," and the same nurse handed Janis the paddles with their long, spiraled, insulated wires connecting them to the defibrillator. "We're on synch."

Savita quickly taped the tube in place.

Janis took the paddles, the nurse moved to get out of her way, and Janis positioned them on the patient's chest. She glanced at the patient's face.

"Oh my God," she gasped. "It's Mark Smith."

The Emergency Room doctor looked terrible. His face had grown gaunt during his long stay in the Intensive Care Unit, and his ribs showed through the skin over his chest.

Savita answered, speaking quickly. "Dr Smith, as you know, has had one complication after another. Now, again, it's sepsis from pneumonia. He coded just now, and we got him right back, but it looks like it didn't last."

"Thanks, Savita. Clear." Everybody backed away from the bed, and Janis pressed the button on one of the paddles. Dr. Smith's body went rigid; his arms flew off the bed, then flopped back down. Everyone looked at the monitor. There was no change.

"Any pulse?" Janis asked again. This time Savita checked.

"None."

Janis held the recharging paddles. "Let's pump him and breath him for a minute." Savita attached the ambu breathing bag to the end of the tube she had just placed in his trachea, and began to squeeze it rhythmically. The nurse who had been helping at the bedside, leaned over the body without hesitation, and began cardiac compressions. Someone had already placed a board under him during the earlier arrest that Savita had spoken of.

A minute passed. "Anything yet?" Janis asked. Savita reached, and again felt for the carotid.

"No."

"Okay, we'll try again." She placed the paddles, announced, "clear" and pressed the button another time.

Smith's body jerked rigid once more, and once more it went slack in the bed.

"Janis, we've got to stop," came a voice behind her.

"Resume compressions and breathing," she told the others, and turned to see Matt Collins standing behind her.

"Hey Matt." She smiled in greeting, but it was without joy. "We've just begun here. I don't think its time to call it quits yet."

"But the family does. I've been following the case since Dr. Smith came here weeks ago. It's been one disaster after another. He's had acute respiratory distress syndrome, pneumonia a couple of times, septicemia, and coagulation problems. His kidneys shut down, and he's been getting dialysis. His renal status has shown no improvement. Last week he had a heart attack and apparently had a large anterior wall infarct. Two days ago, we think, he developed ischemic colitis, and had a large stroke according to CT scan. Today the family told us to back off."

"Damn, Matt, I'd heard he wasn't doing well, but this is dreadful." Her voice was pained, "He's not that old."

"I know, but the family was very clear. They feel he's had enough. They've talked with the attending physician, and they think it's hopeless. They want to let him go. No one got around to writing the 'do not resuscitate' order yet, but that's what they want."

Janis looked at Smith. He was pale and emaciated. He barely looked like himself. She shook her head.

She turned back to the team at work around the bed. "Hold up everybody," she said flatly. "Apparently, we weren't supposed to do this. We have to back off."

For a moment everyone was motionless, time seemingly suspended. One of their own was lost.

"Why?" Savita asked. She had been concentrating on her task, and had not heard the discussion.

"Family's wishes."

The respiratory therapist stood up, withdrawing the needle from Smith's femoral artery by which he had been trying to obtain a sample for oxygen and acid assessment. Savita let go of the ambu bag, and the nurse stopped pumping the patient's chest, stood back, and stretched her back, her face wincing. A nurse who had stood ready at the medicine cart turned to repack it.

Janis shook her head, and stalked off to the little kitchenette adjoining the Intensive Care Unit. She opened the refrigerator, and grabbed a carton of orange juice. As she reached for a plastic cup, she heard Savita's voice behind her.

"Janis, can I talk to you for a moment." Her voice had the musical lilt of her native India.

Janis turned, to see her. "Sure. What's up?"

"That was a tough break for Dr. Smith, but I think, given the circumstances, it was for the best."

"I don't know, Savita. He wasn't the easiest guy to get along with, but he was one of us, and that makes me sad. I mean, all death makes me sad, but this hit closer to home."

Savita nodded her head, then added, "Janis, I was on call last night, and Matt was around. We were talking...and please don't take this the wrong way...he told me about what you're going through."

A sense of dread went through Janis. She did not want the whole world to think she was crazy.

"So what did he tell you?"

"That you believe that you've had telepathic contact with that girl everyone has been hunting."

Janis nodded.

"I don't know much about such things, Janis, but I've heard something in my country that I feel I need to share with you." Her intelligent dark brown eyes were wide and sincere.

Janis smiled wanly. "Okay."

"When I was in my last year of medical school back home I had a mandatory rotation in a rural community. It was a village in a remote farming region, and the education level was poor. Most of the people had had very little contact with modern doctors or anything else modern. At any rate, there was a good deal of superstition there.

"A few months prior to my arrival, there had been some alleged incidents the explanations of which I assumed were just manifestations of ignorance. A young man disappeared one night, and a month later a woman did the same thing. Both times it was around the time of the full moon, and the village...what should I call him?...healer made it known that a demon had taken them. Many of the village didn't believe the old man. In fact, some gossiped that the man and woman had simply run off to be together. However, a lot of the villagers, they did listen to the healer. He also claimed that he knew it was a demon because it had briefly possessed him. He had "heard its words without really hearing" in his head as it spoke to him. In order to drive the demon from him he drank some special tea, and was very sure his treatment had worked.

"As I said I always assumed the story to be nonsense, but when I heard about you last night I started thinking. Maybe this is another example of the telepathy you say you've experienced. In fact, and I checked this out, the attacks here have occurred around the time of the full moon. I'm sure the young woman here is not the same as the "demon" as in the village, but maybe there are people in this world who are wired to operate telepathically, and do bad things." Savita paused, and her eyes looked at the floor. Janis knew that she felt she had taken a big risk by stepping forward. Savita was a very good intern, and even suggesting the possibility that her own story might be true, put her credibility, especially given her junior status, in jeopardy.

"This man thought tea helped?" Janis asked.

"Yes. He believed that it kept the demon out of his head. As I think about it though, Janis, it's not a totally stupid idea. Tea has caffeine and caffeine is a stimulant. Maybe it stimulates neuroinhibitors to telepathic receptors in the brain, assuming, of course, that such receptors even exist."

"Do you believe in telepathy, Savita?" Janis asked flatly.

"Probably not, no, not really, but I have always respected you, and so who knows…I thought maybe this would be of some help to you."

Janis chuckled dryly. "If you asked me not so long ago if I thought there were "telepathic receptors" the brain I would have thought that idea to be totally ridiculous. Now…" Her voice trailed off, then she continued. "Thanks, Savita. I appreciate any help I can get at this point.

Savita…I'm not crazy. I've had some sort of weird experiences with that girl, and I have to say I really mean weird, but they were as real as you or I standing here."

Savita's face was sympathetic. "There are many things in the world that can't be explained. I wish you luck, and I hope that you'll be careful.

"I have to go write a note about what just happened with Dr. Smith. See you soon, Janis," and with that Savita smiled and left.

Janis remained in the little kitchenette a while longer, sipping her orange juice and thinking.

Tea…interesting. I wonder how many folk remedies have come about accidentally, cloaked in myth, but with real healing powers.

She thought about recent events, and had to confess that she did think they had occurred around the time of the full moon. And there had been similar happenings in India? Coincidence? The fact remained that she was confronted with unprecedented problems, and she needed ideas, so anything was worth consideration.

Janis went back to the I.C.U. and headed for the nearest phone. She picked up the receiver and dialed 4471.

On the third ring a matronly voice answered, "Hello, Medical Library. How may I help you?"

"This is Dr. Michaels...Dr. Janis Michaels." Janis smiled as she realized her clarification was not necessary; confusion with her father's voice was not likely.

"How may I help you, Dr. Michaels?"

"I need a literature search done on the stimulatory effects of caffeine on neuroinhibatory centers in the central nervous system, if that even happens."

"Do you want the search restricted to English? I can get material in other languages with English abstracts if you want."

Janis liked the library staff at the hospital. They were efficient, polite, and did their best to be helpful.

"Everything you can get me would be great."

"How fast do you need this Dr. Michaels?"

"The sooner the better."

"I can have most of it for you by the end of the day. Do you want me to send it to the Doctors Mail Room?"

"No thanks. Call me when you have it, and I'll come get it."

"No problem, doctor. Thank you."

"Thank you. I really appreciate your help."

That done, Janis went to resume her rounds. She turned on a computer, and found the record of the patient she was rounding on when she was interrupted by Smith's arrest. She turned to the progress notes. The patient had a recurrence of chest pain last night.

Okay, she thought, let's take this where it's quieter, and she went to the small doctor's dictation room further down the corridor. She pulled the chair back from the desk, and sat down, one leg crossed under her on the seat. She shifted her weight in her chair, and with the fingers of her right hand lightly brushed some stray wisps of hair from her face.

There had been two episodes of pain last night, squeezing in nature and seven out of ten in intensity. It had been thirty-six hours since the patient's heart attack. These last two episodes of pain had not been accompanied by shortness of breath.

"Where's last night's EKG?" Janis whispered to herself, and began hunting through the chart. She found it, and then found an old EKG in the chart. Comparing the two, Janis tightened her lips as her concern grew. There were changes…not good.

Janis went to examine the patient. He was a pleasant man, sixty-two years old and moderately overweight. She had known him from before, and he looked fine on exam today. Still, the EKG was troubling, and the fact that last night's chest pains occurred so soon after his heart attack placed him in the category of post infarction angina. The man was most probably going to need a cardiac catheterization.

Janis thought she had better update Dr. O'Brien, and dialed his number.

"Hello Janis," he greeted her, recognizing her voice. He listened to her present the case to him, then told her he agreed with her assessment. "I'll come over, and see the patient when I'm done here. In the meantime, why don't you give the cath lab a call, and get things going. There was a cancellation of a case later today. We can use that time slot. You can do the case. I'll just be there to supervise." Janis thanked him, hung up the phone, and called the cardiac catheterization room.

Her next several patients were stable. She did the cardiac cath on the post infarction angina patient without incident, and by the time she was ready to go home, she was tired, and hoping for a quiet night.

She had already picked up the library search, and was carrying it sticking out of her pocketbook as she left the hospital through the main lobby. On the ride home she kept the radio volume loud hoping the sensory input of loud rock and roll would ward off mental eavesdropping.

She unlocked the door to her apartment, and startled slightly at the feeling of something soft rubbing against her legs.

"Hey buddy," she said soothingly as she bent down to pick up Elvis. "Did you miss me, baby? I missed you." She cuddled him gently, stroking his head, and pushing the door shut with her shoulder. She walked to the kitchen table, and without relinquishing Elvis, she deposited her pocketbook there, and retrieved her literature search from it. Stretching to reach, she snatched a pencil from her countertop, and then settled down to review the list of articles.

The stack of papers was thick. She scanned them, dismissing some as too esoteric and others as irrelevant. There were some she circled, reading the abstracts when they were available. She would give the list back to the librarian tomorrow to retrieve the actual articles of the items she marked.

As she progressed, she began to feel a creeping sense of disappointment. There was nothing here that was going to open a new clear path for her. Still, there were a few articles of interest.

Her cat remained in her lap, and at length, having finished her printout, she looked down at him. "What do you think about all this, Elvis? Any ideas?"

As if sensing her discomfiture, the cat nestled the top of its head against her, then licked the index finger of the hand she had dropped to her lap.

"Awe...I love it when you try to groom me," Janis cooed as she felt the roughness of the little tongue.

When he was done she sighed, "I hate to disturb you, Sweetie, but I have to check something on my computer." She gently picked him up, placed him on the ground, and stood up. She smiled as he turned and walked away from her as though his dignity had been bruised by some ill-conceived rejection.

Janis went to her computer, and sat down, impatient as the machine booted up. She wanted to search more about caffeine. There was a notice that she had received email, and she quickly retrieved it. She had more or less dismissed the possibility that her email to Rhonda would bear fruit, and she was curious.

She was startled as she read the brief note:

"Hi,

I received your email, and it took me this long to research an answer for you. I needed to check with some other contacts I have." Funny, Janis thought, how much more intelligent she sounds using this form of the media. "There are a few of us who have tried to use and understand our skills carefully. From what I have been able to gather it appears that caffeine dims telepathic capacity. One of us noticed this after eating chocolate, and two after coffee. None of us know why.

Hope this is useful. Let me know if I can help any further.

Rhonda"

Whoa, Janis thought. She sat back in her chair, and pressed her eyes with her palms. It was like fate had entered the game. Had she read this email without talking to Savita today she would have dismissed it given its source, but in conjunction with what the intern had told her…well, who knows?

Janis sent off a brief thank you, and then took a long hot shower. She could not bring herself to take another bath, although that would have ordinarily been her preference.

Toweled off, hair dried she felt a bit more relaxed, and, in her robe, she sat down in the stuffed easy chair in her living room to think.

If she had a cup of tea or coffee now she would not be able to sleep. If caffeine did offer any protection, then there would be times when she would be more vulnerable than others. The scientist in her began to enter the fray: What was the proper dose of caffeine? What about rest? Would chronic fatigue from lack of sleep counteract the benefits? These were all unanswerable at the moment. She set her mind adrift, searching, trying to detect if she was being probed. She did not even know the nature of the sensation she was searching for. If there were no "voice" what indication would there be. It was very frustrating, and in a short while she simply decided to go to sleep.

Before retiring she checked her answering machine, which she had forgotten to do when she first came home. There was one message. Phil had called. His message was brief. He said that he hoped they could go out tomorrow after work, and would she either call him back tonight or page him tomorrow at the hospital.

Ah, yes, Phil. Janis had pretty much come to the conclusion that it was time to end their relationship. He would, no doubt, eventually be the prize catch of some woman, but it would not be Janis. He was handsome, intelligent, and athletic, but he was also opinionated and rather self-centered. She knew he cared about her, and she cared about him, but there was something missing. They would talk…maybe over coffee.

21

Three days into the next cycle of quiescence the creature stirred restlessly. Something was wrong. It did not know why it felt this way really, but there was an ill sense of things gone wrong.

For one thing it had not been able to enter and study more of Janis' mind lately. She simply seemed to have disappeared. What was puzzling was that there had been no preceding sense that she was planning a trip that would take her out of the creature's range. Its connection with Janis had been most useful. Though their minds were completely different, the creature had gradually, over time, become more facile at making useful contact with her. It could do this without her even noticing it, and it could study her thoughts, ideas, language and beliefs. Though it had tried to probe deeply in the past it had never had such a success as now. Perhaps there was something unique about Janis that allowed such a contact, but unique was too restricted a concept. Perhaps there were just not many of the herd with whom such a link could be established. Or maybe it had simply taken centuries for this talent to flower.

Close contact and some interchange with a beast of the herd had always been necessary for the creature to initiate mental contact. For example, at present it was not able to contact Janis' sire. The older male was, for now, not within the hunter's mental range. It thought it would have been able to contact the female it had blinded, but now she had been taken to a special refuge to learn how to cope with the change that had been brought into her life and her current mental status interfered.

It was not just Janis' absence that was troublesome. There was a vague sense of foreboding. Something dark was just beyond the horizon. Something ominous was coming, but it was on an emotional plane without discernable details. Once before it had experienced a presentiment akin to this, and the events that had unfolded had nearly brought disaster.

Several centuries prior, in the old land on the other side of the great water there had been a tracker in the herd. He had been brought to a village of prey the creature had been culling recently, specifically to find and destroy the creature. The members of the herd had held this one in high esteem, and were delighted when he set out on his hunt. A hunt! Almost never did the herd ever even detect the presence of the creature or others of its species. Stealth was their special genius, yet, regrettably, rarely discovery did occur. When this happened stalkers always slipped away, leaving nothing behind but rumors and legend.

This particular time, however, the creature had been detected, but was unaware that that had happened, and so had not disappeared into the mists of time and space, as ordinarily would have occurred. But there had a deep sense of impending danger. It was elusive and nonspecific, and so the hunter chose to ignore this only warning.

It had been one night beyond that of the complete whole moon. The sky was cloudless, and coldly illuminated in silvery light. The winter wind tore at the hair and clothing of anyone who ventured from the thatched roofed dwellings. It had been an open winter so far, yet the ground was frozen hard, and the ice on the stream needed to be broken in order for the women to fetch water for their homes.

The creature had entered the village nearly invisibly, moving, as it always did, from dark shadow to dark shadow. The kill the night before had been easy. A drunkard. It was quite possible that no one even realized yet that he was missing, and if anyone did, then it was possibly with relief. No one would ever find the body, which was, whenever possible, also the custom of the creature's kind. This was instinctive and necessary to help avoid detection. Assumed runaways, adventurers, lovers…all sorts can leave a community without raising a general sense of alarm.

Tonight's hunt looked to be more difficult, perhaps fruitless. The cold weather had now driven all inside, but the creature moved from dwelling to dwelling, furtively peering in through windows, cracks in shutters, unpatched chinks in walls, seeking a house with only a single vulnerable looking inhabitant. Finally, one was found, and on an unshuttered window the creature knocked, standing in plain view of the occupant. The woman inside the house looked at it, and the creature pressed its palms together, fingers straight and pointing up in a gesture of supplication it had seen members of the herd make in special gatherings where they spoke and chanted together. Its strategy was that the female would take pity on it in the dark and cold, and let it in. The creature was, of course, aware of how much it looked like a member of the herd. The fact that it did not wear garments, as did the prey, would serve to make its plight look even more urgent, more desperate.

Anticipation caused saliva to pour into its mouth and it drooled slightly as it watched the woman move quickly to her door. As soon as the door was open the creature would kill her, and swiftly carry her off to be devoured elsewhere.

The stalker was confused, stunned really, for an instant when the door opened, and the woman started screaming.

"The beast is here! The demon is at my door! Help! Help! Come quickly!"

Suddenly the doors of many dwellings flew open, and males armed with farm implements that could double for weapons ran into the frozen night.

This had been a trap. Perhaps they had gotten word of some disappearance elsewhere, perhaps linking it to the disappearance of one of there own last night. Legends sometimes grew around the disappearances of people when they occurred in conjunction with one of the very rare encounters with one of the creature's species. The stories were repeated many times, and grew and distorted with the telling. Sometimes they were spoken in hushed tones among gatherings of town folk, sometimes they were told to children to make them behave, but always they made chills run through the listeners. Maybe these stories had floated through this village.

Perhaps the drunkard had been someone of note after all. It was not clear why, but the villagers had been waiting for danger to appear, and had prepared themselves. The danger of encirclement now was great, and escape was now the only imperative.

Knowing it had been detected rendered a stealthy exit unnecessary. The creature bounded into the main thoroughfare, such as it was, that ran through the center of the town to gather speed, and it bounded swiftly away from its pursuers.

In short order the creature was deep in the woodlands beyond the farm fields. It paused to rest, and crouched behind a dense thicket, nostrils flaring, pupils dilated widely, its head carefully peering just over the top of the scrub brush that concealed it. It knew that the townsmen were still giving chase, though they were not in sight. It could hear with ability far beyond that of human ears and could detect them now through the wind and other sounds of the night.

The moonlight cast a net of dark black shadows across the forest floor, and the creature relaxed. Concealment would be easy.

It found and nestled deep into a recess forming a cave like enclosure under a fallen giant oak. It waited.

A few hours before dawn the voices of its pursuers were gone. It sensed that only one lone member of the group was pushing on. He was moving slowly, examining the ground for signs, and finding them. It was the tracker, yet it was quite doubtful that he would be able to endure the cold for long or follow the subtle signs that showed the creature's route of escape into the darkness.

The feeding cycle was essentially at an end. While it had not dined this evening it was reasonably satisfied, nonetheless, and could feel the torpor of its dormant time creeping into its body. Its current refuge would be safe enough for the next few weeks.

Through the foggy disconnection of near sleep, it sensed the tracker's approach. The eastern horizon was beginning to lighten, but listlessness and the need for dormancy robbed the creature of its acuity. It never saw the man approaching, crouching as he moved forward, holding a spear, his head darting quickly from right to left, and at the ground ahead. The tracker wore leather and fur, and except for his ruddy cheeks most of which were covered with a thick red beard, showed no sign of being affected by the cold.

The creature did not want to be concerned; it would stay where it was. This person would not have the skill to find it, and sleep finally came, a warm swaddling offering sweet escape.

The creature never saw the man stop several yards in front of and to the side of the fallen oak. It did not see him place his hand on the ground, and carefully feel frozen, trampled grasses and crushed frost. The tracker had circled in on the entrance to the creatures refuge, and without hesitation plunged his spear into his quarry. It was a glancing blow, however, off course slightly in the relative darkness. It did no serious harm.

The creature screamed in pain; the man took a precautionary step backward, and lost his footing on ice, falling backward onto the ground.

Its listlessness was dispelled by its instinct to survive, and the creature darted from its failed cover, moving with a speed and agility so startling that the tracker was shaken into a moment's immobility.

In an instant the man was dead, and the creature was able to eat once more after all.

Self-examination revealed the spear wound to be no where near vital sites, but the pain was quite terrible, well beyond that which would be expected from such an injury. The creature took up the spear and examined it. It wiped off the blood, and noticed that the spearhead was made of an ornamental, shiny white metal. The predator thought it must have been dipped in poison to cause pain like that, but it did not feel any ebbing of its life force. It was relieved, and it once again felt its contempt for the herd and its ineptitude. It took the wound much longer to heal than would have been expected.

Now Janis' apparent departure left the hunter with a sense similar to the discomfort it had felt that winter night, so long ago, before the tracker had nearly put an end to its life. But this was also different from then. Yet the foreboding was the same.

22

Janis waited for Phil in a little pastry shop, impatiently. She wondered if it was the greater than usual amount of coffee she had consumed so far today that was making her feel that way. Nonetheless, she felt encouraged. Maybe she now had a way to keep the intruder out of her way.

Finally, Phil entered the shop. He looked invigorated, and, as usual, handsome and self-assured. Maybe this meeting was a mistake. No…it had to be done.

"Hi Jan," he said smiling as he approached her. She was sitting at a little table, and he pulled up another chair, and sat down. "What sinful goodie should we order here?" His smile never left his face.

"I don't think I'm going to have anything. I just want to talk about something."

"Sounds serious," but his tone indicated that he was not.

Janis shrugged, and crossed her legs. "How was your morning?"

"I had an interesting case. Sixty-year-old former smoker presented to his primary care doctor two weeks ago with arthritis and some pleural thickening on chest x-ray. C.A.T. scan showed a small tumor, and it looks like he had pseudohypertrophic osteoarthropathy. At any rate, I just finished his operation, and he is safely tucked away in the I.C.U. It was a good case."

"Sounds interesting," but she didn't sound interested.

Phil Skorian's smile began to dim. "What's up Jan? You seem like something's the matter. Are you just tired or you had more of that telepathy stuff? What's up?"

"It's not that. I need to talk about us."

140

Phil's eyebrows went up a little, and his smile was gone altogether. "Okay," he said, and waited.

As kindly as she could, in a soft voice, Janis told him that she loved being with him, but did not love him. She said she thought he was brilliant and nice, a good person with so much to offer. It was so very hard for her to do this, but it was only fair to both of them. The relationship just didn't feel right. She would love for them to remain friends, but she knew he might feel otherwise. She hoped he did not. She told him how she hoped he would understand, and how this was so difficult for her to do.

For a few moments after she stopped talking Philip said nothing, looking down at his hands folded on the table. Then he looked up at her slowly, his handsome face pained, and for a moment Janis thought she had just made a colossal mistake.

He spoke slowly, also in a soft voice. He asked her if she was sure. She closed her eyes, and nodded her head in affirmation. He looked down at his hands again, and told her he had not seen this coming. Was there anything he could do to make things right? The truth was, he really cared for her, and did she know this? He told her how he had always thought they had been right for each other, and recounted a few of their best memories.

They talked for close to an hour. Much of the time Phil could not meet her gaze. In the end, she stood up, apologizing that she had to go. Always the gentleman, Phil got up too. She held her hand out to him, then thought that much too cold, and moved forward, embracing him. He hugged her back. She kissed him on the cheek, then broke away, turned, and without looking back walked directly out of the shop.

On the sidewalk, among the busy hustle of people hurrying along the treadmills of their lives, a sense of agitation swept her up. Had she done the right thing? She thought so. Would she miss Phil? Definitely. And here she was again, alone. That was going to be tough. For a while she had thought Phil was the one, but she knew now he was not, and she was unattached… yet again. She blinked back tears, and quickened her pace.

Phil remained in the pastry shop a bit longer. After Janis had left, he sat down again at their table. He was hurt and taken by surprise; he already missed her, miserably, but there was more. Phil hated to lose. He had competed in everything his whole life, and this felt like being beaten. She was a pretty and engaging woman; he admired her intelligence, and it had been she who had broken off with him. If the relationship had been doomed he would have greatly preferred being the one to have initiated the end.

His many natural assets…his smile, good looks, athletic bent and his intelligent wit… had always made him esteemed by the women he chose.

Janis was the first doctor he had dated. His being a physician, a surgical resident, had added to his seductive armamentarium in the past with women, but had had no effect on Janis. In fact, he sometimes had the faintest sense that she looked down on his choice of surgery a little, perhaps a thin reflection of the age-old rivalry between the internist and the surgeon. She had come with her own considerable talents and physical attractiveness, which had given Phil the unfamiliar feeling of their being evenly matched. To now be rejected…and yes that was what it had been really, her kindness not withstanding…was confusing. He felt angry, not intensely, but not insignificantly either. He felt something else too. He felt that he had lost something of great value, and that was what was bothering him the most.

23

The creature slept, but it was not a good sleep. Spirits haunted it. They were the spirits of dead prey come to gloat over its impending fate. There was a cataclysm coming. It was not clear what form it was to take, but it was coming. And the spirits were laughing.

No, this is a dream.

Are you so sure, laughed the spirits?

The creature realized, with wonder, that in this dream it was Janis' herd sounds, her language, that was being spoken. It shuddered, and awoke…and for one of the rare times in its life it felt pure deep-seated fear.

24

William Michaels sat frowning. Across from him Matt Collins sat back in his chair, hands linked behind his head gazing up at the ceiling with his eyes closed. Only Janis looked composed as they sat in the sandwich shop half a block away from the hospital. They were in an antique, run down building, but it had been a favorite of doctors and nurses from the medical center for nearly a century. It served great deli.

"This won't work," Bill grumbled. "It's too loose. If your telepath really has the powers you believe her to have, then this is way out of control."

"You're Dad's right," Matt said, opening his eyes, and dropping his arms to the table. "This is a terrible idea. If you try this, and your girl can do the things you think she can, she'll know what you're up to, and you will be royally screwed."

"I don't think so." Janis looked at him unwaveringly.

"Oh please, Jan. Just think about it a little bit," her father said speaking slowly to give his words weight. "You block her ability to read you. Then when you're ready you let the caffeine clear your system so you can contact her mentally to hurt her or make her sick or what ever it was you think happened to her the last time you tried to do that. This is supposed to provoke this psychopath into coming after you so the police, waiting in ambush, can grab her.

"If all that were possible, doesn't it occur to you that as the caffeine wears off there will be a point at which that kid could 'read your mind'… still assuming she can do that…and know what you're up to. You said she claims she can do that without you even knowing it's being done. Don't you think she would come after you, when she finds out? We've heard what you say she's capable of."

Janis nodded. "I know Dad, but the chances of her checking me out at just the right moment is pretty small. I think it's worth a try."

Matt spoke next. "Janis, after you hurt her, she's going to want to know why you did that. She'll contact you as soon as she recovers. How will you hide your thoughts then?"

"Before I make her sick I'll chew up and swallow some coffee beans. That ought to jolt caffeine into my system quickly. I'll keep hitting her… mentally…over and over again if I have to until I think there is enough caffeine back in my blood to block her."

"How do you know you won't have multiple episodes yourself," Matt asked? "It sure as hell looked like you were having a seizure last time. For all you know, repeated episodes like that, might interfere with your breathing, injure you, or who knows what. This is not a good plan."

"Matt's right, Jan. This is not well thought out at all," Bill added.

"Look you guys, I know that you don't really even believe my telepathy ideas anyway. So why are you getting so upset? Why not just say, 'okay let's just humor her. When it's over, we'll get her the psychiatric care she needs?' She sat back, and sipped her soda smiling at them.

"She's got a point, Dr. Michaels," Matt said to the older man. His body relaxed as he returned to his own frame of reality.

Bill's posture also relaxed. His daughter was right. The assumption that her telepathy ideas, and all that went with them, were correct had been a convention of discussion, a counterintuitive concession to help his daughter. He never really did believe any of it, but he struggled with this incredulity because of what it would mean about his Janis' mental state. It was difficult. He could not decide what to hope for, but he had always trusted his own reality, and that being the case, what harm could Janis' experiment do?

"Okay," he said thoughtfully. "But if nothing happens, if there are no tangible results to this, you have to agree to a complete psych eval. I think that's fair."

"There's no time limit, Dad."

"Listen Honey, I…we… went along with you, despite the fact that it seemed absurd to us. We did that for you. Now you do this for me. Okay?" His eyes were pleading, and Janis' heart responded.

"Okay, Dad."

Here father smiled and nodded. His body relaxed even more.

The meeting with Chief Paltini went well. He had remembered her when she called, using the number on the card she had given him.

"Hi Doc. What can I do for you?"

"I have an idea. I think I have a way to get that maniac in the hospital to come to me. You could use that to catch her."

"Really. Why don't you come on down here to my office, and tell me about it?"

Janis agreed without hesitation. She was relieved again that he had not dismissed her out of hand as some crack pot. One of the perks of being a doctor, she thought, smiling to herself.

Twenty minutes later Chief Paltini greeted her at the door to his office.

"Come on in, Doc," and he gestured politely with his hand. "Would you like some coffee?" Janis nodded, and he went to a table in the corner of the messy room to pour two cups. "What do you take?" Janis usually liked milk and sugar, but these were not usual times.

"Just black, please."

As she took her first sip, the chief offered her a chair, and then sat down behind his desk.

"So, tell me about your plan."

Janis reviewed for him her recent experiences, and told him how she had learned a way to block the creature's intrusions into her mind. She explained that she would let the caffeine wear off, then eat coffee beans to assure a quick and heavy return of a blocking caffeine level in her body, but would use the window of opportunity until that occurred to attack the creature mentally. The intent would be to deeply anger the telepath so that she would expose herself attempting to retaliate. Once that occurred, police, prepositioned to do so, could apprehend her, and that would end this little reign of terror.

"And you think you can do this? I mean hurt her enough to flush her out?"

"I'm sure I can. She was furious with me when I contacted her before. She made a real point of frightening me, to let me know I better not do that again."

"Maybe you shouldn't do that again."

"I'll be okay if you guys are nearby and grab her fast."

"Supposing she does something to you mentally instead of physically. Even if we get her she might be able to do that. Have you thought of that?"

"The caffeine will block her. Also, once the police have her she's going to be scared, and I won't be her center of focus. I think we might actually be able to pull this off."

"I think you'll be taking a big risk. I want to get this kid, no doubt about it, but I don't want to put anyone, particularly a civilian at unnecessary risk."

"Have you got any better plans?"

The policeman shook his head. "No. No I really don't. We've been combing the hospital, and we've come up with nothing. Did you know that admissions to the hospital are off by about thirty percent? The Mayor and the City Council are giving me an ulcer, and the press is having a field day with this. They want a scape goat, and guess who that's turning out to be."

Janis answered with sympathy in her voice. "The chief of police. We all have a problem here, but yours is bigger. I can help. Let's try."

"Tell me, how do you know your caffeine theory will work?"

"I've got two totally separate sources that say it will."

"You know, you might be betting your life on those two sources."

Janis sighed, her gaze scanning the office. When her gaze returned to Paltini it was not resolute. Her insecurity was evident.

"I know. I'm scared; but if I don't do something how do I know this person...or thing...will ever let me alone. How do I know what else she might be able to do to me? Could she take permanent control of me, change me, erase my mind...who knows what else. It may sound like I'm ranting, I know, but I'm in totally foreign waters here. I never knew that such mental power existed, and I have nothing to compare this to. I don't know what the limits are here. Not to mention that the death count is up to two, and a nurse has been blinded. Who else is going to get killed or hurt if I don't take this chance?"

"Well, you're right that this is new and weird, and we don't know the limits. Don't forget this girl is a cannibal, and I can't help thinking the disaster in the blood bank is connected to her. It's just too much of a coincidence for it not to be."

"It is related."

The Chief's eye's narrowed as he looked at her. "How do you know that?"

She told him. When she was done, he blew air threw pursed lips as if trying to whistle.

"Jesus Christ, Doc. Do you realize what this sounds like?"

"Like I'm crazy?"

"Yeah, but I know you're not. I've been interviewing and listening to people all my professional life, and I'd bet my pension you're not crazy. But for now, let's just keep this blood bank story between us, so we don't loose total credibility with the whole rest of the world.

"I've been a cop a long time, but I've never seen anything like this." He smiled. "That sounds like a movie cop line, doesn't it? Still, I really never have seen anything like this...I doubt many people have. It's pretty hard to believe this is just a teenage girl."

They both looked at each other, each wanting to expand on that thought, and neither willing to do so.

"So what do we do, Janis asked?

"If you're up for it, I say; let's go for it. One more question though, Doc. When we get this kid, what if she can get to you mentally from behind bars?"

Janis shook her head slowly. "I guess I drink coffee forever. I don't know. Whatever happens I'm sure I'll be a lot safer with her in jail than out free." Then her voice and eyes brightened a little. "So, how do you want to start?"

"First, we plan when we want to do this. I think the sooner the better. We decide exactly how you plan to provoke this kid, and with me right next to you for safety, you do it. We keep two police near you, but out of sight constantly, and with any luck she comes out, and we nab her."

"Simple as that?"

"They got Dilinger when he was coming out of a movie theater."

"How will you get the other policemen to buy into the telepathy stuff?"

Paltini chuckled. "First of all, I'm their boss. Second, we don't tell them anything about telepathy. All they'll know is that we're working on a tip, and that they're protecting you."

Philip Skorian could not get Janis out of his mind. He liked her, more than he was willing to admit to himself, and his new sense of loss hurt. She was certainly what he had been looking for all his life: intelligent, beautiful, fun. How could he have let her slip through his fingers? Had he been too inattentive? Had the intensity of his work been a factor. He doubted the later, given what Janis, herself, did for a living.

Then, there was the ego issue. He was able to acknowledge his discomfort over being the one turned away. In most of his romantic encounters he had been pursued, and to have had the relationship end this way stuck in his throat.

Slowly his competitive self began to emerge. After all, it did not really have to be over. There might yet be a way to blow flames back into the embers. Surely there were embers, for he knew that Janis had and certainly, to some extent, still did care for him. He would start by telling her how much he missed her and how much he wanted them to work things out. He certainly did not want to come across as desperate, but if he did this with a proper degree of restraint, he could pull it off.

He began with a call to a travel agency. A three-day cruise for two at special rates had been advertised lately, and something like that would be impressive and romantic. His moonlighting savings and his resident's salary would cover the trip.

A travel agent, a rare commodity these days, suggested that he come to the office so she could show him brochures, and discuss various options. He complied, and as he sat in front of her desk, the attractive young woman splayed an array of brochures and booklets in front of him for his perusal.

"Now, Doctor, I think either of these two cruises might be exactly what you're looking for." Each of her manicured index fingers pointed to a separate brochure. "The one to the left would require both of you to fly to Miami first. Given your time frame that would probably be tough to do, but of the two it's the best trip."

Phil smiled at her. "I'm looking for something very romantic and fun. We can probably bend the schedule a little if we have to."

The agent looked at him, and grinned. "Why can't I find a romantic guy? With my luck you're the last one...and you're taken."

Maybe I am, Phil thought a little wistfully.

The plans for the cruise were completed shortly thereafter. Janis was going to love this he thought, and he smiled. He thought he would surprise her with the plans tonight. Given her schedule and habits, he very much doubted she would be going anywhere tonight, and he would drop by her apartment to begin the restoration of the relationship he had almost lost. He would not let himself consider it might be truly lost.

25

Once the decision to act had been made Janis wanted to proceed as quickly as possible. The day after her meeting with Paltini she had in place the simple arrangements that would be required. If she was going to have another seizure-like event she wanted all the safety precautions she could muster. She had persuaded Matt, despite his protestations over the entire plan, to help her. They would go to the emergency room and claim that she needed intravenous antibiotics, which he would say he was going to administer as a favor. (She insisted that they avoid room 7.) They would set her up with a cardiac monitor, claiming fear of an allergic reaction. Likewise, they would make sure the code cart for cardiac arrest was near by, although Janis was sure this was not going to be necessary. If a convulsion occurred, the intravenous would allow the administration of antiseizure medicine if such were required. Oxygen, of course, would be readily available. Chief Paltini had insisted that he be present, and Janis really did not object. His utility would, hopefully, come a little later, but it would do no harm to have him present from the beginning. She would simply introduce him, if necessary, as a friend who was keeping her company while she got her medicine.

Janis debated with herself as to whether or not she wanted her father present. It would, without doubt, be of great comfort to have him in attendance, but it would cause him much anxiety. In the end she decided not to tell him she was actuating a tangible plan now. She made this decision for him, not herself.

She, Matt and Paltini walked together down the long Emergency Department corridor, past the cubicles, some of which were empty and some of which were occupied by people of mixed age and gender with various ailments ranging from mild to fatal. Janis' heart was beating hard. She was afraid, but she would not show it.

Iron on the outside, she thought, and jelly on the inside. More than anything she wanted to run away. She wanted this whole mess to have been an aberration of her imagination, a dream, a fantasy. She wanted to be free of the murderous teenager, who had caused the hospital, and, in fact, the city to be swallowed by the dark monster of fear. This was a monster that had quickly spawned its children: rumor, gossip, paranoia and hyperbole with ease, and dispersed them through the population. These children matured quickly, becoming active agents of their parent.

As they entered the cubicle that had been assigned to Janet, Matt spoke tentatively. "Janis, are you sure about this?"

No. No I am most certainly not sure. I want to get the hell out of here now, this second; not in a minute or two; now! That was what she wanted to say to him; rather she wanted to scream it at him. What came out of her mouth was quite different.

"I'm sure Matt. Let's just get this over with. The sooner this kid is caught the sooner we can get back to normal around here." Incredibly she smiled at him, appearing upbeat and confident.

Janis went over to the stretcher, turned, and hopped up onto it, sitting with her legs over the edge. A moment later a nurse entered, and took her vital signs, after which Matt told the nurse that he would take care of things personally from here on; this was simply a visit to begin intravenous antibiotics, and this was one responsibility she could be free of. The nurse smiled at him, thanked him, and left. When she was gone Matt drew the curtain on the front of the cubicle, and the three of them had a modicum of privacy.

"Okay, Doc, I'm gong to sit myself over here, and stay out of the way unless you need me," said Paltini reaching for a stool, and positioning himself in a corner. As he sat down, his open jacket gapped a bit, and Janis got a quick glimpse of his service revolver. She was glad he had it.

Phil was rummaging through an I.V. box he had grabbed when he walked through the E.D. corridor. He had already found the intravenous needle he wanted and a syringe. As he extracted a roll of tape he began to speak to Janis.

I'm going to start the I.V. now. I don't think we need to hook it up to a bag at the moment. It'll be simpler if I just hep lock it."

"What's that," asked Paltini?

"It just means," Janis explained, "That he'll cap the I.V. after instilling it with an anticoagulant. If we need it we just take the cap off, and plug in a syringe of whatever has to be given. That way I'm not tied down by I.V. tubing."

The policeman nodded his head, and watched intently as Matt placed the needle in the back of Janis' left hand after carefully cleaning the area. The chief resident deftly taped down the needle, then stood up.

"Okay Jan. That's taken care of. Now let's attach the monitor leads."

"I'll do it," she said a little modestly. She turned her back on the two men and attached the contact pads to her chest. Then she reached for the monitor electrodes and attached them to the pads. After fixing her shirt to be sure she was presentable she turned towards her helpers again and smiled.

"Well, I guess we're ready." She betrayed not a hint of hesitation.

"You probably ought to get on the stretcher, and lie down to do this," Matt suggested. She complied.

"How long do you think it will take for this nut to do something after you contact it?" asked Chief Paltini.

Janis shrugged, pursing her lips. "I obviously don't know for sure, but my guess would be that she'll contact me telepathically as soon as I stop the noxious stimulus. I don't know if she is capable of doing that while I'm doing it. I'm sure she is going to be furious with me if this works. How soon after that will she come after me physically I don't know, but I don't see her as the type to let much time go bye when she's very upset."

The chief smiled wolfishly. "Well, I'll be right here with you, and like I promised, there will be a minimum of two officers assigned to keep an eye on you after I leave twenty four hours a day until we nail this little psycho's ass."

"Okay, guys. I need you to be real quiet now," and Janis pulled up the guardrails of her stretcher and placed blankets over them so as to add padding should she thrash about.

"Matt, would you hand me the airway?" Matt held out a short curve tube that could be inserted into an unconscious person's mouth to be used to prevent the tongue from falling back into the airway and the teeth from biting the tongue. Janis placed it into her own mouth.

Then she laid back and closed her eyes.

With a worried look Matt retreated to the corner where Paltini sat, and took up a standing position by his side. Neither man looked at the other, both watching Janis intently.

Nothing happened. Janis lay supine on the stretcher, her body relaxed, her breathing slow and regular. As in all episodes of extreme anticipation, time seemed to shift gears into a slow and plodding rate. Matt shifted his weight from leg to leg; Paltini coughed a few times. The myriad of sounds of the E.D., barely noticed, became a soft homogenous blend, like a mist softening the surroundings.

It was difficult to wait. Matt was not sure how much time had passed. He had not wanted to move at all for fear of distracting Janis, but he finally looked at his watch. He felt foolish when he did this, as he had not noted the time when they began.

As he let his arm fall back to his side, Janis arched her back, and a guttural sound escaped her throat. Matt took a step forward, but the policeman gently placed a restraining hand on his forearm, and he stood still again.

Janis' limbs went rigid, and the veins on her neck began to bulge. Her face took on a plethoric hue in an unhealthy blotchy distribution. Rigid, and with her back arched she held this position for many seconds. Matt's concern grew as her face changed to a dusky tint of blue; and then she went limp, air escaping her lungs in an audible rush from her mouth.

She did not open her eyes, but lay very still, and both observers flinched when she began to convulse again. Matt's eyes flicked from his watch to Janis and back again repeatedly. If she took too long to break the seizure he would remove the vial of anticonvulsant from the pocket of his white coat, and administer the contents.

He looked a Paltini, held up an index finger briefly to indicate the other man should have forbearance, and moved quickly to Janis' bedside. He reached for the green tubing coiled on the wall above Janis' head and applied the oxygen mask. Then he stepped back to where he had been standing.

"In case she gets cyanotic again," he said to the police chief, his voice clearly reflecting his tension. Paltini looked blankly at him. "Turns blue," Matt added by way of explanation.

Janis collapsed limp on the stretcher. Matt and Paltini could see that she was breathing, and neither man moved. They waited to see if it was over. A minute passed...two.

"Doctor Michaels?" The policeman asked as he stood up. "Can you hear me?" He moved closer to the stretcher. "Are you okay?"

"She may be postictal," Matt said.

"What's that?"

"After a seizure, sometimes a patient has temporary neurological deficits."

"I wish you guys spoke in plane English."

Matt smiled. He glanced at the monitor, and except for a rapid rate the heart tracing looked normal.

"You think it's over?" Paltini asked.

"I have no way of knowing."

Then, as if in answer, Janis stiffened again, this time more violently than before. The rigidity lasted only about half as long as the others, but was rapidly followed by yet another seizure, more severe that any of the others. Rapidly Janis' face and neck turned dark red, and then began to turn blue. Her heart rate was extremely rapid.

"Christ," Paltini murmured, eyes fixed on the woman who was now so arched and stiff that she appeared to be supported only by the back of her head and the heels of her feet.

"Oh, man, I don't think she's breathing," Matt said, true alarm rising in his voice. His hand dove into his pocket, and he quickly pulled out the syringe. He stepped to the side of the stretcher, and reached for the cap on the end of Janis' I.V., but as he did so her body collapsed back into the stretcher. She lay motionless briefly; then, to the great relief of both men, she drew in a deep draught of air, after which her breathing resumed a regular cadence.

Matt replaced the syringe into his pocket, and in its place produced his stethoscope. He placed it on Janis' chest, pushing it under her shirt.

In a moment he stood up and announced, "She's moving air well on both sides, and her heart sounds fine." He glanced at the monitor again. "Rhythm is sinus tach. That's good."

Janis' eyes fluttered open. She looked around, seemingly confused. Her visage quickly cleared, and she rose up on one elbow. She coughed, then her eyes carefully looked at each of her companions.

"I definitely made contact," she said with a raspy voice. She coughed again, and cleared her throat. "How did it look to you?" she asked, her voice clearer now.

"You had a series of tonic seizures," Matt told her simply. Janis nodded her acknowledgement, and struggled, groaning, to sit up.

"Everything hurts,"

"Your seizures were very rough," the chief resident explained.

She was able to sit up finally. "Did anything else happen?"

"No." This time it was Chief Paltini who spoke. "Did you experience anything while you were out? How do you know you made contact?"

"I wasn't able to communicate with her really. I think my mind doesn't really 'fit' hers, in the sense that while I can make crude contact all I really do is jam her circuits and cause her to suffer somehow. But I was able to perceive some of her feelings. I could feel surprise, then shock. She probably was sure she had intimidated me into never trying this again. Then there was anger, and it grew to rage very quickly. And there was something else that she tried to hide from me, even though our connection was rudimentary. I think it was fear."

"Were you able to get any idea when she might try to retaliate?" the chief asked.

"No, not really, but it's a sure bet, just like I said before, it'll be soon."

The policeman bit his lip, shoved his hands into his pockets and looked at the floor. He was frowning.

26

Phil sat in his car, the cool night air bracing him through the open window on the driver's side. He was parked outside Janis' apartment. In his back pocket were two cruise tickets. The travel agent had assured him that if the dates did not work, they could be exchanged for a different date. Now he worried not so much about scheduling problems, as he did about whether or not he could repair his relationship with Janis. He was not good at this. Initiating reconciliation was something he had had minimal experience with. It had been his lot that women were usually more attached to him than he to them, and so he was almost invariably the recipient rather than the initiator of overtures for reunion.

Notwithstanding, he wanted this to work. His sense of loss was heavy, and he was going to try hard, and, if need be, he was going to try hard as often as it took...up to a point.

On the passenger seat of the car laid a dozen red roses trimmed with white Queen Anne's lace, the stems gathered and wrapped in green florist's paper.

He looked at his reflection in the rear-view mirror. Not totally satisfied, but enough to proceed, he blew a little air through pursed lips, and reached for the flowers.

"Hear goes," he murmured to himself.

He pushed the car door open, and stepped out of the car. Pausing only for a moment to straighten his clothing, holding the flowers in his left hand, he headed for the door of the apartment building.

After she, Matt and Paltini parted company Janis did a little light work, but found it difficult to concentrate, her fatigue and aching muscles oppressing her. She signed out to another of the cardiology fellows early, and went home.

Once in her apartment, she was a little surprised that Elvis did not come to greet her as he always did. She had wanted to gather him up, go to her bedroom to lie down and stroke his soft fur.

"Elvis,' she called. There was no sound. "Elvis, where are you, Honey? Come here buddy." She clicked her tongue rapidly against the roof of her mouth; still nothing.

Oh great, Janis thought to herself. Did he sneak out when I left earlier? The cat liked to do that, and once out of the apartment he would wait by the front door of the building until someone opened it, and then he would quickly scoot into the wide world.

Janis did not want to go on a long outdoor hunt for him. She was tired, sore and worried, and she wanted some peaceful down time until things got intense, as she knew they soon would. She felt comforted that two policemen, as promised, were guarding both the front and back doors of the building. They were doing so discretely from their cars, but they were positioned such that they could rapidly be on the scene when the crazy girl appeared. Hopefully this whole mess would be over soon.

Janis wondered if the girl's legal defense would be insanity. Stupid, she thought to herself. How could it be anything else?

Janis poked her head into the bathroom. "Elvis?" When no little fuzzy presence appeared, she moved to the kitchen.

"Come on, little guy. I'm tired, and I don't want to have to hunt for you." Most of the times when Elvis did not appear as expected, it had been because he was sleeping, often in an unlikely location such as the top of the refrigerator up against a wall warmed by an internal hot water pipe. Thinking of that, Janis got on tiptoes to investigate that particular location, but the cat was not there.

"Damn," she thought.

There was a knocking at the door. Now what? She walked to the door, looked through the peephole, and her body relaxed somewhat. She undid the safety chain, cleared the dead bolt, and opened the door.

There stood Phil. He looked drawn and nervous.

"Hi. What are you doing here?" she asked.

He had hidden the flowers to his side and out of sight, and as she asked him this question he pulled them forward.

"These are for you."

Janis spoke first. "How lovely. What is this for?"

"Look Jan, I don't want to lose you. The flowers are for you, but they're symbolic. You're my only *real* rose." This was so unlike Phil, Janis almost giggled. He looked so uncomfortable.

Janis smiled. "So, I see you have a poetic streak you've been concealing from me. Please…come in." She smiled again. "Thank you. The flowers are beautiful. It wasn't necessary."

"Yes, it was," Phil said slowly.

Janis went to the kitchen, found a vase in a cupboard, filled it with water and placed the flowers in it. She brought them back to her little foyer, where Phil was still standing. She placed the flowers on a table, and turned to him. He could feel her lovely eyes looking him over quickly.

"So, you don't want to break up, and you want to woo me back?"

Phil nodded.

"Sit down with me," she said softly, and gestured toward the couch. "You need to know that…"

Phil interrupted her. "If you don't mind, I'd really like to talk first. I think I've been an idiot. You and I are very right for each other, there's no question in my mind about that."

"Why do you say that?"

He told her why he thought so, and she told him, with real tenderness, that she really didn't see them getting together again, except as friends. The discussion went on for about twenty minutes when Janis, who had appeared progressively more concerned the last few minutes, stood up unexpectedly.

"Phil, we need to take a break. I haven't seen or heard Elvis since I came home. That's very strange, and I'm worried about him."

Phil felt his face redden. He was hurt that she would bring this up now, but did his best to conceal it.

"Okay," he said wanting to please, "let's see if we can find him, but I'd like to talk some more afterward."

Janis nodded.

Phil started by looking under the couch, and Janis went to her bedroom. It was not as tidy as she would have preferred, so she shut the door behind her.

"Elvis, if you're in here come on out, baby," she whispered.

"Janis," came the voice in her mind. "I've come for you."

She froze. Some how the caffeine must have worn off without her knowing it.

"What do you want," she whispered icily, taking care to control her thoughts, trying to conceal the trap she had laid.

"I thought I made it very clear to you that you were never to do what you did today." The voice was hard, menacing.

"Go to hell, bitch," Janis whispered, hoping to be provocative, hoping to incite carelessness, and fearing for her life.

You dare to call me this? You dare to defy me? You have no idea who I am. You have no appreciation of my power, my lineage, or of what I am capable. You are an idiot. I had thought you were more intelligent than most of your pitiful species, but you are not. You are contemptible."

"My species? Listen you crazy bitch, you and I are both the same species. You're not powerful, you're sick. You're just some pitiful, paranoid psychopath. What you need is confinement and medicine. You're..."

"Shut up!" There was white-hot rage now, still controlled, but just barely. "It doesn't matter what you think. Your time in this world is over."

"Come get me you pathetic nothing." Janis was incredulous that she could produce such words given how frightened she was.

"I have already arrived."

Janis felt ice suddenly encase her heart. She had already arrived? Where?

"Here." The creature had read her mind. Janis shut down verbal thought. She spun around the room, but there was no one there. Suddenly, as if by impact, her eyes fixed on her window, or rather what was just outside her window.

There, framed by the darkness of the night, just beyond the glass, somehow hanging upside down, was the creature. A scream rose part way up the young doctor's throat only to be choked off by the very fear that had created it. The creature's squinted eyes focused hatefully on her. Its arms were crossed over the front of its chest, and its shoulders drooped downward towards the ground, giving it the appearance of a huge malevolent bat, with the notable exception of its pale color.

"Stay; away," Janis whispered.

"But I thought you wanted me to 'come get' you?" The voice in Janis' head spoke with irony and slow heat, reflecting the passion of unmitigated anger. There was rage piled up like a giant wave against a cracking dike. The danger was imminent, overwhelming and remorseless.

Without knowing it, Janis backed up a little. Sensing the retreat was enough to release the hair trigger of the creatures overwhelming need. It swung its body in a kind of somersaulting arc, its feet smashing through the window, shattering glass into the room.

This time Janet did let out a short cry, as she reflexly jumped back further from the window. She had never been this frightened in all her life.

The creature was in her bedroom! Only a few feet away was an entity, she was sure wished her dead, and was prepared to do its best to make that a reality.

The creature had landed in a low crouch, and now it stood up slowly, like some serpent uncoiling. Its eyes were fixed on her, and the muscles in its cheeks were moving visibly. Janis, who had been with Dr. Smith when he was envenomated, knew what was coming, and was able to dart to the side, avoiding being hit as the soft slimy glob of paralyzing poison shot from her assailant's mouth.

What kind of oral device did she have that could do that, Janis wondered? Her puzzlement was interrupted by the horrifying realization that her two policemen were outside the building.

When he heard the sound of the window shattering, Phil's head snapped toward the closed door of Janis' room.

"You okay?" he called with concern. He heard nothing, and quickly went to the door.

"Jan?" Again, there was no answer. He gripped the doorknob, and opened the door. For a moment he stood transfixed by the tableau he encountered, his pupils dilating as adrenalin poured into his system, giving him an instant sense of nausea.

"Christ," he exclaimed in a low voice. The creature's eyes met his. The three of them stood as if positioned at the points of a triangle.

"Jan, can you get behind me?" Phil asked softly, quietly, edging towards her.

"It doesn't matter if she does that or not." The creature spoke out loud this time. Because of its gruesome history, Phil was surprised that its voice and tone were those of an adolescent girl. The voice sounded almost callow, and the incongruity made it all the more horrible.

"Why not," asked the Phil, still moving towards Janis, his eyes unflinchingly fixed on the creature.

"Because you can not protect her. You and she are no match for me, and no matter what either of you do I will be drinking your blood and dining on your flesh in a few moments just as I have done with your kind for centuries uncounted."

These were not the words of a child. These were not even words of a sane mind. For an instant Phil felt a sense of unreality and dizziness, but it cleared almost instantly.

"Get away from her." Phil's neck had lowered, his shoulders hunched a bit and, although he did not know it, he had balled both hands into fists. It was becoming a paradigm scene of predator and prey. The male was positioning to protect the female quarry. The female was alert, frightened, but holding ground, and the predator was scanning both of them with its eyes, looking for a weakness, ready.

"I will kill you first," the creature said to Phil. "So she can watch you die. I will disable her before that so she cannot escape...she'll stay and watch. Then, Janis, after I kill you, I want you to know that I will kill your father, too, because I know how much you love him. It will cause you pain to know this before you die, and therefore joy for me. Know that this fate will come to him...and all because of you."

Janis' cheeks flushed. "You're not going to hurt my father, or us either. There are two of us."

The creature made a chuckling sound, and shifted its weight. That little motion was all it took to trigger Philip's lunge. It was, by far, preferable to him to be on the attack than maintain a defensive posture. The scrawny adolescent looked to be no match for him at all, and he wanted this ended. He would clear the danger that had disrupted the hospital and agitated the city. Dimly, but not out of his consciousness altogether, he knew that a hero's role would also surely enhance his status with Janis.

He had underestimated the creature's strength. He had judged it by its size and muscle mass, and would have been correct if it had been of human substance, but evolution had placed more power in smaller volumes in this species.

Phil's motion hurled him to the front of the hunter, and he curled both hands around its throat, squeezing as hard as he could. He felt the soft tissues collapse under his force, and felt certain this would all be over in a moment. He would not strangle this maniac child to death, just render her unconscious, then bind her, and let the authorities take her away. He noticed as her cheeks began to work, but he had heard what she had done to Smith, and he head-butted her forehead, before she could deliver the poison. He watched as the girl's eyes went blank, stunned, and as they cleared, he moved his body to his left, and used his hands to torque her neck and head to his right. He was no longer in her range.

The creature had not expected a direct attack, and certainly was surprised by the fierce blow to its forehead. It had underestimated this bull, and was annoyed because it knew better. A male would always ferociously defend a mate or potential mate. It should have slaughtered him immediately. The creature raised both its hands, and brought its claws into play.

Phil made a rasping noise of pain as four slashes were dug into each side of his face. The blood came quickly, and with his peripheral vision he saw it had spattered his arms. With his legs he pushed forward, driving the creature backward. Then four more slashes ribboned each of his cheeks, and he tasted blood, realizing that at least one of his wounds had gone right through a cheek.

While it delivered the second set of slashes the creature twisted hard, trying to free its airway. The two of them turned counterclockwise, and Phil, his face close to the creature's, became disoriented as to direction. He bent his knees, and redoubled the force of his drive to push the hunter backwards. He hoped to pin it against the wall for the end game. What he succeeded in doing was to drive them both toward the broken window.

Janis saw what was about to happen, and cried out a warning, but Phil never heard it, so engaged was he in the combat.

Both man and monster were completely confused as they found themselves engulfed by emptiness, falling. Phil released his grip from the creature's neck, and tried to position himself somehow to break his fall. That was his last thought.

"No! Noo!" Janis cried out as they fell out of the room. She ran to the window, and gasped at what she saw below. Phil was lying prone, his left profile towards her, arms and legs spread. One leg twitched meaninglessly, and then he was totally still. The creature, on the other hand, was still conscious, despite the three-story fall.

"Help," Janis cried, hoping to bring forth the waiting policemen. "We need help here. Now!" What Janis did not know was that the two policemen had both heard the breaking glass, had a quick exchange on their two-way radios, and had run toward where they judged the noise to have been.

They arrived, just as the creature was struggling to stand. Each had come from around a different side of the building. Their guns were drawn, and they took up positions in a manner that would not allow them to shoot each other if shooting became necessary.

"Get down," one of the men cried out to the monster that looked like a young woman, who froze at the sound of the voice. The two men were each about twenty feet from her.

"Get back down, Miss. Face on the ground. Now!" Why is she naked, he thought? He had read the reports of her appearance, but was surprised anyway. And why isn't she more injured from what had been an obvious fall from a dangerous height?

The creature did not 'get down.' It turned its head; first towards one officer then towards the other.

"I'm not going to say this again. Get down on the ground, and spread your arms and legs."

The creature had one imperative: escape. Its back was to the building, and on each side in front of it were the two men with weapons. To run through the spaces would be hazardous, so the creature decided to overpower the smaller of the two, and escape through him. If it could do this fast enough the other would not shoot for fear of killing his comrade.

Despite the pain of its injuries, the creature hurled itself forward, but in the confusion of what had just transpired it misjudged the policeman's reaction time. The man aimed his gun, and pulled the trigger.

A force hit the creature's left shoulder, spinning it in a half circle. Confused, the hunter tried to rush the other policeman who also fired his gun, getting off two shots. One bullet entered the creature's right chest, and the other grazed its right forehead. The hunter staggered back, paused, and then its knees suddenly buckled, dropping it straight down in a heap.

An hour after all the people had left the scene and quiet engulfed Janis' now dark apartment, a frightened cat, the first to have appreciated the danger that evening, slowly and cautiously left its hiding place behind a shoe box in the bedroom closet. It walked carefully; its tail still slightly bushed out. It looked for Janis in search of solace, but could not find her, so it let out a little mew of misery, and curled up on the living room couch to await her return.

27

Janis was beyond miserable. She sat on a couch in the doctor's lounge of the hospital. Next to her sat her father, his strong arm around her shoulders. She had insisted on riding with Philip in the ambulance that took him to the hospital. Technically he was still alive when the EMTs arrived, but he never regained consciousness, and died shortly after arriving at the hospital.

The death count had ratcheted up again, Janis thought. On the other hand, that damned teenager was still alive. She was in surgery now, where Phil's colleagues, true to their medical oaths, would do their absolute best to save her.

She and her father said nothing for quite some time. They did not have to. They were communicating with the silent unspoken language of grief and dismay often employed by people in distress, bound to each other by love. It was a language used universally after car crashes and battles, and, in reality, it expressed something in its wordless physical way that words could never convey.

Janis finally straightened herself on the couch, and turned her tear-streaked face towards her father's kind and sympathetic face.

"I can't believe any of this, Daddy." Her voice was a choked whisper.

"I know, Honey. This whole thing has been terrible. I know Phil Skorian was important to you, and I am truly sorry for your loss."

"I recently broke it off with him. It just wasn't going to work out with us, but, still, he was a great guy, and he really didn't deserve this."

Her father nodded. "I don't know why things like this happen, Jan. I've seen death my whole professional life, but I haven't found the answers.

I do know that time helps, and with that maniac in custody the healing process can start."

"Sharon's eyes aren't going to heal. Jimmy's not coming back, and neither is Mark Smith. I just can't believe Phil is dead. How is that possible?"

The older man shook his head. "I don't know. But I'm talking about you. For that matter, I'm talking about all of us who knew the victims. There'll be a lot of talking that will need to be done. Grieving and nightmares too. But I do know that with time all of this will dim a bit, and the pain will begin to quiet down."

As they talked, in another part of the hospital, the surgical team working on the creature was finishing the surgery. As the last skin sutures were being placed, and the tension that usually accompanied big trauma cases was ebbing, each member of the team was dealing with his or her private thoughts.

Their thoughts ran along similar lines: "This was the killer. It would have been nice just to let her die...maybe even help the process along a bit... No. I don't really mean that...I don't think I do" ... "I've known Phil since we were interns. I can' believe this bitch killed him. I can't believe he's actually dead" ... "Why wasn't there more blood loss from the bullet wounds...She didn't even need a transfusion"....."What was with that accessory lobe of the right lung? I never read about that in any anatomy book."

The members of the team did not share these thoughts. There had been a minimum of chatter during the repair, and they could not shake the funereal aura that had enveloped them. They didn't really try to shake it.

From the operating room the creature was moved to the recovery room. It was attached to a respirator, and had a large caliber intravenous line inserted into the great vein under its left collarbone. A tube exited its chest to drain any blood or other fluid that might collect post operatively, and emptied into a large complex clear plastic collection receptacle. A catheter drained urine from its bladder, and one or two people had wondered if there had been an odd faint green tint to the liquid in the bag. No one commented on it, as it was very subtly visible, if at all.

Three nurses transferred the still unconscious stalker from the O.R. stretcher to a recovery room bed, and all of them felt an odd, faint sense of revulsion at the pallid ivory color of the patient's filthy skin. They noticed the dark thickened nails, and while they all thought them grotesque, they all attributed them to bad teenage taste and appliqué.

One of the nurses left with the O.R. stretcher, and the other two remained at the patient's bedside to settle her into their routine. One of them listened to her lungs with a stethoscope as the other attached new monitor wires.

These tasks done, they stood up, and for a moment looked at each other across the bed.

"It's hard to believe this little thing did all that damage around here," one said.

The other raised her eyebrows, pursed her lips and sighed. "All I can say is I'm glad she's still out. If she were awake, I don't know if I would even dare to get near her."

A policeman, having been notified of the arrival, entered the recovery room.

Several hours later, shortly before dawn, one of the two surgical interns on call at the hospital, sat down at a nurses' station in the surgical intensive care unit. He placed the cup of coffee he had been carrying on the counter in front of him, and turned on the computer, clicked his way to the new patient's chart, and began to read the record. Jane Doe he read, and he knew he had the right patient.

"Only one nameless person here tonight." He scanned the operative note and then the anesthesia note; the later to look at the operative vital signs.

Okay, let's go see her, he thought to himself. He hauled his tired body out of the chair with a little groan, and walked over to the patient's cubicle.

Post op check. Once he finished this he would be able to grab an hour's sleep before the new day began. A shower would be great, but it would have to wait. He was always too afraid of an emergency call while he was all soapy and wet to dare to do that.

At the bedside he scanned the patient. His eyes fixed on her right ankle to which was attached a set of handcuffs. One cuff encircled the ankle, and the other shackled her to the vertical steel bar that made up the far end of a bedrail. In the corner of the cubicle sat a police officer. The man sat straight in his chair, and was flipping casually through a magazine, but there was nothing else casual about him. His eyes took in the intern, coolly appraising him and his intentions despite the scrub suit and the white coat with the hospital nametag.

Won't mess with this guy, thought the intern, smiling to himself, because he knew he would never "mess" with someone like him anyway.

With one hand he removed the sheet that covered the creature, and the creature's eyes snapped open. It turned its head to look at the young doctor.

"Whoa," the intern exclaimed. "Sorry to startle you. How do you feel?" There was no answer. The hunter, still with a tube in its throat by which it remained connected to a respirator, could not, of course, talk, but it made no effort to communicate in any other way. Its squinted eyes looked straight into those of the intern, and the man felt the hairs on the back of his neck prickle.

She gave him the creeps, and in this case that was completely justified. The intern had known Phil Skorian, though not well. He had also known Sharon Calder, and had liked her a lot. He had the sudden fantasy of smothering the girl with her pillow as she lay helplessly in the bed in front of him.

He shook his head slightly to drive the thought away. The dressing on the chest was dry. The left shoulder was also dressed, and no blood had oozed through to the surface of the gauze. The left arm was in a sling. A gauze pad was taped to the creature's right forehead.

"Well, you seem to be doing okay," the intern said. "We'll do some pulmonary tests, and if everything checks out, maybe we can get that breathing tube out."

His patient only looked at him with preternaturally alert eyes, and again the doctor felt a tingling on the back of his neck.

At ten o'clock in the morning the same surgical intern found himself at the doorway to the Surgical Step-Down Unit. It was located midway down the main general surgical floor, and was a place for patients who no longer needed intensive care, but who merited watching more intensely than that which would be possible on a general floor per se.

There was only one patient there, and the intern knew who it was. He had transferred the creature there a couple of hours earlier.

He was aware that the girl had tolerated extubation of the breathing tube without any problems. Her vital signs afterward had been stable with the exception that her pulse had been too slow. He had been told that she had had an even slower pulse when she had been in the emergency room sometime before, so he was not very alarmed.

The doctor picked up the clipboard with her vital signs on it. The pulse was still slow, but the blood pressure was good. Urine output was excellent.

No fever. Good. This kid ought to come through this without a hitch. One or two more days here, and then the authorities would probably take her to their own facility hospital. That would be good. This kid was creepy.

He walked to the bedside to check the wounds. The shackle on her right ankle still held her to the bed, and the same guard sat in a corner of the room. This time the intern would remove the dressings, and replace them after directly examining the wounds. He reached toward a box mounted on the wall by the kid's head, and pulled out two examining gloves. After putting them on he spoke to her.

"Miss, I'm going to remove your bandages, and check your wounds now. I'll be as gentle as I can."

The hunter did not respond. It was awake, but it looked only at the ceiling above it. The intern became aware of the unattractive mouth, and thought of the bizarre teeth he had heard were noted when the breathing tube had been placed. Why would anyone file all their teeth to points? As to the rumor that she had way too many teeth, he dismissed that as exaggeration. Nevertheless, with the tube out, he had no desire to put his hands within biting range. He wanted to be done with this bitch.

The doctor asked one of the nurses if she would stand at the head of the bed, and fix the sides of the patient's head between her hands to restrain her if she decided to bite. His hands were his future. The nurse agreed.

He would examine the chest wound first. When the nurse had secured her head, he withdrew the bed sheet, and frowned. There was a problem. The chest tube had become detached from her. There was a small amount of bloody fluid in the tubing and the receptacle at its other end, but the end that was supposed to be inside the creature's chest lay free in the bedding.

"Damn," the doctor whispered to himself. The nurse could see what had happened, and said nothing. The intern knew an open hole in a chest was a serious hazard, and quickly removed the gauze and tape that had held the tube in place so he could fully examine the opening.

"What the hell?" He looked at the nurse. This time she could not see what he was reacting to.

"What is it?" she asked.

"There's no puncture wound. At least I can't see where the tube entered her." The nurse arched her eyebrows, and leaned forward to look as he searched more carefully.

"Well, that's just weird," he said, and just shook his head.

His hands then moved to the bandage that covered the large incision through which the lung had been operated on. As he removed the dressing, he looked more puzzled, and he began to be annoyed.

"There's no damned incision." His words were said softly, but rose in pitch as he spoke. The nurse frowned as her eyes confirmed what he was saying. There were no sutures, save a few little fragments that lay stuck in the gauze of the dressing. Most impressive, though, was that fact that under the dressing, there was only intact skin.

"Is this some sort of joke?" the intern asked no one. The creature's eyes flicked towards him for a second.

He had not been in the O.R. for the surgery, and he wondered if he was the victim of a prank or, more likely, some sort of bizarre drill or quality control test.

He looked at the nurse. "Let's check the others." He removed the shoulder dressing: no operative wound. He looked under the dressing on the head: again, no injury. Next, he removed the sling, and gently moved the arm. The creature evinced no sign of pain.

"This is ridiculous," he said, shaking his head.

"I don't get it," the nurse said to him. "What do you think is going on?"

"I don't know, but I'm going to find out. I have too much work to do to be dealing with this sort of crap. I'm calling the attending to ask him what this is all about."

Angry, he stalked out of the Step-Down Unit to use a phone on the general floor, so as not to be overheard by the patient.

The attending surgeon did not conceal his annoyance at the intern's call.

"What are you talking about?" he grumbled after the training doctor finished describing what he had seen...or not seen.

"There are no wounds."

"That's ridiculous. I was in the O.R. It was my case. I don't know what you're trying to do here, but you better cut it out."

"I'm telling you, I'm not 'trying to do' anything. The girl's got no wounds, no sutures, nothing. I think we should move her out of the Step-Down Unit, and probably just have the police take here out of here."

"You're not going to do anything until I get there, and check all this out for myself. If this is a prank, and I have to go there for nothing, God help you." The staff surgeon's voice had grown more ominous as he spoke.

There was a brief exchange of cold goodbyes, and they hung up. The surgical intern looked up, and through the door of the Step-Down Unit could see that the mystery girl's curtain had been drawn around her bed. The policeman had left the room, and was now quietly standing a few feet away from the intern.

"What's going on?" the doctor asked, nodding towards the curtain.

"Kid had to use the bed pan, so the nurse set her up. She's not going anywhere, so I though I'd stretch my legs."

The intern nodded, and his thoughts turned back to the angry surgeon he had just talked to. For one cold moment he doubted what he had seen, and felt fear over what would happen when the senior doctor arrived. But that was ridiculous. There had been no wounds. It was preposterous, but that is, in fact, what he had seen.

Let the old man come. In a few minutes he'll be as confused as I am.

The nurse who had helped the intern a moment ago returned to the closed curtain, and spoke to her charge.

"Are you finished?" There was no answer. "Are you all set in there?" Still no answer. She put her hand on the edge of the curtain, pulled it back slightly, and peaked in. Quickly she dropped the curtain, and turned to where the policeman stood. Her face had tightened with concern.

"Officer, you better come here."

The man did not hesitate, and nearly ran to her side. He said nothing, as he reached for the curtain, to take a look.

"Oh shit," he moaned with emotion.

The intern, curious, began to walk towards them, as the policeman pulled the curtain completely out of the way. The bed was empty.

"Are you kidding me?" the young doctor, said.

"Oh my God. You better look at this," said the nurse with new alarm. Both men followed her gaze, and each then made his own sound of incredulity.

Near the foot of the bed among tussled sheets lay the handcuffs, one end still attached to the vertical pole at the end of the bed rail, the other still around the ankle. However, the ankle was free. It had been severed from the rest of the leg, and left behind. There was some blood around it, and it was even paler, as it lay there, than the creature's skin had been before.

The two men and the woman crowded the bed where the remnant lay, amazed and sickened by what they saw.

"Look at this," said the intern pointing at it. "It looks like it was friggin' chewed off."

"That's exactly what it looks like," said the officer.

"Like an animal in a trap," the nurse said very softly.

"This is a girl, not some damned wolf," the doctor grumbled. "Where is she?"

The policeman looked up. "There maybe?"

A tile of the drop down ceiling had been pushed up and to the side, leaving a hole just above the bed.

"You've got to be kidding me." The doctor whispered this. "You got a flashlight?" he asked the nurse.

"Are you nuts?" the policeman asked, aghast. "You're not sticking your head up into that hole."

28

In a dark, obscure recess of the hospital, secluded from the eyes of the herd, the creature sat motionless, knees drawn up to its chest. It felt weak and sick. The healing of its surgical wounds had cost it energy and nutritional reserve. Now more was being consumed in the healing of its leg. It looked listlessly at the stump, which now caused it considerable discomfort from intense itching. New skin had already covered the open area, and the bud of a newly forming foot was clearly visible. The leg would be totally restored soon, but the cost would be very high. There would not be enough of the reserves it had worked so hard over the last feeding cycles to accumulate for the mating to be successful. So much energy would be depleted by the time this last injury was healed, that it would be doubtful the creature could even survive the violent act of copulation.

It was more agitated than it had ever been in its long life. The frustration was, and would continue to be for some time, a force that took it to the limit of endurance. And then there was the rage. This was growing and spreading in the creature's spirit like a conflagration, consuming its capacity to think calmly, building smoky clouds of passion that would suffocate lesser concerns.

The creature began to plan. It would avenge itself on that which had brought all this trouble to it. It would destroy the entity that had, for the first time in its life, thwarted its most basic and powerful drive, procreation. It would seek vengeance on the source of this terrible disappointment. Janis was to die. It would not be quick, it would not be easy, it would be as protracted and miserable as the creature, with all its skill, could make it.

The hunter ranted silently. How could it have been so stupid, so naïve, as to have had even a modicum of fondness for that female? She was of the herd...prey...nothing more. The creature's kind did not respect prey; they simply ate it. What could it have been thinking?

The hunter tried to ease its mind, tried to convince itself this had been a valuable lesson, but it could think of nothing redeeming. Its self-contempt and its hatred for its cause were unabated. Hatred and frustration were the dry wind of a summer day that fanned the fire of rage, making it grow into a roaring wall of destruction.

Janis would die, but more importantly she would suffer. She would plead for mercy. She would happily accept the mercy of death, but it would be denied her for a long time. In the end she would want nothing more but release from that which was soon to befall her. The creature would see to this.

Its leg would be whole soon, and then the hunter would bring Janis what she deserved. The time was coming. It would be soon.

29

Bill Michaels startled when his phone rang. He had been sitting at his desk reviewing lab results, lost in the work. He picked up the phone, and it was Melinda who greeted him.

"Dr. Michael's I have Dr Antonio on the line for you. Do you want to talk to him?"

"Yes. Yes, I've been waiting for him. Thanks."

"Okay, hold for just a moment."

The line went silent, and then an exuberant voice came on the line. "Hey, Bill, how you doing?"

"I'm fine Dale. How are you?"

"I'm fine. I'm good. I have some information for you back from the genetics lab."

"That was quicker than I thought it would take." It had been the senior Dr. Michaels who had had the idea to send a specimen from the amputated foot for chromosome analysis. The girl's behavior had been so extremely bizarre that he had come to suspect they were dealing with some genetic aberrancy. Perhaps they had encountered a new mutation. It really did not take any arguing to get everyone involved to agree that the testing was worth doing. The surgical attending physician, who had been the doctor of record, was eager to explore the possibility once the question was raised, and so the tissue had been sent.

"Well," the pathologist said, "We won't have everything for a few more days, but I got them to do some gene probes, and some other tests before doing the full karyotype, and guess what. They called me up all pissed off. They let me know that they were too busy for 'stupid practical jokes,' as they called it. Bill, they told me that tissue block wasn't human."

There was silence. Then Dale Antonio spoke again. "Bill, you there?"

"I'm here. Are you serious? Did they really say that?"

"Yeah, I'm serious. I got mad when they said that, and told them we would never waste their time like that. They got a little calmer, but told me that someone here must have screwed up, because their sample is definitely not human.

"Now I'm going to tell you, no one here screwed up. We were busy that day, and I was doing clinical to help out. It was me who prepared, and sent your tissue. I dissected off the piece, and processed it myself. There was no mistake."

"Maybe they messed up the specimen," Michaels offered.

"No, I don't think so. When we were getting a little hot I accused them of that, and judging from what they said, I don't think they mixed anything up."

"So, okay, what do they say it's from?"

"They don't know. All they can say is that it's not human. Once I got them calmed down, I got them to agree to send some pieces to some of the other prominent genetic labs around the country. We'll have a lot more information soon, but I didn't want you to wait. I thought you ought to know that we've got a major piece of weirdness here."

"To say the least," Bill mused. "So, what do you think?"

"I don't know. Obviously, I've never seen anything like this before. The scientist in me says they're wrong. The dreamer in me says we just made a big discovery."

"How so?"

"Did you ever hear of co-evolution?"

"No."

"It's like when animals of different genetic backgrounds inhabit the same type of environment they can evolve similar features. Obviously, there is so much variation, this doesn't usually happen, but think of this for example. There were dinosaurs that lived in the oceans, and according to fossil records some of them...I forget the name of the type, ...got to look an awful lot like porpoises of today. The two types of animals were very different genotypically, but because of evolutionary convergence they were phenotypically quite similar." Again there was silence on the phone.

"So our girl just looks human?"

"Yup."

"Do you realize what this sounds like?"

"Yeah, like I went over the edge, and if you buy into it, you're going to look like that too. But think out of the box for a minute. Everyone thought Lister was crazy when he proposed his germ theory. Darwin himself stirred up a ton of controversy. Biology, just because it's a science, doesn't escape resistance to change. It's comfortable to think you've got the answers. But over and over again change rears its little head, and science gets to grow some more."

"So, this human looking thing evolves with us, and escapes detection because it looks like us."

"Maybe. One thing I think…maybe we've found something incredible. As this stuff develops we need to keep our hands in it. This could be career making stuff."

"Or career breaking stuff if there's a mistake we're missing, and we end up looking like idiots."

"Hold on a minute, Bill." The sounds on Dale's end of the line became muffled, and Michaels thought he must have put his hand over the receiver to talk with someone.

"I gotta go, Bill," Dale resumed. "They need me in the other room. We'll talk more soon. How do you want to handle this?"

"I don't know. If you're right, this is a very big find. I need to think about it, and I need to see the reports as they come to you."

"No problem. I'll fax them to you as I get them. Also, I would suggest that for now, at least, we keep this only among a few people we trust. Before we present this to the public, we need to have a strong tight body of evidence."

Bill agreed.

They said their goodbyes, and Michaels sat back in his chair. If this were true, then many things were possible…including Janis' claims at telepathy. That thought made him feel guilty for having doubted her…but who would not have, given his knowledge…or perhaps it would be better to say lack of it…at the time.

Janis stood in the hospital corridor leaning with her back against the wall. In front of her stood her father and Matt Collins. They were speaking in hushed voices.

"Whoa," Janis said in a long drawn-out sigh. "This makes everything fit a lot better. Co-evolution, eh? This is amazing. No one gets a chance to make a find like this." She shook her head slowly.

"Too bad the thing's got to be dead by now." Matt said.

Both father and daughter looked at him.

"What makes you so sure?" Bill asked.

"I doubt it could have survived these many days with that wound untreated. We know it didn't make it to another emergency room. The police have been crawling over this place, and I've asked them that more than once. For it to have holed up some place here is what probably happened, and without medical attention, or maybe it would be better to say veterinary attention," he smiled without mirth, "it would have either bled to death or died of infection."

The senior Doctor Michaels nodded, frowning, and added, "That's what most likely happened. I agree. Still, this is a newfound entity. It seems to be telepathic, and who knows what other abilities it has. I don't think we should assume anything about its survival with certainty."

"Dad's right," Janis said. "Who knows what this creature can and can't do? If it's still alive, obviously it has to be found, captured and studied, and if it's dead, we still need to find it and study it. This is probably the biologic find of the century."

A resident, two interns and a nurse, making rounds, walked by them, and all three stopped talking until they were past.

"So now what do we do?" Matt asked.

Bill smiled. "We do what we've been trained to do. We act like scientists. We consult the literature, combine it with our observations, make a decent hypothesis and decide what actions."

"What medical journals do you think are relevant to this, Dad?" Janis asked, a mild touch of irony in her words.

"Not medical journals, Jan. Nature journals maybe. We think out of the box and include things like reports on big foot, the abominable snowman, and stuff like that. Not from tabloids, but only reputable scientific sources. What I'm saying is we check out things having to do sightings of human-like creatures."

"No offence, sir, but that isn't just out of the box...it's out of the building. All of that stuff has never been proven, and most of it is nonsense." Matt was trying not to sound irritated.

"I know what that must sound like to you. I'm not saying we only look for reports on the fringe. I mean we include them. We're dealing with an unprecedented finding about which we know nothing, so I think we better not exclude anything at first."

There was a silent moment, and then Janis started to speak. She did so slowly, fearing a much stronger reaction to what she was about to say.

"Guys, you know, I have an idea. I think looking those things up is a good idea, but what about more ancient legends. If this thing co-evolved with us, then it's been around with us for a very long time. Sharing turf with us like that...this couldn't possibly be the first time one of these creatures has been encountered. Obviously, this species is incredible at blending in, avoiding detection, but still...Look, this kid, or thing drank nearly everything in the blood bank, and she hangs upside down like a bat. That sounds like a damned vampire. In fact, vampires were supposed to be great seducers...That part of the legend could have come from the telepathy part, including the ability to physically control the movements of someone else.

"Also, Savita Reddy told me, some time ago, about a village she was assigned to in medical school in India. There were some disappearances that had occurred around the full moon, and there was a village shaman who claimed something that sounded a lot like telepathy. When our own little monster started doing her thing here, she was active the first couple of times she struck around the time of the full moon too. Savita had checked that out before she told me, and after she told me about it, I checked it out myself, and she was right. That, and the fact this thing eats human flesh hints at the werewolf legend."

"Oh, come on Janis," Matt interrupted, his words showing his distain for this whole line of thinking. "We can't go off the deep end on this or we're going to get hopelessly lost. We need to reign this in a little, don't you think?"

"No. Matt, listen to her," Bill said. "There have been countless legends that've had their roots in fact."

"That's right," Janis continued. "For example, the whole story of the siege of Troy was thought to be just legend for millennia ...until one day someone actually found it!

"I'm not saying that we have a real vampire or a real werewolf here. I am saying that we need to consider all possibilities. If there were encounters, say even a few centuries ago, the people who would have experienced it would have had no scientific knowledge to help them. It would have been like ancient people who looked up at night, saw the moon, couldn't explain it, and so came to believe it was a goddess. There was a moon, but the explanation was wrong.

"We've got no precedent for our monster, so we take our leads where we find them. If we look into these ancient legends, maybe...and I concede it's a long shot...but still, maybe, we might find some kernel of truth that will help."

Matt was not convinced. "How do you know that vampire and werewolf legends are ancient?"

"I don't," Janis answered. "And it doesn't matter. What does matter is that our case has elements that sound like those things; so maybe, sometime in the past our friend's ancestors, or she herself for all I know, gave rise to legends that tried to explain what was unexplainable?

Matt shook his head. "So her species could be the dark root of two of the scariest legends we have in our society. Shit, this is incredible."

"It is," said the Janis' father. "Or, maybe, it's actually credible."

"I have a plan," Janis announced. "We have no other leads. We need to do something, so I propose we go to the library, the computer and wherever else we can find information, and work with the vampire and werewolf legends. I think we should work backward in time, following the development of the stories, if possible, to their origins as best we can. Maybe we'll find something useful. Maybe we'll find the truth that led to the myths, and from there we might gain some advantage on this thing. There's nothing else for us to do, anyway."

"We could help the cops try to find her." Matt said, still resistant.

"How would you do that, Matt?" Janis was evincing just a touch of impatience with him. "Are you a policeman, a skilled tracker, a psychic? Tell me what else you can come up with to do."

"It feels so stupid. Vampire, werewolves, bull shit."

"We are not talking about the actual mythical monsters. We're talking about what led to the dawn of the legends. Did something historical cause these stories."

"Why not tell the cops your idea, and let them run the stories down?"

"They have their own routines. I doubt Paltini has the manpower to spare for literary work. But you have a point. I can bring it up to him, and see if he goes for it, but we're the scholars, and it would be wrong not to help.

Matt looked at his feet saying nothing.

Bill broke the pause in the discussion. "I can have Melinda cancel out the rest of my day. I'm willing to give it a try. You're right, Jan, this is all we can do for the moment, and I sure as hell won't be able to just sit around doing nothing. Think of it…a new species that may have been with us, virtually undetected for as long as there have been people. You know there's another twist to this. That sea going dinosaur that looked like a porpoise, never came close to meeting its look alike. They just evolved to look alike in a similar environment separated by millions of years. Our doppelganger is a contemporary."

Matt made a throaty sound, and then said in a voice that showed both resignation and a touch of amusement at himself, "Well, Piano owes me a favor. He can cover my clinic today. Count me in."

Yeah, Matt! Janis thought.

"Okay." Janis' voice was energized. "Let's divide up. I'll go to the city library. Matt, would you check out the library at the University, and Dad, can you work on the Internet?"

Matt nodded, and her father said, "Sure." He was pleased that his daughter had taken the lead, but, after all, that was what he would have expected from her.

An hour later all three had begun the arduous task of trying to grasp what amounted to quick silver in history, events hidden in the mists of time that might still be indirectly impacting on the drama of human experience. All three searched relentlessly, until their backs ached, and their eyes burned.

Bill had not come close to exhausting the Internet, and was beginning to have doubts that he ever could. The legends were popular. Movies, novels, short stories, all engaging for some, but garbage for him. He did come across some references that purported to be authoritative, and he wrote down their titles and authors, planning to check them out himself in the library at a later time.

Chat rooms were, for the most part, ridiculous. However, in one of them he did come across someone who seemed to have both feet on the ground. The person claimed to be a professor of mythology at a university in the midwestern United States. Impatient to make some sort of progress, Bill did not inquire as to which university it was, but just plunged into dialogue.

"Can you tell me a bit more about your area of interest?" he typed, and hit the send button.

Very quickly the response came back, "I have published and lectured on myths of current day Europe."

"Have you studied anything about the legends of vampires or werewolves?"

Brief pause.

"Why?"

"It's personal."

Slightly longer pause.

"Personal? I'm a scholar of mythology and I take it seriously. If you think you have a problem with one of those two things, I can't really help you, except to tell you they don't exist. That's why they call them myths."

Feisty, Bill thought, smiling. Probably quirky too.

"I agree with you," he typed. "I don't think they exist either, but you might be just the person I'm looking for. I'm looking for the origins of these particular legends." He pressed the send button with a bit of vigor. Maybe this was going to be a real lead.

"Who are you? Are you a student? Tell me why I should spend time online with you?"

Bill took a moment to design a properly phrased response. After all, this person wasn't being forced to be in this chat room.

Then he typed, "I'm not a student. If you are concerned that I might not be taking this seriously, let me assure you that is not the case. I have a..." Bill paused here for a moment, then continued. "Keen interest in how people come to formulate beliefs, and if you could help me I would be grateful."

He sent it. There was a long pause, and for a moment Bill was afraid the man had dropped him.

New message on the monitor: "You don't sound like a kid. You sound like you might be an academic yourself."

"I am."

"Tell me about it." No, no, Bill thought, irritated. I don't want to be your friend; just give me the information I need.

But he wrote, "I am a professor of medicine and a chief of medicine. I would be very grateful to you if you would help me for a moment."

Another long pause.

"I hate doctors."

Oh great, Bill thought. This isn't going to be pretty.

There was no way out if he wanted this man's help.

"Why?"

"I think you are all a bunch of damned quacks."

Now it was Bill's turn to pause a bit too long before responding. He had to be careful. This fellow obviously needed handling, and not offending him was important.

"I can't speak for others, but I try to do my best." He wasn't sure how that would be received, but he thought it best to be brief and unprovacative.

Quick reply: "Maybe. Okay, tell me just what it is you want to know."

"Good", Bill sighed. Then he typed a long note.

Again, there was a long pause, and finally a response appeared. The professor would type a few sentences, send them, type some more and send again. His response was long, and he did not want to be silent for such a time that his new disciple would give up, and sign off.

"These legends are very complex. In part they reflect aspects of psychology. They express the carnal needs and conflicts that are part of humanity. They deal with the eternal struggle between good and bad. In the stories good always wins, and that's comforting. We get scared, but we prevail."

Bill enjoyed his eloquence.

"One of the things that make these two legends, the vampire and the werewolf, so compelling is the constancy of the stories. That suggests, in my opinion, that they are, in fact, based on historical events. Whatever happened, I would suggest it happened more than once. The legends are ubiquitous all over Europe and parts of Asia, and appeared during times when news moved slowly. Yet the stories are similar, no drift from the core despite different times, places and cultures. Forget the happy endings. Those are just products of wishful thinking. But the nature of the monsters, and what they do, is always the same. There is very little variation in the tales. The appearance of the stories in the Americas was probably just the result of their being brought along by European immigrants, but who knows...There are suggestions that the Mayans had similar legends, but these indications are quite vague and inferential.

"My suggestion is that you consult a book that I and my colleagues believe to be quite authoritative. It is entitled 'The Blood Myths of History.' Despite the rather gothic title it is very well researched. It was written in the mid nineteenth century by an historian from the Netherlands by the name of Martin vanBrent. He tracked down contemporary and near contemporary sightings, debunking most of them...but not all. You have to remember that in his time there was widespread European concern with these things. It was not at all uncommon, for example, for travelers to carry 'vampire kits,' equipped with crosses, vials of holy water, etc.

I, myself, wonder what happened in those times that caused this flare of concern. Anyways, vanBrent also consulted archives in universities, churches, monasteries, etc. His work was massive. Unfortunately, he died, after years of labor, before he finished his second book which was reputed to have contained very relevant and very real information, but no one can verify that, as the work was lost...mysteriously. The first book still exists, and has been translated into many languages including English. I suspect you could find it in any large university library."

The writing stopped.

Then: "Does that help?"

Bill typed quickly, "Yes, thank you. It may be just what I need. I really appreciate your help."

The professor, for reasons that were not clear, abruptly signed off, and Bill sat back in his chair and stretched.

This might be a major break, he thought as he pulled his shoulders back and extended his arms. This guy might just be nuts, but maybe not. He took his cell phone out of his pocket, and dialed Matt's mobile number.

Matt's voice came on after the second ring.

"Hello?"

"Hi, Matt. It's Dr. Michaels."

"Hello, sir. Any luck?"

"Actually, yes...maybe."

Matt, said nothing, and Bill sensed this reflected doubt, and a desire to remain polite. It was Bill who broke the brief silence. "Are you still at the university library?"

"Yes."

"Okay. See if you can get hold of a copy of a book from the mid eighteen hundreds called 'The Blood Myths of History.' I've gotten a lead that this might be an important reference for us."

"'The Blood Myths of History?'" Matt said with a deprecatory sniff. "Doesn't sound very solid to me."

"Matt, I know you don't have much faith in what we're doing, but it's all we have to do." Despite himself, Bill chuckled and quipped, "Besides you can't judge a book by its cover...or its title." He paused, then went on, "Will you try to get us the book?"

"I'll try, of course. You're right about my not having much faith in this. Just the same, don't worry about it. I agreed to help, and I will. Who's the author?"

Bill told him.

In the mid evening the three doctors met in Bill Michaels' office. They sat around his conference table, each with a set of notes. Matt also had a large old tome.

Matt appeared in good spirits, and, for the first time since the investigation had begun, he looked animated, his eyes flicking from time to time to the book he held. Yet it was Bill who was speaking, finishing an account of what he had done that day.

"...and that's what I was able to find. I have the citations written down as I showed you." He fished a paper out of his shirt pocket. "I have some notes from some references I was able to check out, but I have to tell you I think the best lead I got was from a rather odd professor who gave me what is supposedly the title and author of a definitive text. Matt, you brought it, right?"

Matt held up the book. "Yup, right here. I've looked through segments, and considering the subject, it's not too bad."

He's getting into it maybe, Bill thought, then said, smiling, "Coming from you that's pretty high praise."

Matt grinned, then turned toward Janet. "You've been pretty subdued since we got here, Jan. What's going on?"

Janis looked at her lap, and for a moment said nothing. Then she cleared her throat, and looked up, first at her father and then at Matt. Her face was strained, and she looked tired.

"I've heard from our friend."

"The creature?" Matt asked.

"Yes."

"So it didn't die," Bill said softly. "Weren't you able to block contact with caffeine?"

"Yes, but I assumed it was dead or dying, so I backed off that."

"Is it dying?" asked Matt.

"Hardly. The damned thing was practically gloating. It claims to have amazing regenerative powers, and says..." She paused for a moment. "And says it has essentially regrown its foot."

"That's not possible! Are you sure it said that...or thought it to you or whatever the damned thing does?"

"Oh yeah."

"Christ."

Bill stood up, and began to walk about the room, agitated. "What did it want, Honey?"

"It wants us dead." Her voice quavered almost imperceptibly. "It wants to kill you, Dad, and then me. It's furious. It was rambling in half sentences about something having to do with a ruined mating and having to wait a whole bunch of 'moons' until the next 'time'. I think it may be psychotic."

"Is it after me too?" asked Matt.

"It didn't mention you." Janis' face was grim.

Bill was standing still now, looking at his daughter. "It plans to kill us? Could you get any read on where it was? You know…where it's holed up."

Janis shook her head.

"Any idea how it plans to try to do this?"

"I can't be sure, but I think I sensed it wanted to do it through me. Control my motions, and make me hurt you, and then myself, but that's a half guess. The good news is, regardless of what it wants, it seems it never had a strong telekinetic ability, and now it's way too weak to even seriously consider it. I think it'll try to get us directly."

"How could this thing be in any shape to come after anyone?" Matt questioned. "It recently bit its own foot off for God's sake! It's got to be very weak, if not moribund."

"There are a lot of things that haven't made sense lately," Bill said taking over. "Okay, we're not going to get overly excited just yet. We can't make it go away, and we can't make it love us, so let's keep on brainstorming. Matt, you want to tell us what you found that was so interesting in that book?" He didn't want his daughter to dwell too intensely on the threat.

"Sure. The book attempts to trace some of the scary legends we all grew up with. Werewolves and vampires are included. The interesting thing is that it doesn't try to impress the reader with magic or gore, but it's an honest attempt to trace back the roots of the legends. At any rate, it was a slow read, but I did find something of interest. There was an archbishop in thirteenth century Wales who had established a personal library. This was pretty unusual for the times. Anyway, the library was destroyed in a local war, but there were people who valued it, and they managed to save a little of its contents. One of the things that was saved was an account by a local baron of what sounds, for all the world, like our girl, right down to bite marks that showed excess pointy teeth, drinking blood, eating human flesh, and something about it that made people think of a bat. It certainly sounds like it might be an ancestor of our problem.

"What's cool is that the author was, in fact, able to trace both the werewolf and the vampire legends of Europe backward in time to this particular account. That means there was a divergence of the two legends going forward in time at that point, which to the author, and, quite frankly, to me too at this point, suggests that this really might be the actual origin of the two legends as separate and discrete beliefs. The author makes it clear that there are other theories about the roots of these myths, but he definitely believed that this one was the most likely.

"Pretty interesting don't you think. I doubt many people know the real origins of those stories."

"I always thought Vlad Tepish, the Romanian king, was the origin of the vampire stories," Janis said.

"No, he was the origin of the Dracula legend. The legend of the vampire preceded him."

"How do you think this helps us?" Bill asked.

Matt beamed. "Okay, let me go on.

"Soon after the encounter I just mentioned with this creature, stories of its reappearances with a mate arose. This part of the story was not a part of the archbishop's library, and survived for a long time only as oral tradition, so it's not as authoritative an account as the first one. This story, however, states, for the first time, that this type of creature could be killed by a spear through the heart, and that silver was apparently toxic to it. Oh yeah, they seemed to be most active during the full moon. Without the baron's account in the archbishop's library there would be no corroboration of this story, but the baron's account does exist, and that, I think, makes the second story more plausible"

"This is incredible," Janis said. Her face mirrored her relief.

"It is," Bill said softly. "It is not much of a leap after hearing this to see how the stories developed. Sharp bite marks and the full moon suggest some horrible wolf, so the werewolf was born. Sensitivity to silver could have later become the silver bullet to kill werewolves. Hanging upside down like a bat, sharp pointed teeth, drinking blood…a no brainer: that became a vampire. Spear through the heart: the fatal stake through the vampire's heart. I also think…"

Agitated, Janis interrupted him. "Okay. This is good. We take our lead from the legends. This may be a newly discovered species for us, but we need to remember that it's an ancient breed, and obviously has been seen before. More than that, some people obviously learned how to successfully fight it. Silver, a stake through the heart. Gentlemen, I think we have a breakthrough." She smiled broadly, sat back in her chair, and visibly relaxed muscles that had long been tense.

30

It sensed motion. It was not itself moving, but it could sense it anyway. Tonight would be the night before the full moon, and its powers would be charged, not nearly as they had been, but rather the best that could be given what had transpired. But now, in its torpor, it struggled to understand what it was feeling. What was this movement?

Janis! Janis was moving. The creature was instantly certain of it. She was going to run, to try to escape.

Go ahead, Janis. Try to run, it thought, malice dragging the corners of its mouth downward. I will follow you. I will make you suffer. Your suffering will be sweet, and I will make it last a long, long time. You have cost me much, but I have learned much from you, and I will be satisfied.

The time was close enough to the monthly season of hunting that rousing itself was not very difficult. It crept from its hiding place, slowly, cautiously. It crouched in the shadows, and its gaze darted to and fro. There was no threat, and it moved on in a quick loping stride, from one dark shadow to another.

Unseen it made its way to Janis' home. There was an ebbing of tension when it saw that Janis'…what was the word for it?…car…was still in front of her dwelling. She had not yet left!

Quickly it darted to the car, crouched, and slid supine under the vehicle. Then, in its strange way, it effectively gripped the irregular surface of the car's underbody with its toes and its fingers, and drew itself up flush to the bottom of the automobile. It did this none to quickly, for no sooner was it in place than it heard the voices of Janis and her father. They were leaving the building, talking softly to each other, and walking quickly. No human would have been able to discern what they were saying from the creature's vantage point, but the creature was not human, and its preternatural hearing picked up every word.

They were planning to run. They would go to a friend's "cabin." The creature did not know this word, but whatever the meaning, it would go with them, undetected, waiting. When the time was right it would begin its pleasure. It would be the warm, sensuous joy of slowly and skillfully killing an enemy.

Its foot was fully regenerated now. There was barely any discomfort from it, and, all things considered, the creature was satisfied with the recovery. All that remained now was to wait.

31

The flames danced on and around the wood, threatening to engulf it. They and their shadows gave the illusion of major and minor devils leaping, and grabbing in an orgy of sacrificial lust. The occasional hiss as steam broke free into the air reinforced the illusion. Yet the warmth of the fire felt good. The evening was cool, and it was good to be sitting in front of the large hearth.

There were no other lights on in the room, and so it was lit in somber flickering shades of yellows and russet. The man and the woman sat back in their padded high back chairs on either side of the hearth, diagonally facing the fire and each other. Each held a mug of coffee, and neither spoke to the other.

Both people felt the relief of sanctuary. The tension of the past many weeks had taken its toll, leaving both spent and hungry for this sense of security.

The light of the flames made it difficult for them to read each other's facial expressions. The moving shadows across their faces gave the impression of an unstable myriad of changing moods, but that was only illusory. It was just as well. Being unable to read each other made the effort useless, and abandoning the effort added to their sense of escape.

They had agreed that it was imperative for Janis to maintain caffeine intake until they could sort out and execute their next strategic action. Neither knew the range of the creature's strange mental power, and so it was imperative that they not allow the enemy to discern their whereabouts. If they could remain undisturbed for a while, both were confident that they would eventually be able to formulate an effective plan to rid themselves of the threat that had come to them unbidden and so forcefully.

Thus comforted, both father and daughter stiffened visibly at the sudden sound of movement behind them. Adrenalin slammed into both of them making each feel as though there hung a dark vacuum where a moment ago had been their hearts. Their eyes shot fearful glances toward each other, and they began to rise from their chairs.

Both sank back into their seats, nearly giddy as they realized what had happened.

Elvis had quickly stepped out of the shadows, and now stood between them, verbalizing, in his own insistent way, his need to be held.

Janis laughed softly. "Come on baby." She patted her thighs with both hands. "Come on up. Come on, sweetie. You scared us, you silly cat." As if he knew the words, the animal turned to her, took a couple of steps, and silently, gracefully, leapt into her lap, instantly beginning to purr as the fingers of Janis' right hand gently scratched behind his ears.

After an indeterminate period of time, Janis gently lifted the now sleeping cat, curled in her lap, and carefully placed him on the floor. As she got out of the chair Elvis woke up, and swaggered out of the room as if disgusted with his mistress' ill-conceived displacement of him, while he slept.

"I'm going to do the dishes, Dad, and then try to get some sleep," Janis said sleepily.

"I'll help you, Honey."

They walked to the kitchen, flicked on a light, and moved toward the sink where they took up positions, and went to work.

"I was thinking, Jan, you must be pretty tired from sleep deprivation after all the caffeine you've been consuming in our little war," the man said.

"Yup, but there's no way around it I'm afraid. I'm sick of it, though. I go to bed, and I can't sleep. When I do fall asleep, its shallow, and I wake up tired. And I'm scared. If I let up, and the creature picks up my thoughts, we're sunk. I really can't wait for this to be over."

"Don't worry Jan. We'll get the bitch. Tomorrow morning we'll come up with a plan, and we'll bring an end to this crap."

Janis met his gaze, and she smiled. How she loved this sweet middle-aged gentleman. Her father. He had always seemed so strong to her. And kind. From her earliest childhood he had always had the answers. Growing up she had been able to confide in him at times when her friends would not have even wanted to be in the same room as their parents. He always listened, accepted her, and did his best to help. Now here he was again, at her side, unflinching in a crisis.

He looked older now. The stress was wearing on him too. She felt protective of him, and at the same time she felt protected by him. She was glad he was with her, but she worried.

Bill had begun wiping the dishes and utensils, and placing them back in drawers and cabinets. Janis washed the dishes with an unwarranted intensity, moving fast and scrubbing too hard. Bill frowned; her anxiety was leaking out in many ways, but he knew his daughter. She was strong, and he was confident she could hold it together until this was over.

"Go to bed, Jan. I'll finish up here."

She took a step towards him, and stood on her tiptoes to kiss him on the cheek.

"Good night, Dad. Thanks."

"Sleep well, Sweetie. If you get nervous just wake me. I'm going to bed soon too."

She smiled at him again, and left the room, happy memories of childhood goodnights blending into the jumble in her mind.

As she climbed the stairs to the second landing where the bedrooms were located her thoughts were roiling. The creature wanted both of them dead. They were in hiding, and there was no plan at present, except to lay low, and block the creature from her thoughts.

Her mind continued to jump from topic to topic. She hoped she had not taken in too much caffeine, fearing sleep would elude her altogether. She held out her hands, and groaned slightly when she saw the faint tremor.

Okay, big deal. There's nothing I can do about any of this right now, she thought. I'm going to lie down. If I sleep, good; if I don't, then at least I will have gotten some rest. Her body ached for sleep, but her mind was racing.

She entered the room that was to be hers during their stay at the cabin, and was walking toward the bed, when a movement caught her eye. Her heart seemed to seize up, and her head snapped towards the window.

There had been motion there, she was sure of it. She walked towards the window, and looked out. The dense, primal forest that surrounded the cabin except for the path that led up to it from the unpaved road was totally still. The moon was a sliver away from being full, and everything was bathed in silver moonlight and shadows. Janis almost opened the window to look out, but thought better of it, fearing that she would be too exposed.

It was good that Janis made that decision, for unseen outside, gripping the exterior wall with spread fingers and toes, positioned upside down with its face just above the window, was the creature. It had purposely attracted her attention. It had hoped Janis would open the window, and lean out for a better look. It would have then snatched her, using surprise and a ruthless application of pain to stun her; then it would have dragged her through the window, and taken her away to fully even up the debt it was due.

It must have been a night bird flying by, or a bat, Janis thought. The thought of the latter gave her a shiver.

I need rest. Time to lie down, and try not to think about anything for a while…and to stop being so jumpy.

Nevertheless, even though there were no neighbors, Janis pulled down the shades of both of the room's windows. That done, she laid down on the bed, not bothering to remove her sweater, jeans or hiking boots.

She drew the covers up to her neck, rolled onto her side, and as she rued the caffeine and her excess wakefulness, she fell asleep.

Bill finished tidying up the kitchen. Then he snapped out the light, but stood in the doorway for a moment looking back. Under normal conditions this kitchen would have been the scene of great fun. They would have made simple feasts during their stay, and they would have talked incessantly, and laughed a good deal. He loved being with his daughter. She seemed to give off a special invisible radiance that made his spirit glow when he was in her presence. She had been a bright, curious little girl, and she had grown into a lovely, intelligent, sensitive woman. A physician. He was proud of her accomplishments, and he was proud of her as a person.

I'm lucky, he thought. But the realization that there was an entity afoot that wanted to destroy all that made him feel shaky inside…and furious.

They would need to be careful and resourceful. Tomorrow, after a night's rest, they would brainstorm, and invent a set of plans. For now, he was exhausted. He knew he had to sleep, or he would be of little use in the morning, and with that he left the room, and found his way to the stairs, turning off lights as he went.

He thought he heard a scratching sound on the outside of the house. He paused on the stairs, not moving a muscle, listening intently, holding his breath. There was no further noise, and after a long moment he relaxed, and climbed the remaining stairs.

Squirrels, he thought, and forgot the episode.

In a few minutes he had washed, and gotten into bed. He too, slept in his clothes. If there were to be trouble tonight, he would feel better fully dressed. Soon, lying on his back, while staring at the ceiling, and trying to put together preliminary strategies, he drifted into sleep, unaware that he was doing so. A few minutes later, lying there peacefully, he dreamed of sailing in the afternoon with his little girl so many years ago.

The dream mutated. He was lying in a bower in the shape of a bed and woven with rose vines. It was in full bloom, fragrant and lovely. The red roses grew all around him, and felt soft where they touched his skin. As he lay there, he realized no thorns pierced his skin. He was totally comfortable. In fact, it was a sensation beyond comfortable. His eyes were heavy, and they closed, and when they did, he felt a gentle touch on his neck. A soft cloth was being applied over his throat. No pressure was applied, and the cloth increased his comfort even further. He did not open his eyes, but wondered who was being so gentle, and in his dream, as in reality, he slept.

Janis, too, dreamed. She was in a small sailboat, reclining in the stern. Her father's hand was on the tiller, and she felt safe, even though the seas were more rough than usual. As the boat sailed on, her father's hand disappeared, and she realized she was alone. Someone else, unseen, was steering her vessel. She looked all about her, but could not discover who or what it was, and yet whatever was controlling her course was quite skilled at the task.

The sunny weather was changing, and clouds seemed to converge from all directions. Of course, that was not meteorologically possible. It would have required a ridiculous combination of winds. Nevertheless, it was happening. The sky grew steadily darker, and Janis sat up straight in the boat now, worried.

Where is my father, she wondered? He would know what's happening. He was here a moment ago, but now he's not. Where did he go? In her mind her voice was that of a child, the child she had once been. But somehow that seemed natural, and as she looked down at her hands and legs, she realized she was, in fact, a child again.

A voice whispered in her ear, "You will never grow up. You will not get past this storm."

Janis' worry turned to full on fear, and as she looked around to see who had said this to her, the boat began to be rocked by increasingly choppy water. The air was cold and wet, and it felt as if danger had swooped down over her, and dropped a net on her. She was trapped.

Somehow, she should have seen this coming. She should have anticipated it.

And then her eyes flew open.

She was lying on her back, awash in tall grass and silver blue moon light. Just above her face two squinted eyes set in an unearthly ivory white face peered at her. The eyes were cold, but intelligent, and Janis gasped as she realized to whom, or rather, to what they they belonged.

She tried to sit up, but two lithe, slender arms pushed her back with a strength that greatly belied their appearance.

"You!" Janis gasped.

"Yes Janis, it's me. Are you glad to see me?" The voice was that of an adolescent female, but the tone was aloof and ironic.

"I know you're not here. This is just another dream. You can't be here because you don't know where I am. This dream will change, or I'll make myself wake up; but, one way or the other, I'm getting rid of you."

The creature laughed, its stark purple red lips drawn back, and her many pointed teeth showing. For a moment Janis feared she was about to be hit with paralytic poison, but it didn't happen. Good. Even in a dream that thought was devastatingly frightening.

"Janis, I'm distressed. We have shared so much, and you say something like that to me?"

Was this a dream, Janis began to wonder? The creature's touch, when it had pushed her back, had been tangible.

Well, couldn't that happen in a dream?

Janis tried to sit up, and this time the creature did nothing to impede her. When she sat up, she noticed that her gaze was higher than that of the hunter. This thing is so small. How could it have done so much damage?

"Janis, you know this is not a dream."

"I don't know that. I've had weird dreams since you intruded into my life. As far as I know this is just another one," but Janis, becoming more awake, was rapidly beginning to doubt the truth of what she had just said. She could feel the ground beneath her, and the moisture on the grass under her hands. The air was cool, and everything was vivid.

"Ah, I see it in your eyes, Janis. You know. I am here, and so are you, and now we can begin our final farewell."

Janis said nothing.

"Nothing to say? Good. I have many things planned for us this evening. You have robbed me of my reproductive cycle, my offspring. You have no idea what that means to my kind, or how rare an event it is, or how much work goes into storing enough energy, or what it feels like to have the gestational sensations coursing through your veins. I cannot teach you these things, nor do I want to. What I will teach you is the price that must be paid for the great evil you have done. You will learn by the magnitude of your pain. You will realize it as you gasp out the last of your life." It paused, appearing breathless and emotional, its face reflecting the tides of anger, rage and sorrow that raced in circuit through its psyche.

"I have robbed you of nothing." Janis sounded more awake and more focused.

Abruptly the creature slapped her face. The blow was powerful, and Janis' face snapped sideways causing her first thought to be concern as to whether or not her neck had been injured. It had not, but the sting in her face was severe.

"From this point on," the stalker snarled, "you will not contradict me. You will listen and learn before you die, but if you speak, even one more time, it will go much worse for you."

Janis had no doubt that her enemy meant it. They had never been pitched against each other physically, but judging from the push a moment ago, the ferocity of the slap, and this hideous thing's past history, she was not at all certain that she could physically best it, despite the fact that it looked so much like a frail teenage girl. And there was the venom to be considered. Janis said nothing, and thought it prudent.

"Good," the creature whispered. Now I want you to..."

Janis was running. She had suddenly turned to her left, and begun to run as fast as she could. She was in shape, and she thought there was a chance she might get away. She had been to the cabin many times since childhood, and was familiar with the forest in which it was nestled. Although she could not immediately identify exactly where she was, she was confident that she could do so quickly. She kept to the denser shadows for concealment, and changed direction as often as she could without slowing herself down. She carefully watched the ground in front of her as she pushed on trying to avoid anything that might trip her. To fall now, or worse yet, to injure herself, could quite possibly make the difference between life and death. She had no doubt of this.

After a time, her breathing became somewhat more labored. Janis still had plenty of reserve left, and she began to take stock of her flight. She quickly came to an exciting realization. There were no sounds of pursuit. Though she continued to run, she listened carefully, probing the woods for signs that would tell her where her pursuer might be. There were no sounds of footfalls; and there were no sounds of another's labored breathing. Could it have been so easy?

A couple of minutes after this, she stopped, her breathing now coming harder. She quickly looked around, but the light of the moon and the sounds in the air revealed no threat. Janis bent at the waist, placing her palms on her thighs in an effort to catch her breath quicker.

She was surprised. With all its bizarre abilities, she found it hard to believe that she had actually evaded or even out run the creature.

Okay, safe for now, she thought. She noted a huge tree, darted towards it, and quickly squatted at its base, choosing the side she estimated to be away from where she had just come. Keeping low she leaned her back against the tree, and, still working to catch her breath, she continued to listen. There was nothing.

Think, think she thought urgently.

First, she would lay low here, and when she believed it was safe to do so, she would try to ascertain her location. That would not be easy to do that if she could not readily find any familiar landmarks at ground level. Of course, were that to be the case she could climb a tree, check out the topography and identify her location that way. From that point, she would be able to return to the cabin, but would do so using a circuitous route for security reasons. She would then wake her father, barricade the place, and call the cops. Or maybe they would just pile into the car, and get the hell out of there as fast as they could.

Her anxiety became mixed with bewilderment. How had she come to be lying in the moonlit grass in the forest? Had her somnambulism returned? Possibly. How had she come to be in the presence of the creature again? It would be too coincidental for these events not to be related. Had the creature carried her here as she slept? Was the slight figured thing powerful enough to do that? When Janis thought of the carnage the creature had wrought, and remembered the strength of those thin arms as they pushed her down a few minutes earlier, she thought that might very well be the case. And if the beast could have carried her here, not even arousing her from sleep, then Janis knew even more the power and control of her foe.

There was a scuffling sound above her. She looked up, and a thin sound escaped her as she saw a pale vertical form hurtling down at her. It struck her hard, each foot landing on a shoulder.

However, in attacking its prey thus so the creature had seriously underestimated the reflexes of the young athletic woman it was pursuing. Instinctively, at the instant she realized what was happening, Janis had jerked her body backwards, and was, therefore, in motion at the moment of impact. The creature lost its balance, then tumbled to the ground, and the strength of the attack was blunted.

Janis did not waste a moment. Sensing there was not enough time for her to get to her feet and flee, she lunged at the creature. She struck it hard with her body as it had just begun to rise, and both figures fell to the ground rolling, locked in an embrace of mortal struggle.

Janis found herself on top. She had never been in fight in her life, but she acted as if she had been in many. Something primordial was at work from deep within her, something bred through countless generations of survival and success.

The fingers of both her hands closed around the creature's throat, and squeezed with all their strength. The creature emitted a squeaking sound that ended abruptly, and Janis knew that she had closed off the beast's airway. Enraged, the creature, lifted its head, turned and bit Janis' left forearm. She saw it coming, and moved her arm so the bite was only glancing, but the skin was torn by several teeth, and Janis grunted with the pain. In so moving her arm, her left arm loosened its grip slightly on the hunter's throat, and it could move air again. To Janis' surprise it spoke to her despite their physical struggle.

"Please Janis, don't hurt me. Please. I need help. Please help me." The voice was unmistakably that of a teenage girl. It was agonized and plaintive, and for just a second Janis hesitated. In so doing she failed to tighten the grip of her left hand again, and the creature's hands suddenly snapped into action struggling frantically to pull Janis's arms apart from each other and off of its neck. It worked.

Her grip gone and angry that she had fallen for a rouse, Janis foolishly straightened up, shifting her weight, and allowing the creature the opportunity to topple her. She fell to the ground, her head striking something hard. She was dazed only for an instant, but it afforded the creature the opportunity it needed to straddle Janis as she lay on the ground. It grabbed both of Janis' wrists and drew them together. Janis was astonished at the unbreakable grip in which her wrists were held; she could not move them at all.

"Lay still Janis," the creature snarled, its voice now loud and compelling. For reasons she did not understand, Janis obeyed.

The creature looked at her for a moment, never releasing its hold. Then it spoke.

"Janis, don't you wonder about your father? Don't you want to know what..."

"Leave my father alone, you bitch," Janis screamed.

The creature laughed heartily. Finally, its pleasure was to begin.

"Janis, you need to know about your father. Maybe you can still help him. I will tell you about him, and I will let go of your wrists if you promise to sit still, listen and not run." There was no response. "Do you agree?"

Janis nodded.

The stalker let go of her wrists slowly. Both rose to their feet, neither removing their gaze from the other. They stood facing each other, and then Janis spoke.

"Tell me about my father." Her voice was now contained and measured. She was struggling to control herself.

"Your poor father." The creature shook its head in a parody of sympathy. "He is still sleeping back at the cabin, but he is in peril, let me assure you. Before I took you here..."

Janis' eyebrows went up slightly.

"Yes, I carried you here. The stupid beasts of the herd always make the mistake of assessing my strength by the standards of your own inferior bodies.

"But that is a digression. Before I took you here, I visited him as he slept. As I know you are aware, my kind has the gift of being able to produce wonderful venom. One of its many qualities is that it slowly erodes the fabric you call cotton. I stripped some from one of your father's shirts, folded it several times and moistened one side with my nectar. Then I gently placed the dry side against his neck, and left the cloth there. Even now the cotton is slowly being eaten away, and the venom is drawing closer to his skin. Soon it will reach him, and while the skin does not absorb the poison as efficiently as the eyes or mouth, it does absorb it, nonetheless. Depending on many factors it can be produced so as to stop respirations, as well as paralyze the rest of his body. He will die slowly. But then, if you are clever, maybe you can save him. His life is in your miserable hands

"Just think, my friend, if you can escape me …who knows? But if you don't get to him before the poison perforates the cloth completely or if he rolls over and spills it onto his bedding then…" The hunter shook its head, its face burlesquing sorrow with grotesque exaggeration.

Janis became agitated, and sensing that she might run again, her captor spoke once more.

"Before, when you ran, I let you because I felt it would be pleasurable to watch your face when I suddenly reappeared. Let me assure you that if you try to run now, I will slash you to death with my teeth and claws in an instant. I prefer not to cut you as I intend to drink your blood as you remain alive and conscious. It would be a shame to waste any of you."

Janis shuddered, and was swept with a wave of lightheadedness.

The creature continued, "In fact you will be aware of everything. I will drink your essence slowly, and I will watch as you grow cold and weak. I will assure that it will be a long time before it happens, but you will beg for water. That's something that happens with severe hemorrhage, Janis, but you know it from the useless ministrations you carry out for the other dumb brutes of the herd. The victim gets thirsty. The coldness and the thirst will go on and on for you, and in the end I will watch as your eyes dim and the life ebbs from your body, and when you are no more, I will eat your remains.

"You look puzzled. I am going to punish you like this because I had allowed you a degree of respect that I have never given to one of the herd before. But in the end, you showed that you, like the others of your species, have only one real value: nutrition for my kind. You betrayed me, and I will have revenge. I will have your life, and I will take it as I wish."

While shaken badly, Janis was still quite functional. "How could I have betrayed you? We had no relationship. I didn't betray you; you attacked us."

"Be quiet!" the creature screamed. "I don't want to hear your evil thoughts. Don't say another word or I will make your death worse that it is planned to be."

Janis remained quiet, but kept her eyes on this malevolent member of a strange and predatory species. She could easily understand how it, or one like it, could foster the development of dark legends.

While she dared not speak, she was thinking quickly. There was no panic now. She was angry, and she knew that her life and that of her father hung on what she did in the next few minutes. Panic would have been an indulgence.

Drink my blood? Did this thing really say that?

The creature was confident in its ability to subdue her. It was allowing her to stand here unfettered. That confidence could be a weakness, and maybe, if she was shrewd, Janis could exploit it.

"Why didn't you use your poison on me?" Janis flinched as she realized she had just defied the command she had been given.

To her relief, the creature did not act on this breach.

"If I had done that you quite likely would have died much too quickly. You see, yours is to be a particular kind of death, and it will not be an easy passage into eternity."

There was silence between them. The hunter seemed to relax, and Janis believed it was actually assuming the mind set for recreation, and that gave her another wave of light-headedness.

An owl cried out in the night nearby, and the creature's eyes tracked the sound by reflex. Janis had never taken her eyes off her captor's face, and saw the eyes flick. That was all she needed. The adrenalin and fear exploded in her, and before the stalker could react Janis was upon her, her fists balled tightly. She struck the creature twice in the face with all her strength. Her knee came up into her opponent's abdomen, and Janis could hear the air escaping from its mouth with the force of the blow delivered. The tone sagged in the creature's body, and Janis knew it was stunned. She saw a rock, quickly bent to grab it with her right hand, and came back up swinging. It hit the hunter in the side of the head, and it went down. It was not unconscious, but its face was vacuous as it lay in the silver-blue light that soaked the earth.

Without thought Janis ran. She knew somewhere in her terrified brain that she was missing an opportunity to finish off the monster. But she was no killer, and her urge to flee was overpowering.

Her flight this time was reckless. All she could think was to put distance between herself and this murderous sadist who craved her death. She heard a screech of rage, and knew it was recovered enough to know it had been injured, and its prey had again escaped. Its pursuit would be fevered, and Janis knew this. She could not formulate a plan at all. All she could do was run.

She was dimly aware of a subtle change in the terrain. There were fallen tree trunks and limbs of trees scattered about. Beavers. She was near the beaver pond, which meant she now knew exactly where she was. She had been there many times over the years, and in fact, she was not very far from the cabin. This was of little comfort to her. Given her circumstances it might as well have been a thousand miles away.

But then she remembered her father was there. He was sleeping with poison slowly making its way toward him. She refused to consider that it might have already killed him. She had to make it to the cabin. She had to…

And then there was a plan. It seemed to simply come to her without effort. The legends gave a clear road map, and nature was to be her assistant. She stopped running, and reached into a pocket of her jeans, her fingers seeking what she needed. They found it, and she withdrew it in her clenched fist.

Next, she looked about her, not immediately finding what she needed. Tension mounted to a crescendo, for she knew the creature was in hot pursuit, and again she could not hear it. It could appear at any moment from any direction.

Suddenly her eyes found one. It was a tree branch about an inch and a half to two inches in diameter, and about three feet long. Both ends were pointed from where the beavers had been at work. Janis picked it up, and tested its heft. It would do fine. She found a large tree, and crouched at its base as before. The shaft remained in her grip, but she let it rest on the ground so as to camouflage it.

Then she waited.

It was impossible to tell from what side the creature would attack, or if it would come from above as before. All she could do was wait, knowing without doubt that she would be found, and knowing without doubt that she would have only one chance. It felt to Janis as if every nerve were on the threshold of firing, as if the least stimulus would cause her to explode into diffuse action.

She didn't move. She barely breathed. The forest had an unearthly quiet, as if even the small animals of the night knew a terrible drama was unfolding. Each of the millions of shadows that surrounded her could contain death. Each rustling leaf above could be a harbinger of the end. It was unbearable.

And still she waited; not moving.

There was a flicker of motion in her peripheral vision.

Real or imaginary? Janis could not tell, but her heart was pounding again enough for her to feel it in her ears. She placed the object from her pocket in her mouth to allow both her hands freedom.

A slight rustling. Another fleeting movement half seen; then again nothing. Silence.

There was a noise above her, and she shot a glance upward. It had begun. Again, the attack was aerial. Once more a pale form descended towards her, but this time spread eagle, a clear attempt to blanket her, avoiding hitting feet first with the risk of being toppled again.

Janis brought the stake up vertically, bracing it in both hands, aiming it as best she could.

Her aim was good. The creature was impaled. The branch pierced its chest, and Janis felt a surge of triumph, hoping it had gone through the heart.

The stake had entered the front of the chest, gone straight through, and extended from the back, the blood glistening and purple in the moonlight.

The creature screamed, and Janis leaped backward, stumbled and landed in a sitting position supported by her arms. She was several feet away from the creature, who, to Janis' disbelief, now stood up. It was impaled through the chest, and it was standing. Worse, it was trying to grin.

"Janis. Poor Janis," it said, through clenched teeth, trying to conceal its pain. "You don't have any idea of what I am capable of. I have regenerative powers you can't even imagine."

With its own two hands it firmly gripped the stake in its chest and steadily, slowly began to withdraw it.

Good, Janis thought. The second it's out of the heart there won't be any plug, the internal hemorrhaging will become overwhelming, and death will be quick. It's saving me the effort.

The stake was out now, and the creature let it drop to the ground. Still, it stood, showing no signs of collapse.

"You look surprised, my stupid friend. Right now I am already beginning to heal. It will take a while for full recovery, but I will be able to deal with you in a moment."

And the hunter was correct. Its heart muscle cells were contracting locally to seal off the perforation, as well as globally to maintain circulation. Clotting proteins not contained in the human circulation were beginning to aggregate at the edges of all the torn tissues, and Janis could see that the bleeding from the chest wound was already stanched.

The creature took a deep breath, then a single step towards the woman sitting on the ground.

"Janis, already I am less weak. If you are religious pray, because you are at your end."

Janis retrieved the item from her mouth, leaped to her feet, and rushed the creature, issuing a cry from the deepest part of her primal soul. She forced herself to crash into the hunter, and as she did so pushed the item in her hand into its chest wound. She remained against the monster for an instant, and with disgust, quickly used her index finger to push the dime deep into the chest cavity.

The creature gasped. Its squinty eyes widened, and its mouth gaped. All confidence and anger vanished from its countenance. There was unabashed fear, for it felt what it had never felt before in its life. It was mortally wounded.

"What?" it gasped.

Janis backed away, breathless. "A wooden steak through the heart and something like a silver bullet. Straight from the myths. Did you know that your species is the origin of the vampire legends and the werewolf legends? Horrible stories, but they hold clues."

The creature looked dreadfully sick. It was even paler than usual. A dark liquid, perhaps brown, but difficult to be certain in the moonlight, was issuing from its nose and mouth. It looked at Janis, its lips moving, but saying nothing. It fell to its knees, teetered for a moment, and then fell straight forward, face down. It twitched twice, and then Janis gasped as it burst into flames.

"What the hell?" Janis whispered. Some chemical reaction had obviously taken place, but she had no idea what it could have been.

The body was rapidly engulfed. Janis did not move. She was hypnotically transfixed by the sight, needing to see it through to the end.

For at least two minutes the fire burned intensely, then died down, finally going to ashes, which fluttered up in the nearly imperceptible night breeze, dissipating into nothing.

Janis rose, and slowly, cautiously moved to the site where the creature had been incinerated. Except for a blackened stain on the ground there was nothing left. Again, she thought of the legends, but another urgent thought came roaring back into her consciousness. Her father.

She knew how to get to the cabin from here, and she ran. She jumped an occasional low log, and sprinted the straight-aways. Dodging trees, she ignored her intense breathlessness, and pushed on.

In a short while she could make out the cabin. The air seemed to burn as she dragged it into her lungs in anguished gasps. Her left arm throbbed, but she ignored all of these discomforts. The cabin and her father were all that mattered.

She took the front steps in twos, and found the door to the lodging ajar.

"Dad," she cried out? "Daddy, don't move. I'm coming, stay still. I'll explain."

She reached the top of the interior stairway in seconds, and rushed along the landing to her father's open bedroom door.

Her heart sank. He was lying motionless on the bed. She was sure she would have awakened him if he had been sleeping, and then she saw something even worse. The cloth draped over his neck had a hole in it, and bare skin was showing through it.

How could she have lost her focus like she did as the creature's body burned, she thought. Valuable time irretrievably lost. Oh, please let him still be alive.

She rushed to his side, and nearly grabbed the cloth. She froze, arm outstretched, then turned, reached for a pencil on the bedside table, and used it to flip the cloth to the floor. With corner of the bed sheet, she wiped off the glistening slime from his skin, then placed the index and middle fingers of her right hand over her father's carotid artery.

"Thank God!" she whispered. There was a pulse. His lips were not dusky. He was breathing. His eyes were tracking her face, and she believed he was conscious.

"It's going to be okay, Dad. It's going to be okay." Tears ran over her cheeks, and she moved to grab the phone on the bedside table. She pounded in three numbers: 911.

32

The hospital room was set up for single patient occupancy. The sunlight coming through the window made the light blue walls look almost cheery. Next to the bed was a small electric machine that maintained the intravenous flow at a steady rate as it ran into the man in the bed. At the side of the bed sat two people, a man and a woman, waiting, not speaking, looks of concern spread across their faces.

The patient's eyes fluttered, then opened, and they showed instant recognition of the others.

"Hey, Dad," Janis said softly, smiling gently.

"Hi, baby," he said, smiling back. He had arrived at the hospital, the same one in which he was the Chief of Medicine, two nights before, and to everyone's surprise the paralysis had reversed quickly. That had not been the case when Smith was stricken, and it was the opinion of some, that Bill must have inherited some enzyme or other substance capable of denaturing the poison that was lacking in Smith. At any rate, Bill Michael's had stable vital signs, and had even fed himself lunch, albeit with a shaky hand.

"You look better than you did even this morning, Dr. Michaels," Matt Collins said. "Obviously you needed that nap."

"Thanks, Matt. The nap felt good." He looked at his daughter and stretched a bit weakly. "When one of the nurses is free, I'm going to see if I can go for a walk."

"Great Dad. It will get the juices moving. Incidentally, in answer to what you asked me to find out before you dozed off, toxicology still doesn't have an I.D. on the toxin."

Bill smiled. "Well, they certainly took enough blood to run the tests. You know I feel like a patient," and his smile turned into a full grin.

There was a moment of silence, and then Matt spoke, his voice upbeat. "I'll say one thing; it's going to be great just going to work, and not having to look over your shoulder. I'm glad that, whatever it was, is gone, but, to tell you the truth, it would have been really interesting to have had a body to study."

"Well," Bill said, his face clouding a little. "There are others. If this thing 'co-evolved' with us there had to be a population large enough to assure survival and reproduction."

"Yup, I agree," Janis added. "But these things apparently appear to humans, at least those that are not victims, so rarely that their very existence has been cloaked for eons. They've only been known, really, from rare accounts buried in legends. I doubt we'll ever see another."

"Unless they're vengeful."

"I doubt that. I bet these things are hard wired by evolution to live by fading into the woodwork."

"Then it's over," Bill said, his voice both tired and relieved.

Janis was looking at the floor, and in a surprisingly glum voice she simply responded, "Maybe."

"Why do you say that, Honey?" her father asked.

"The vampire and werewolf legends, like a lot of legends, sprang from reality, but they were molded by retelling and lack of exact history. I think if both legends shared something in common then the odds would be that that particular item might be one that was factual."

"Okay. That's possible...but not proven. What about it?"

"So..." Janis held up her bandaged left arm. "Both legends are very explicit about what happens to someone who survives a bite."

There was a brief, heavy moment as comprehension of what she had just said took hold.

"Oh my God," Bill gasped.

Matt looked at her, and his jaw went slack.

Janis' eyes darted from her father to Matt then back to her father. No one said anything. Their faces said everything; and tears welled up in Janis' eyes.

Made in the USA
Monee, IL
28 December 2022

23581913R00125